M000033597

Mike Faricy

Russian Roulette

Published by Credit River Publishing 2011
Copyright Mike Faricy 2011

Russian Roulette
ISBN-13: 978-0615521060
ISBN-10: 0615521061

Acknowledgments

I would like to thank the following people
for their help and support:

Special thanks to my editors, Kitty, Donna
and Rhonda for their hard work, cheerful
patience and positive feedback.
I would like to thank Dan, Roy and Julie for
their creative talent and not slitting their
wrists or jumping off the high bridge when
dealing with my Neanderthal computer
capabilities.

Last, I would like to thank family and
friends for their encouragement and
unqualified support. Special thanks to
Maggie, Jed, Schatz, Pat, Av and Pat and
Emily for not rolling their eyes, at least when
I was there, and most of all, to my wife
Teresa whose belief, support and inspiration
has from day one, never waned.

To Teresa

**"The very first kiss she gave him was electric...
and he was toast."**

Mike Faricy
Russian Roulette

Chapter One

I was sitting in The Spot bar, minding my own damn business, content in a mild and steadily growing alcoholic haze. A client had paid me. The check was enough to cover my overdrafts and fund a night or two of partying.

I saw her come in the side door and look around for fifteen seconds. She was blonde, hot looking, thirty something, maybe wearing a little too much makeup, dressed in a delightfully slutty sort of way. Conversation didn't stop, but heads turned as she walked past. She headed toward an empty stool. There were four on either side of me. Her chest was like the prow of a battleship and plowed a firm, bouncy course down the length of the bar. She passed the first three empty stools and pulled out the one next to me. It was red vinyl and edged in worn duct tape.

"Is anyone sitting here?"

I caught the slightest hint of an accent.

"Not that I can see."

"You are Mr. Devlin Haskell, right? The private dick?"

She batted her eyes a few times, which at the moment struck me as extremely sexy. Her perfume wafted over me like a plastic dry cleaning bag and forced me to gasp for breath. It was strangely spicy.

"Yeah, that's me. Although it's not all that private," I joked.

Incredibly she smiled, but didn't comment. After a moment she said, "Mr. Haskell, I've been looking for you. Of course, the other places were a little nicer than this." She gazed around at the dingy brown, smoke-stained ceiling. Maybe she caught the two bullet holes in the front door now filled with putty and supposed to have been painted sometime just before Obama took office. Maybe it was the 60s-style cheap wood paneling on the walls, or the eau de beer reek of the place. Maybe it was the worn wood-grain Formica tables in the booths or the twenty-watt bulbs in the light fixtures. Or maybe it just didn't matter. She sat up straight, spun toward me on her stool, and thrust her death-defying cleavage in my face.

"You were looking for me?" I asked, wondering if my luck had finally begun to change.

"Yes, a friend gave me your name."

"Really? What can I do for you?" thinking maybe a getaway weekend to a quiet lake, a bed and breakfast with a Jacuzzi in the room, or just your basic tawdry night at my place.

"Well, I hope you won't think I'm strange."

At this point Grace, the bartender, stepped in front of us. An experienced little voice inside my head said '*Just smile, finish the drink and get the hell out of here before you get in real trouble.*'

"Buy you a drink?" I asked.

"Will you have another?"

That experienced little voice whispered '*no.*'

I nodded 'yes' toward Grace who rolled her eyes.

"Yeah, okay, I guess I'll have a double vodka martini, two olives," she ordered quickly, then smiled at me.

A double, my kind of girl.

"So, I was about to think you're strange?" I said.

"What? Oh yes. Look, I wanted to hire you to sort of find someone. I'll pay you," and with that she dug in a small beaded handbag suspended on a chain over her shoulder.

I hadn't noticed it before, but then I'd been otherwise engaged making careful notes as to her physical characteristics.

"Oh, sorry," she said as she snapped the handbag closed with an audible click and then reached into her front pocket. She pulled out a small wad of hundred-dollar bills. I was actually more amazed there was room for anything thicker than a dime in her pocket. The jeans looked to have been sprayed on over her perfect thighs.

"Here is five hundred dollars, I can get you more if you need it."

"You still haven't told me who you want me to 'sort of' find. A name would help, for starters. Not to mention you know my name, but I don't know yours."

Grace brought our drinks, and grabbed a ten off the bar from the small pile in front of me.

"Oh yes, sorry, I'm Kerri." She held out her hand to shake.

"Nice to meet you, Kerri. Call me Dev. Your accent?" I asked.

"Ahhh, French."

She nodded, batted her eyes innocently, then proceeded to drain nearly half her martini glass.

"Mmm-mmm, that is a very good vodka," she gasped. "Yes, French, but from a long time ago. I was just a little girl. Dev, I hope you'll help me find my little sister."

"Your sister?"

"Yes, she is called Nikki."

"Hmm, Kerri and Nikki, sisters. Anyone else in the family? Mom, Dad, brothers, more sisters?"

"No, we are the only ones. My, I mean, our parents passed away eight years ago, maybe six months apart." She made a quick sign of the cross, in the Orthodox way, reverse order to the Irish Catholic I grew up with then washed it down with a hearty sip of martini.

"Oh, sorry."

"Don't be. My father killed himself, one drink at a time. And my mother was a religious crazy woman. She wore herself out trying to put a stop to anyone thinking of enjoying himself. You know the old question? Which came first, the alcoholic husband or the long-suffering wife?"

"Can't say that I do, but I know a couple or two it might fit."

"Yes, well."

"So, Nikki?"

"Oh, right. I have not seen her in maybe two months. Not that we were really close or anything, but she hasn't been home for quite a while as far as I can tell and her phone is disconnected. Her car remains in the same place, in her driveway. I have a key to her house. I went through it, but nothing seemed unusual, you know? It was not trashed or ransacked or some-such."

"Husband, boyfriend, kids?"

"Not that I know about. She had a boyfriend about a year and a half ago, but he did away with her. Actually, he was keeping her on the side and had a regular girlfriend. He married that woman last spring. Nikki read about it in the newspaper."

"That's a tough way to find out."

"Yes. I think he was maybe four years older than Nikki, Bradley Cadwell. Brad the Cad we called him. He is a lawyer now. But I must be honest, she only spoke of him, I never really met him."

"But a lawyer?"

"Yes."

"Say no more."

She didn't. Instead she drained her glass and left the olives. With a nod, I had Grace mixing a new double just after her empty glass hit the bar. Things became a little bit bleary after that.

I remembered checking the rearview mirror constantly on the drive home to make sure she didn't lose me, although I couldn't swear to the exact route we took. I remembered she could drink vodka like a fish, and that she had a gorgeous figure.

9

She was trimmed as opposed to shaved and had a little Victorian-looking angel with wings sitting on a cloud tattooed on her right butt cheek. I was too drunk to read the writing that encircled the angel.

I've got a bite mark on my left nipple, scratches on my back, my bed's a mess, and the place reeks of stale spicy perfume. My head is pounding and I just finished reading a note that says she only took a hundred dollar bill from the five she gave me out of "professional consideration".

She penned her phone number at the bottom of the note, just after she wrote to hold onto her emerald green thong from Victoria's Secret should I run across it.

I needed aspirin, coffee, and a sauna. Any phone call to Kerri could wait until after those things were accomplished. And, ever the professional, I made a mental note to find out her last name.

Chapter Two

While recovering I sat in a back booth at
Moe's a little after one in the afternoon. Moe's was
my morning office at least three days a week. The
earlier sauna and aspirin were working their magic,
and the third cup of coffee kept me going until
breakfast was delivered. I was just finishing up the
last of my hash-browns, dragging the remnants
through a slick of heart-stopping hollandaise sauce
as I phoned Kerri. Her phone message kicked in, but
the voice didn't sound like her at all.

"Hey baby, thanks for calling. Sorry I'm all tied
up at the moment. Leave your name and number,
and one of us will get back to you just as soon as we
can, bye-bye."

My guess was Kerri didn't work for a
pediatrician. I checked my watch as the beep
sounded to leave a message.

"Hi, Kerri, Devlin Haskell here. Please give me
a call when you can. I'd like to schedule an
appointment so we can review some facts on your
case and I can begin my investigation. It's
Wednesday afternoon at one-thirty, you can reach
me at …."

I'll be the first to admit it was a bit presumptuous to suggest I'd be able to review facts on her case. I really only had four facts, Kerri's first name, her sister's name - Nikki, Kerri's phone number, and five, make that four hundred dollars cash in advance.

A half hour later I was behind the wheel of my car, debating about starting it up or going back into Moe's for a couple more aspirin when my phone rang. I glanced at the number coming through like I always did and just like always couldn't read the numbers.

"Haskell Investigations."

There was a very long pause on the other end before a female voice sounding somewhat confused said,
"I think I must have the wrong number," then hung up.

The phone rang again less than a minute later, I did my routine of looking at the incoming number, just like before I was unable to read the damn thing.

"Hello," I said in what I thought passed for pleasant, considering my hangover.

It was the same voice from a minute before, female, young sounding.

"Yeah, I'm calling for Devil."

"That would be me, Devlin, actually," I said, enunciating the last syllable in my name.

"What do you need, baby?" she asked, sounding decidedly unimpressed with my attempt at correction.

"I need to speak with Kerri, actually. Is she available?"

"She can't do nothing I can't do better, honey. You don't need her, do you?" She hissed the word nothing, suggesting maybe there was a space between her teeth.

"Actually, yes I do, I need to talk with her. Is she there or is there a number I can reach her at?"

"You a cop?"

"No, I'm not. But look, I'll call the cops and give them this number unless you have Kerri call me in the next half hour. If I don't hear from…" Whoever she was, she was so impressed she hung up.

I decided to venture home, grab some aspirin, maybe close my eyes for a few minutes. My mood improved as I considered I could be sitting on the easiest four hundred dollars I'd ever made.

I had just put my feet up for the briefest of moments when my phone rang. Yes, I looked at the number. No, I still couldn't read the damn thing.

"Haskell Investigations."

"Oh, no wonder Da'nita thought you were with the police. Do you always answer like that?"

I recognized her voice immediately. A hazy, torrid scene from the previous night replayed in my mind.

"Kerri?"

"Dev?"

"Yes."

"Dev, I'm returning your call. Remember? You wanted to set an appointment. I think we should. No drinks please. At least not until we're finished with the serious business," she chuckled.

"You tell me where and when."

"How about your office?"

"My office?" I swallowed, the throbbing in my head returned with a vengeance.

"Yes, that is okay, no?"

It would be okay if I had an office, so I dodged the question.

"No, I mean, look, I think I owe you at least dinner, after last night and all. You free this evening?"

"I can be."

"Okay, tell you what. You know Malone's?"

"It is a place on the corner, with the black awning."

"Yeah, you got it. I'll make reservations, say seven, seven-fifteen, no alcohol. At least not until we're done discussing. Sound okay?"

"Yes."

"Great. Oh, Kerri, can you bring some pictures of your sister? And I'll need her address and if you have a spare key to her place that would help too."

"Maybe I should just bring her."

"Huh?"

"Joking, never mind. I will see you at Malone's."

I was pretty sure I wouldn't need a reservation, but phoned anyway.

"Yeah, I'd like a table for two at about seven tonight."

"Not a problem, you won't need a reservation."

"Let me make one anyway, so I look important."

"A reservation here is gonna make you look important? Jesus."

"See you at seven."

14

Chapter Three

I had a nap, cleaned up a little, and actually changed the sheets. I stole some flowers from the neighbor's after I remembered I was supposed to water the garden while they were out of town. Showered, shaved, found a clean shirt, and some fairly clean black jeans. I topped it off with my black leather jacket that a former girlfriend once described as making me look 'incredibly sleazy'.

I was at Malone's five minutes early and then waited twenty minutes nursing a Coke before Kerri arrived. Malone's is one of those restaurants with passable side dishes, great steaks, a nice bar, and no surprises. It was about half full, which seemed rather good for a Wednesday night in the midst of the Great Recession. As far as I was concerned, it was a good steak place with a limited wine list and cheap drinks. Ambience was not its strong suit. The placemat was white paper sporting purple script that spelled out Malone's and looked like it was designed by a fourteen-year-old girl serving detention after class.

I was seated in the back, close to the kitchen door, which pushed in or out, depending, thumping loudly every time it swung closed. So much for reservations.

Even the women sitting at tables cast an appraising eye for a brief moment when Kerri sauntered through the front door, stopped, and scanned the room. She was wearing some sort of black stretch pants which, were indeed stretched, wonderfully. Sling back heels, dangerously high, clicked across the oak floor. Conversation halted as she strutted past.

She wore a black strappy T-shirt, emblazoned with stretched, bouncing white letters that proclaimed 'St. Paul Girls Are Hot!' I could only imagine the thing must have shrunk in the wash. She smiled and nodded in my direction as she made her way to my table. Two waiters fought to pull her chair out, then lingered over her, fawning and leering down her top as she sat.

"Oh, thank you. Nothing for the moment," she said, dismissing them before turning her attention to me.

I waited until the two were in full back pedal. Her perfume began to waft around the table before I spoke.

"Do you always have that effect?" I chuckled.

"Effect?" She seemed genuinely unaware.

"Nothing, nice to have the service I guess." I'd never seen a waiter pull a chair out for someone at Malone's before.

"I guess you did not need a reservation?" she said, looking at the handful of empty tables then stared past my shoulder as the kitchen door thumped closed.

"That won't do. Excuse me." She smiled at the waiter hovering in the shallows of her perfume. "Is there another table we could have, please? This door banging will drive me cuckoo." She smiled, her accent suddenly stronger. I thought she set her shoulders back ever so slightly, batted her eyes, and maybe added a slight bounce or two to her request.

"I can take care of that for you. Is there a table you'd prefer?" He smiled down at her, then quickly stepped to the side to pull out her chair, hovering again to catch a glimpse as she bent forward. That was twice in the same night with the chair pulls.

"How about that one in the corner?" she said, crinkling her eyes and grabbing his forearm.

"Not a problem, ma'am. Please, allow me," he said, leaping across the room.

"I don't believe it," I said once we were reseated and he'd danced off, attending to a table that had been attempting to get his attention for the past few minutes.

"What? I would have lost my mind with that door."

"No, I mean the chairs pulled out for you, the waiter fawning all over."

"Is it not what they are supposed to do?"

"Yeah I get that, but here? At Malone's?"

"At anywhere, Dev, there's nothing wrong with a little manners once in a while. Oh here, a picture of Nikki," she said handing a folded manila envelope across the table to me. "I placed a house key in there along with her telephone bill and a credit-card bill. That man, Brad the Cad, his phone number is in there, too."

I unfolded the envelope, reached in, and began to pull out what felt like a photo.

"It may be wise to wait," she said nonchalantly.

I glanced down at the photo and focused on two naked women standing on a beach. One of the women was Asian. I attempted to focus on the other. I registered red hair, boobs, and tan lines before I shoved the photo back into the envelope.

"Thanks for the warning, I'll study it later."

"Ma'am, sorry for the inconvenience." Our hovering waiter placed a glass of wine in front of Kerri. "Compliments of the house," he smiled.

"Oh, that is so sweet. Is that not sweet, Dev?" Again with the hand to his forearm, only this time rubbing up and down.

"Really sweet, Kerri. Could we see some menus, please?"

"A very nice wine. Perhaps you should try a glass. Did you have to send him off like that? He was only being nice."

"He can be nice to someone else's client."

"Jealous?" she asked looking evil for just half a second.

"I thought we weren't going to have anything to drink until after we discussed business?"

"Yes, that was your idea, no? But I think everything you need, at least to start, is already in the envelope." She took another sip and set the glass aside.

"What's with the naked photo?" I asked.

"The envelope has her address. A key to her front door. It is a duplex, she has the top one. Her name is on the mailbox. Her last name is Mathias."

"Kerri. The photo?"

"Ma'am." The waiter suddenly hovered from out of nowhere, carefully presented Kerri with her menu, then quickly discarded another in my general direction.

"I can get you something not on the menu tonight. We have a wonderful steak, stuffed with smoked oysters and served with a special red wine sauce. Comes with whatever else you'd like."

Kerri giggled, shrugged her shoulders, smiled sexily and said, "I'm sorry, the smoked oysters, they give me the shits. I think maybe just a salad, oil and vinegar. Does that come with maybe a cracker?"

"If you want it to."

"I do."

"Very well, ma'am," not even blinking.

"I might try that steak, what was it again?"

"Actually I think there was only one left. I can check and see if someone hasn't already taken it," implying it was no longer available.

I stared for a long moment.

"Give me the rib-eye, rare, hash brown potatoes, French dressing with blue cheese on my salad. I'll take a Jack Daniel's on the rocks. A double." Then gave him a nod that suggested '*Got it?*'

"Very good, sir. More wine, ma'am?"

"That sounds very good, thank you."

I watched him saunter away, then took a deep breath to put him behind me. I didn't mind him hovering, for a bit, but he was close to becoming a pest, and I was the schmuck who was going to get stuck with the bill in the end.

"Are we not happy after last night?" Kerri's eyes flashed over her wine glass.

"No, I mean yes, yes, I'm happy. And by the way, thanks. That was very nice," wishing I could remember more of what had happened as I thanked her.

"Nice had nothing to do with it." Her eyes flashed.

Over the course of dinner and more wine, Kerri effectively dodged my question of the naked photo at least half a dozen times. Nikki didn't seem to have had any full-time employment. A couple of vague cleaning jobs, some house-painting gigs. She'd been a waitress, a bartender, done childcare.

"Did she file taxes?" I asked.

"Taxes?"

That spoke volumes, about both women, actually. As enjoyable to look and leer at as Kerri was, I felt there was something, or maybe, just something missing.

Chapter Four

Eventually we finished up the small talk. Even optimistic old me caught on that nothing was going to happen tonight beyond dinner. The bill dutifully washed up on my shore, five glasses of wine for Kerri at twelve bucks each.

"You like the wine?"

"It was just okay."

"Okay?" I tried to maintain my composure at sixty bucks worth of okay. My steak was a bare two dollars more than one of her glasses of wine.

"Well, he was so sweet and I didn't wish to hurt his feelings," she said, then drained her glass. The waiter was nowhere to be seen so I signed the tab and pulled Kerri's chair out all by myself.

"Thank you, Dev. Shall we talk again, maybe in two days time? You should find her by then, no?" She was walking toward the door at this point, half talking to me over her shoulder.

A waiter nodded, then smiled at her from across the room, called out what sounded like genuine thanks. The bartender waved good night to her like Oliver Hardy, a large paw up at shoulder height, fingers wiggling next to his idiotic grin. Other heads turned to appraise her from the rear then nodded approval as she strutted past, heels clicking, hips inviting.

"I'll see what I can learn. Who knows, maybe she just went to Disney World or something."

"Do you think, maybe?" she asked, sounding serious, as if she might actually be entertaining the suggestion.

"Well, maybe, but I doubt it. Let's see what I can come up with."

Once outside I asked,

"Where are you parked? I'll walk you to your car."

A little dark blue sports car, a BMW actually, suddenly pulled to the curb. I had no idea what model it was, other than out of my price range.

"Oh, no need, here is my car." She nodded at the BMW and walked around the front to the far side just as the driver's door opened and the hovering waiter jumped out. The car came up to just above his knees.

"All set to go for you, ma'am. I left my card on the console," he added half under his breath, glanced at me, then said, "In case you need anything or forgot something, ya know."

"Oh, you are so kind." She smiled and continued to stand just a little too close. He had to brush against her, heavily, to get out of the way so she could crawl behind the wheel.

"I'll call you later, Kerri," I said to her tail lights as she drove off, signaled, and took a quick left around the corner. I repeated her license plate number over and over in my head until I reached my car and wrote it down on the back of a dry-cleaning receipt. I toyed with going down to the Spot, thought better of it, and went home. The last vestige of Kerri's lingering perfume hit me as I opened the front door.

Chapter Five

The duplex where Nikki lived was located on the East Side in a corner of town dominated by the stark, imposing edifice of St. Simpert's Catholic Church. Simpert was an eighth-century Benedictine abbot, nephew of Charlemagne and patron saint of Augsburg, Germany. I'm sure he was unaware of the embarrassment his name would bring to generations of American grade-school kids playing on his teams.

A solid blue-collar neighborhood up through Lyndon Johnson's presidency, the East Side had been in a gradual downward spiral for the past fifty plus years. Drafty, old, two, and three-story wood-frame homes had been cut up and sectioned into rental units on block after block. A number of the old neighborhood bars still catered to the locals, but the locals had changed and now the bars sported metal detectors, hip hop, and bouncers. In the ecumenical spirit of the times women of all races hustled themselves on street corners. Child thugs in hooded sweatshirts offered a pharmacy of escape options. The police cars traveled in pairs.

Nikki's duplex was second from the corner and sported shabby, brown asphalt siding that was supposed to look like brick. Eighty years on and in the afternoon drizzle it just looked like shabby asphalt siding. The floor on the wraparound porch had apparently been painted gray years back, but the paint had pretty much peeled off exposing bare wood, which accounted for the buckled floor. A post supporting the leaky roof stood dangerously close to a rotted two-foot hole in the porch floor. A rutted, muddy driveway turned to weeds toward the rear of the house then just disappeared altogether beneath the rusting remains of a green Bonneville. The car, or what was left of it, sat on cinder blocks. The hood and the engine were missing, and five year's worth of dead leaves rotted beneath the thing. Kerri had mentioned that her sister's car had been parked in the driveway. I hoped she wasn't referring to the Bonneville.

The front door had probably been elegant at one time. The glass, long gone, was replaced with weathered plywood. A jagged hole had been drilled through the plywood, slightly off center, presumably to look from the inside out. Although closed, the door was unlocked. Two black metal mailboxes were mounted just to the left of the front door. The top one had a faded, handwritten piece of cardboard taped to the front. #2 Nikki. No last name.

I pushed the door open and followed the squeak inside. There was a small hallway that led to a grimy door beneath a staircase. The number 'one' had been drawn on the door in black marker. The staircase, sporting a railing of 2x4's painted flat gray ran up the right hand wall to a landing where it turned left and went up another half dozen steps. The wall was stained and dingy from years of grimy hands running up and down. The 2x4 railing wiggled dangerously as I began to climb the stairs. The air held just the slightest hint of mouse.

Nikki's grimy apartment door sported four panels that had been painted an icy flat white a very long time ago. You'd have to look hard to find an uglier color. On the door a haphazard 2 had been drawn in black marker. The door was locked, although by the look of the frame and the panel next to the doorknob, the door had been kicked in more than once.

Surprisingly the key turned the lock, and I pushed the door open then stood on the small landing with my ears perked. I heard nothing. Eventually I stepped inside and closed the door behind me. The place was soulless, nothing on the walls. A single recliner looked orphaned in what served as a living room. No carpet or rugs, just dull, worn wooden flooring. No end tables, no lamps, no television, not so much as a radio or a clock. The kitchen was much the same, an old refrigerator, bare. Empty cabinets, one plate, a coffee mug, no silverware. No pots, no pans, no food, no soap.

Amazingly, the bedroom sported a bed and a dresser. The dresser drawers, more empty than not, held a pair of jeans, and a T-shirt. In the small closet a cheap, dark blue rayon robe hung alone on a nail. I could still detect faint perfume from the robe.

What looked to be a full roll of toilet paper hung in the bathroom. A white plastic shower curtain was draped across the shower entry. A full container of Soft Soap sat on a corner ledge in the fiberglass shower. No toothbrush, no toothpaste, no makeup. No shampoo or conditioner for a redhead with hair down to her shoulders.

There was no wastebasket to go through. No computer with files to copy. No stacks of mail to sort. No phone with a message light blinking. Nothing. So had Nikki lived here and moved everything out? Recently? I couldn't imagine someone living like this for very long, say more than an afternoon, and then only if she had a good book and at least a six-pack.

I did a brief walk through twice more and came up with even less. There was nothing there. It was like the place was a sleazy hotel room and somebody forgot a couple of things in their haste to just get out. I thought maybe Brad the Cad, the ex-boyfriend/lawyer, might be able to shed some light on things.

Chapter Six

Bradley Cadwell answered on the third ring.

"Hi, Brad," was actually how he answered.

"Brad Cadwell, please," I said.

"You got him," he said, still pleasant but the hint of a question in the tone.

"Mr. Cadwell, my name is Devlin Haskell. I'm hoping you might be able to help me with some information. I'm …"

"Concerning?"

"A woman by the name of Nikki Mathias."

There was a pause. In retrospect I think Brad was choosing his words carefully.

"I haven't seen Nikki for at least a year. More than that actually, much more. No, I doubt I can be of any help to you."

"I wonder if we could talk, anyway, at a time of your convenience. I'm attempting to locate her and…"

"I told you I haven't seen her in maybe two years. I wouldn't know where she was. I'm married now. Happily. I really don't think …"

"Could I just get five minutes of your time? That's all I ask. Or, I could come to your office?"

Another pause, a little longer.

"Okay, but not here. I could meet you tonight I suppose, but I really have no idea where she is. It's been over two years since I last saw her."

"I can appreciate that. I promise I won't take more than five minutes of your time. You just name the place."

"A place. Okay, there's a bar in downtown. You familiar with St. Paul?"

"Yes," I replied.

"You know where Henry's is, across from the Hilton?"

"I do. Would six be too early for you?" I asked.

"I'll make it work. Tell me your name again?"

"Haskell, Devlin Haskell."

"All right, Mr. Haskell."

"Thanks, I appreciate your time. Look, you'll be able to recognize me. I'm a dapper guy, stunningly handsome. I'll be wearing a black leather jacket, St. Paul Saints baseball cap, and blue jeans. I'll be sitting at the bar in Henry's at six o'clock tonight."

"I'll find you," he replied and hung up. If he was smart, I figured he would be checking me out right now.

I phoned Aaron LaZelle, a cop I know, and ended up leaving a message. Then decided to drive to the BMW dealership out on I-94 and look at little sports cars. If the note I wrote on the dry-cleaning receipt could be trusted, Kerri drove a Z4. I looked at one at the dealership. A roadster with a retractable hardtop. Twenty-four miles to the gallon, as it turned out. Three hundred thirty-five horsepower, and I was right... it was way out of my price range.

They started at sixty-one five and headed north based on extras. I've owned houses that hadn't cost that much.

Chapter Seven

I was sitting at the bar in Henry's fifteen minutes early, nursing a root beer and waiting for Brad the Cad to show up. A few minutes before six, two guys entered through the side door, passed eight or ten open stools, sat down beside me and proceeded to work hard to ignore me. They ordered beers, Summit Extra Pale, then embarked on a forced conversation involving what could only be a fictitious office tryst. They had the look of college jocks, former college jocks. The muscle had, if not quite turned to fat, been at least downgraded from prime A category. I waited a few more minutes and at ten past six, Brad the Cad arrived, stylishly late.

He had the former college jock look too. Maybe a little less extra weight, say ten to fifteen pounds as opposed to the twenty-five apiece the guys next to me sported. I guessed they had probably all played on the same hockey team. They had that hockey look noses broken at least once, scars along the chin three to five stitches long, skater's thighs. Being oh so clever, they all made eye contact for a brief nanosecond as Brad walked past and stood next to me.

"Excuse me, Devlin Haskell?"

I was the only guy in the place wearing a black leather jacket and a St. Paul Saints baseball cap, so it wasn't really rocket science. Brad the Cad stood about five foot eleven, short cropped blonde hair, blue eyes, nice-looking guy about thirty-three, thirty-five tops. As he held out his hand to shake mine, he smiled.

"Brad? Thanks for coming. Hey, please call me Dev. Very nice to meet you."

He had a solid grip, but he wasn't giving me the I'm a real man squeeze. He looked me in the eye, confident but not cocky.

"Yeah, well like I said… I'm not sure I'll be of any help."

"You never know. Look, I promised I'd take just five minutes of your time. Would you feel more comfortable if we got a table?" I asked.

"No, here will be just fine." He didn't look at them, but he'd included the two ex-jocks in his comment, whether he knew it or not.

"We can get a table for four if you'd prefer," I said.

"Huh?"

"Your pals, not a problem with me." I nodded in the direction of the two. The larger one slid off his stool, about six four, chin jutted out a bit. He glanced at Brad.

"Hey, did I see you skate somewhere? Not Minnesota," I asked, making it up as I went along.

"Fighting Sioux," he answered before he caught himself.

Every once in a while I guessed blindly and it panned out.

"Yeah, North Dakota," his pal added almost simultaneously.

"We all played together up there," Brad replied. "Look, Dev, like I said I haven't seen Nikki for almost, well, for a very long time. And, I'll be honest, you probably already know the last time we parted it wasn't on the best of terms."

"Actually, no, I know no such thing. In fact, I'll be perfectly honest, I know absolutely nothing. Except that she's supposedly missing and her sister wants me to find her."

"Her sister?"

"Yeah."

"I didn't know she had one," Brad said.

"You dated her, I mean Nikki, awhile back?"

"Dated? Yeah sort of, look here's the deal. We met her, we all did. She was the entertainment for a bachelor party we attended. I called her on a couple of occasions, maybe a month, six weeks apart. But that was before I was married," he added hastily.

"Me too."

"Me three," the pal on the stool added with half a chuckle.

"So this was a professional arrangement?"

"Initially." Brad frowned and nodded. The two friends nodded as well.

"Any of you seen her in the past year?"

They all shook their heads. The one who'd stood initially, reached for his beer, took a long sip, then set the beer down. We were just guys talking now.

"So how'd you leave it with her? Did you just not call?"

They looked from one to the other, and Brad answered.

"That was sort of the deal breaker. See, I met her to sort of end things. She had started contacting me, and I didn't need any trouble. She went ballistic, crying, screaming how could I do this to her? Not fun. And I purposely set our meeting up in a public place. Mears Park, about three o'clock on a sunny Saturday afternoon. I thought it would be safer. God, el wrongo! People were grabbing their kids and hustling out of the park. She was swearing. She even took a swing at me. Jesus, I'd just passed the bar exam. I was about to be engaged, not the sort of attention I wanted or needed."

"When I heard that, shit, I just never called her again," this from the pal still sitting.

"Me neither. She was fun, but who needs it? Plus, the whole hooker thing. I mean I got a kid." The pal standing took another sip, a long one.

"She phoned me about a week later," Brad said. "And she threatened to post pictures on the Internet, tell my girlfriend, all sorts of threats. She wanted ten grand. I mean, she was blackmailing me, or trying to. I just let her rant and then told her I'd taped the call."

"Did you?"

"No, but she'd left a message on my phone earlier that day a couple of minutes of her screaming about the same sort of shit, you know, posting pictures, but she never mentioned any money in the message. Anyway, I told her I taped the call and I'd send her a sample. I sent her the phone message she'd left, and that was the last I heard from her, ever. So anyway that's why Barry and Greg are here, I or we thought maybe this was a setup too, you know? Blackmail me or us, again."

When Brad mentioned their names, Barry and Greg nodded, like they were just being introduced over a casual beer instead of being fingered as call girl's customers and potential blackmail targets.

I reached into my pocket and pulled out the photo of Nikki and the smaller Asian woman, both naked with tan lines. There were two guys standing alongside and behind them on a beach, maybe a lake, maybe the ocean, hard to tell. The Asian woman had a sunburst or something tattooed around a pierced navel.

"Is this Nikki?"

"Yeah." Brad nodded, but looked deadly serious. Barry and Greg passed the photo back and forth. They nodded as well. No one joked.

"You know either of those guys in the photo? Or maybe where it was taken?"

Barry looked at the photo again, shaking his head 'no' as he stared.

"Any of you happen to know who the other woman is?"

Head shakes all around.

"Did you ever meet at Nikki's?" I asked hoping to get a line on what was up with the place. They all shook their head 'no' again.

"I always met her in a bar. Then, well... I'd have a room lined up somewhere and we'd go there," Barry said.

"To tell you the truth I was always a little leery about getting bushwhacked," Greg smiled at the term. "You know, some guy hiding in a closet with a baseball bat or the cops come knocking on the door and it was a set up and now I'm really screwed. I, well, I paid her and then just took her back to where her car was once we were finished. We never spent the night together or anything."

I couldn't help but think, 'oh well, since you didn't spend the night together I guess that makes it okay', you idiot.

"Did you know where she lived?"

All three shook their heads.

"What kind of a car did she drive?"

Three completely blank looks from one to the other.

"What did she charge?"

"Usually about two…"

"Don't answer that," Brad interrupted, cutting Greg off.

"Okay," I said.

"Look, Dev, like I said before. I don't think we can be of much help. None of us have seen her for quite a long time. We've no idea where she could be or even who would know." Greg and Barry nodded in agreement.

I asked Brad, "What about the pictures of you she threatened to post on the Internet?"

"That was the screwiest part, or one of them. She never took a photo of me, not even with her phone. The places we got together, I arranged them so it's not like she could have had them bugged. She never knew where we would end up. I don't ever recall so much as holding her hand in public. It was strictly business, very private and yeah, believe me, I know it was really stupid, on a number of levels."

I had to agree.

"Sorry, wish I could help you more but that photo you passed around, that's the first time I've even seen Nikki in almost a year and a half, God's honest truth. After the blackmail threat, I purged all my records of anything to do with her. I wouldn't know how to contact her if I wanted to, which I don't. Look, we're expecting. My wife, Linda and I. The last thing I need, or any of us needs right now is Nikki coming back and holding us up. God, I'd go right to the cops."

More nods of agreement.

I left shortly after that. Nice enough guys who'd been really stupid and instead of giving me any answers just left me with more unanswered questions. I shook hands all around, threw a twenty on the bar and told them the next round was on me.

Chapter Eight

Aaron LaZelle's call woke me up at 8:45 the next morning. Okay, I was awake but I was in the lounging mode, still in bed staring at the ceiling.

"You dipshit, don't tell me you're still in bed!"

"Mom, is that you?"

"Look, dopey, I'm about four blocks from that flophouse you live in. Meet me at the Donut Hole for lattes and French donuts. I'll start without you. Oh and you're buying!"

"Give me twenty minutes."

"Make it ten, I don't have that much time," Aaron replied and hung up.

I levitated out of bed, threw on a semi-clean golf shirt, last night's jeans, and a sport coat from a few nights back, that I hadn't hung up yet. Just to be nice, I tossed four or five Tic Tacs in my mouth and chewed them up as I stuffed the Nikki beach photo in my pocket and walked down the block to the Donut Hole. It was barely past nine in the morning and the cloudless sky held the promise of becoming beastly hot.

The Donut Hole occupies the corner of a five-story red stone building built as a hotel in 1889. The building sat derelict for most of the 1970s before getting revamped into designer condos in the '80s. The place, the Donut Hole that is, has excellent latte's, fantastic high-cholesterol pastries, and a pleasant female staff more tattooed than not. Aaron had just finished ordering when I walked in.

"Make it a double latte, and two of those French donuts. He'll pay." He nodded in my direction.

I nodded back to the girl at the counter. She was pretty without makeup, and might have been prettier had it not been for the sky blue hair, a five-pointed star tattooed on either side of her neck, and what looked like a bouquet of a dozen roses covering her chest.

"Another double latte and one French donut," I said.

"On a diet?" Aaron asked.

"You must be working undercover this morning. You're dressed so nicely. Or, are you appearing in front of Internal Affairs again?"

"Jesus, don't even joke about those guys."

I'd known Aaron since we were kids. He'd been working vice for the past three or four years. One of those cops on the way up, destined for bigger things. He made lieutenant a year ago.

"You called yesterday," he said once we sat down. The donut in his hand fluttered close to his mouth, and he inhaled almost half of it before I had a chance to answer.

I nodded, my own mouth full.

"These things are great," Aaron said, spitting crumbs.

"Yeah. Hey, I'm looking for someone. A woman, but…"

"You giving up on dating guys?"

I ignored his comment and continued.

"But it's gotten screwier. I have that funny feeling I'm not being told the whole story."

"This professional or personal?"

"You think I'd call you on a personal deal?"

"Never stopped you before." He stuffed the last half into his mouth, then picked up the second donut.

"Yeah, true, but this is professional. Maybe in more ways than one. Looking for someone's sister, supposedly." I wiped my hands off on a napkin, pulled Nikki's photo out of my sport coat pocket, and handed it to Aaron. I felt something else in my pocket, reached in, and pulled out the corner of a green thong. Kerri. Small world.

"Nice tan lines on the boobs. You know these people?" Aaron commented as he studied the photo.

"The redhead's name is Nikki Mathias. Her sister hired me to find her. Supposedly been missing for a couple of months. According to her sister anyway. But things aren't adding up. Maybe a bit of professional working girl, here. I don't know anyone else in the shot."

"That's why you called me?"

"Not at first. I called you for this." I opened my wallet, took out the dry cleaning receipt with Kerri's car description and license number written on the back, then handed it across the table.

"I suppose you want to know who this is? Not caring that I would jeopardize my career were I to give you this sort of information."

"Something like that. Actually, it's my client, Kerri the sister. That's her car, or at least the car she

40

was driving. I just wondered who it was registered to that's all."

"And you think it's not hers?"

"I don't know. Like I said something's just not adding up."

"Nice set of wheels. When did you become a car buff?" he asked, reading my note.

"I was at the dealership yesterday. By the way, sixty-one G's and some change worth of nice wheels. Just wondering if it's hers. What about the photo? Recognize anyone?"

"Where'd you get this?"

"From my client. Like I said, I'm supposed to find the redhead."

"And this is the only picture she had of her sister?"

"Makes you sort of wonder, doesn't it?"

"Cash in advance?"

"Well, a retainer, and then she…"

"I don't want to know," Aaron shook his head.

"You recognize the other woman?" I indicated the photo with my chin.

"The Asian gal?"

"No, the other woman you can't see. Yes, the Asian gal, the only other woman in there."

"Oh sorry, I hadn't looked at her face yet." Aaron reappraised the photo.

"Jesus."

"Actually, I do recognize the two guys."

"Really? Great, maybe they can point me in the right direction. Any direction would help."

"Well, not unless you're clairvoyant. They're both dead," Aaron said glancing up at me from the photo.

"Dead?"

"This guy, in the back, he's Dennis Dundee." Aaron pointed to the heavier of the two men in the photo.

"Should that mean something to me?"

"Kind of a player, heavy into girls, some drugs, but always a step or two away from the action if you get me. Then, remember the meth lab that blew up, maybe late February?"

"Vaguely."

"Well, it blew the front of the place halfway across the street. Burned down what was left of the house. Luckily no one was killed. At least that's what we thought. Turns out your boy Dennis was in there. Only, the postmortem suggests he was dead prior to the explosion. It's inconclusive because there wasn't a piece of the guy big enough to properly examine."

"Great, and the other award winner?"

"Humph, Leo 'Pugsley' Tate. Man! A real sweetheart, with an alleged appetite for underage little girls. He was never too far away from whatever the latest bit of sleaze was rolling into town. Your girl here can sure pick 'em."

"You said he's dead, too?"

"Yeah, assisted suicide."

"Assisted suicide?"

"Back in maybe late March, early April of this year. He apparently blew his brains out with a colt .45, then put a second round in what was left of his skull just to be sure. The .45 still in his hand, an unsigned, typewritten note stuffed in his pocket."

"That said?"

"That said some bullshit about seeing the error of his ways, a life of sin, asking forgiveness. If I recall it was about three sentences long." Aaron licked donut crumbs from the tips of his fingers.

"And you're not buying it?"

"Well, for starters, all the words were spelled correctly and it wasn't written with a color crayon."

"So, what do you think?"

"I think the guy intended to keep the hot date he'd arranged for the following weekend with sixteen-year-old twins and the .45 slugs ruined his plans."

"For real, the date I mean?"

"Yeah, they were regulars. He'd paid their druggy mother in advance."

"God. Suspects?"

"You kidding? We'd have to rent the Xcel Center just to hold 'em all. Both of these guys aren't exactly missed by anyone. Like I said, your lady friend here could set the bar a little higher when it comes to guys she wants to stand around with when she's naked. These guys were mid-range players in the whole Internet escort-service thing. They were killed before we got a chance to nail them. You find this girl, you'll be lucky if she isn't really messed up." He handed the photo back to me.

"Huh?"

"If she's involved with these two clowns or anyone like them, be lucky if she's not dead from an overdose in twenty-four to thirty-six months. That's the upside. These creeps, they'd look at gals like this, just fresh meat as far as they're concerned. They'd want to get them out there hustling just as fast as possible."

"Charming."

"That's why I love my job. Every once in a while we nail one of these bastards."

Chapter Nine

Sitting at The Spot I decided it might be time for a little Come-to-Jesus chat with my client, Kerri Mathias. I didn't necessarily mind looking into things that were on the far side of the law, but it would be nice to know what I was getting into before I got into it. I didn't like surprises in my business.

"Let me talk to Kerri, please." I added the please as an afterthought.

"She's busy right now. Perhaps I could share a few items of interest that might allow you to broaden your horizon…" she said, a couple of telltale hisses in her pronunciation.

"Da'nita?" I guessed.

"Who this? Wilson, is that you?"

"No, actually it's me, Dev?"

"Dev? Oh, Devil, how you been, baby?"

"Thanks for your concern. I'm doing just fine."

"Look, I'll have Kerri call you back. Unless, like I said, you might want to broaden your horizon, you know."

"Sweet of you, Da'nita, but I need to get hold of Kerri. If you can just have her call me that would be fine."

"You sure? I could show you things that…"

"No doubt you could. I appreciate your effort. But I just need to talk with Kerri. Okay?"

"All right, if you say so. I'll give her the message. She's got your number?"

"Yeah, she does. At least I think she does. You got a pen? Let me give you my number just in case."

I gave Da'nita my number, then hung up, and tapped my fingers on the bar wondering what next. I didn't have to wait long. My phone rang before I had another sip of beer. As always I attempted to read the incoming number and as always, failed. I was going to have to get a pair of cheaters.

"Haskell Investigations."

It was Kerri. I thought I could smell her perfume through the phone.

"How are you, Dev? Have you found Nikki?"

"Amazingly no, I haven't. At least not yet. But I've come up with a lot of questions. Can we get together and go over some things?"

"What kind of things?"

I wasn't going to get into anything with Kerri while I was in The Spot bar. And I certainly wasn't going to get into anything with her over the phone. I like to watch people when they lie to me.

"Just some general background info that might speed things up. Can we get together tonight?"

"I wish we could but I have an appointment that will probably run late, very late."

I didn't need any detail on the appointment.

"How about breakfast tomorrow?" I asked. I thought I detected the slightest pause.

"Yes, I guess that would work."

"You just tell me where and when," I said, trying to hide my surprise.

"You know Bon Vie?" she asked.

It took me a moment, but I did. It was almost within sight of my front porch and didn't have a bar, which may have explained my pause. Other than McDonalds, I don't frequent many food establishments without a bar.

"Yeah, sure, perfect. What time?"

"Noon would be best," she said.

"Noon?"

"Yes, twelve o'clock, noon. Does that work for you, Dev?"

"It does, I'll see you there."

I hung up and phoned Aaron to check what he had found out on Kerri's car. I ended up leaving a message.

A few beers later I thought about dinner and then after dinner. Fortified by the beer I placed a couple of calls and ended up leaving messages at both numbers. I wasn't exactly feeling like Mr. Popular.

I woke up sometime after three the following morning. Bourbon and a book will do that to me. I'd been sleeping in my favorite reading chair, which was great for reading and not the best for sleeping. My body felt like a bent piece of plumbing pipe and I stretched and groaned on the way to bed. My joints sounded like a bowl of Rice Krispies; snap, crackle, and pop.

I stumbled out of the bathroom sometime after nine in the morning and noticed the message light blinking on my phone. The first voicemail was from Pam, one of my attempted post-dinner dates from the night before.

"Hi. Look, Dev, thanks for the invite, but I really wish you wouldn't call me... umm... ever again. I'm very happy with my life now that you're not in it, and I would prefer that I never, ever hear from you. Hope everything is going okay. Bye."

I pushed the delete button and made a mental note not to offer Pam the opportunity to enjoy an evening of my witty comments followed by mad, passionate debauchery. Which was screwier, Pam's message or my calling her in the first place?

Next message.

"Hey dipshit, you there? Call me I think I got something that might interest you. Grab that photo you showed me too, will you?"

It was Aaron. I called him back, left a message in response to his, then padded into the kitchen and made some coffee. He phoned back a minute or two later, just as I was pouring my first cup.

"Haskell Investigations."

"Christ, you sound barely awake. You keeping banker's hours over there? How soon can you meet me?"

"I'm just finishing up a meeting," I said.

"Yeah, right. Look, get dressed and meet me at the morgue in thirty minutes. I got something for you."

"The morgue? That doesn't sound good."

"Don't forget to bring that photo with you. See you there," Aaron said and hung up.

I poured my coffee into a travel mug, sipped as I got dressed, topped the travel mug off and headed out the door.

Chapter Ten

The old St. Paul morgue used to sit just below the river bluff from downtown. Perhaps, not ironically, it was built directly over the ruins of the old Washington Avenue red-light district. In the days when brothels provided clean shirts for regular customers to wear home, served decent liquor, and featured a piano player banging out ragtime. At least that was the perception.

The new, more efficient, Ramsey County Medical Examiner was a state-of-the-art facility located on the edge of an industrial area off University Avenue. If you were looking for romance, this probably wasn't the place, but time marches on. I entered the comfortable waiting room done in various tones of beige with overstuffed chairs, a flat-screen TV, and somewhat current magazines.

I sipped from my travel mug as I walked up to the nice-looking receptionist.

"Good morning. I'm supposed to meet Lieutenant LaZelle here."

"Mr. Haskell?" she said after glancing at a yellow Post-it note stuck to her computer screen.

I nodded in mid-sip. She was a fairly attractive brunette, darker skin tone. Maybe Italian, Greek, Hispanic, Israeli. It didn't matter, I'm an equal opportunity admirer of women.

"Aaron said to send you back to the cooler. Do you know the way?"

As a matter of fact I did.

"Down the hall, right?"

"Yep, all the way back," she said giving her hair a shake and a quick raise of her eyebrows.

I headed down the long hallway toward the examining area and the walk-in cooler. I think they can house up to forty or fifty bodies at a time. The few offices I could see were done in off-whites bordering on the beige side of things. The occasional tasteful framed print hung on the wall, and one got the sense this was not the sort of place for levity or office clowns. I wouldn't have fit in very well.

Once through the heavy metal door, things became very industrial. The autopsy suite, in all its clinical chill, was straight ahead. Off to one side stood a large, low-dose radiation scanner. To my immediate left, Lieutenant Aaron LaZelle was chatting with an attractive blonde of about forty with her hands stuck in the pockets of her white lab coat.

"What'd I tell you, Doc? Doesn't he look like he should be in your cooler?" Aaron said.

She chuckled but didn't say 'no'.

"Oh, I'm sorry. Pretending to look like you're working? You must be undercover," I replied.

"Let's get started." Aaron gestured toward the massive walk-in cooler, all stainless steel, not that the occupants cared.

"Oh, Doc, the world's top crime investigator, Devlin Haskell of Haskell Investigations. Dev, Dr. Mallory Bendix, medical examiner extraordinaire and big fan of mine."

"Dr. Bendix, nice to meet you," I said then waited for her to say please call me Mallory or Mal or Doc or Snookums. She didn't.

I'm going to blame a walk-in cooler full of bodies to her not being bowled over by me. There are some things even my charm can't overcome. I thought it might be wise to hold off on the stiff jokes, at least for the moment.

"You got that photo?" Aaron asked, following sexy little Dr. Mallory into the cooler. It was obvious the two of them had already gone through this drill. They walked directly to a stainless-steel drawer, number seventeen, labeled Doe, Jane. Aaron stood to the side as the good doctor pulled the drawer open, then unzipped the heavy, black body bag, gradually revealing a small dark-haired female.

"You gonna hang onto that photo all day?" Aaron asked, breaking me out of my trance. He grabbed the photo from my hand as he asked, "You okay, Dev?"

I nodded, taking a deep swallow. The fans were running continually so that you had to raise your voice slightly to be heard over the noise. Even with the fans, there was still that hint of decomposition in the air. The woman laid out in the drawer was the Asian beauty in the photo on the beach standing naked next to Nikki. Only now her lips were blue, the left side of her face was bruised purple, and her nose had been broken. There were bruises up and down her arms, and a larger one on her rib cage. Her

52

breasts, once the pride of the beach, looked like damaged fruit resting on her chest. The sunburst tattoo surrounded her navel.

"Well Doc, at least we got a photo of her in happier times. No name?" Aaron looked at me for a possible update.

I shook my head no.

"I'd like to make a copy of that photo if I may, and add it to our file," Dr. Mallory said.

"Make two, one for you, and one for Dev, here. I'll keep this. It's evidence," Aaron said, then smiled as he handed her the photo once she pushed the drawer closed.

I could have protested, but it wouldn't have gotten me anywhere. There's nothing like looking at a dead body to take the wind out of your sails.

Just outside the door of the building Aaron paused next to his car resting in a no parking zone.

"Man, the old Doc there is a little cutey, isn't she?"

"I don't know. It must have been the setting. I didn't pick up any vibes."

"You just don't know a good thing when you see it."

"And you're working Vice?"

"Oh Jesus, relax will you? Doesn't mean I can't enjoy a couple of the finer things in life. Anyway, I ran down that license number you gave me. You really struck pay dirt with this client of yours. You got a photo with a Jane Doe homicide who's been cooling her heels in the meat locker here for six weeks. Two former lowlifes, one blown up and the other blown away. And it's all tied together with a beautiful redhead who seemed to just vanish into thin air. Meanwhile her sister's driving around town in a car leased to Lee-Dee Enterprises."

"Lee-Dee? Never heard of 'em. What do they do?" I asked.

"Well, for starters they don't do anything, anymore. Lee-Dee, Leo Tate, Lee and Dennis Dundee, Dee, ring any bells? Most likely bogus from the start, just a tax dodge so they could write off the wheels."

"The two guys in the photo?"

"Yeah, the two dead guys in the photo, Lee-Dee. Now this gal, and by the looks of her I'd guess she didn't exactly go peacefully."

"You think that photo will help ID her?"

"Can't hurt. What might help a lot more is if I talk to the sister, what's her name, Kerri?"

I nodded.

"You gonna see her anytime soon?"

There was that little voice in my head again, saying *tell him you dope, yeah, I have a lunch date with her in about forty-five minutes. You should come along.*

Instead I said,

"I don't know when I'll see her next. How 'bout when I do, I give her your number? She can give you a call."

Aaron gave me a long look, then shook his head.

"You can do what you want, free country and all that. But you've seen some of the action you're getting involved with stretched out in the cooler here this morning. That body bag didn't get your attention. Nothing I say will. Just know, if someone else gets hurt and I find out you're holding back on

54

me because you thought you could take care of it or some bullshit 'my client's rights' brain-fart sort of thing, then you got me on your ass, big time." Aaron gave me a slight nod then pulled his car door open and climbed in.

"I'll keep it in mind. Try and stay on your good side," I said, hoping I didn't sound too worried, depressed, anxious, cocky, or just plain stupid.

Chapter Eleven

It was eleven-forty, I'd just sat down at a
corner table in Bon Vie. I stared out the window at
the traffic. Bon Vie is a nice place, small, maybe
just eight or ten tables, fourteen-foot ceilings
covered in stamped tin and painted flat black and
gold. Marble topped tables, pastel walls dotted with
original artwork, a trendy sort of place, no bar. I was
twenty minutes early for my Kerri breakfast at noon.
I ordered a mug of coffee, remembering I left my
travel mug on a stainless-steel counter at the
morgue. They could keep the damn thing. It wasn't
worth going back there just to get the mug. I could
steal another one anytime I wanted.

I think I was on my third refill when Kerri
waltzed through the door a good thirty minutes late.
I'd been withering under the stares of the rather
large hostess who must have concluded I was some
sort of groveling, love-sick puppy about to get stood
up.

Kerri's appearance did nothing to help. She was
eye stopping in some sort of white knit top, about
four sizes too small, jeans that fit like a surgical

glove, and hair damp with that fresh out-of-the-shower look.

"Oh Dev, I was out late last night," she said bending her head down so I could kiss both her cheeks before she sat. Once seated, she shook her hair back and forth a few times. I thought the two guys at the table next to us were going to have heart attacks. I didn't mind them staring and ogling, but the least they could have done was pay for our breakfast.

"Meeting last night go into extra innings?" I asked.

"Meeting? Oh no, just running late ever since I got out of bed this morning."

I was going to say something about the long drive home once she got out of bed but decided instead to be clever.

"Oh, found something of yours," I said reaching into my pocket and pulling out the green thong, then cleverly handed it to her across the table. I heard a fork bounce off a plate, one of the guys next to us.

"That certainly is not mine."

"Come on, it's green." I forced a laugh, my hand still extended across the table, the thong hanging out either side of my fist, face reddening by the second.

"Yes, I see that. Do you not listen? My thong was Emerald Green, from Victoria's Secret. My God, that thing looks like it was on special at one of the Dollar Stores. You are either sleeping with high school girls or you should find perhaps a little higher class woman."

I quickly stuffed the thong back in my coat pocket. If I'd had a tail, I could have tucked it between my legs.

"Just black for me," she said to the waitress who poured coffee while I sat there red-faced.

"Give me a minute to look at the menu." I didn't add and collect myself.

The waitress gave me a look that wondered what in the hell I'd been doing for the past fifty minutes, nodded, and turned to the two guys at the table next to us, both of them leaning in our direction with their ears cocked.

After a long moment of scanning the menu, Kerri looked up at me, did a sexy little hair shake again just in case I'd forgotten who was in charge.

"So, Nikki?" she said, raising the coffee mug to her lips.

"Yeah Nikki. Where to start? I guess the beginning. The first thing would be I talked to your friend Brad the Cad."

"Actually, I think I said I had never even met him."

"You did as a matter of fact, and he more or less confirmed that. I feel fairly certain that he hasn't seen Nikki for quite some time. He told me he hasn't seen her or been in contact with her for well over a year and I've no reason to doubt him."

"All right," she said with a nod.

If I was getting to her in any way, she gave no indication.

"I'll get to her apartment in a moment, but first tell me what kind of a car did she drive?"

"Her car? I don't know. I mean, it was blue. I really don't know cars, to tell you the truth. Didn't you look at it when you were over there?"

"You mean the one in the driveway?"

"Yes."

"There wasn't a car in the driveway. Well, except for this rusted green hulk without an engine, up on blocks in the back…"

"Dev, that was not her car. It is a pile of junk, no? That is the landlord's car. It has been there for as long as, well, it has been there forever. So, where is her car? Someone must have taken it." She sounded genuinely concerned.

"I don't know. I don't know what kind of car it was. I don't know if she even had one."

"I told you she had a blue car."

I didn't add, since it was blue, it could be that little Z4 you're driving around in, compliments of the deader-than-a-door-nail Lee-Dee boys.

The waitress returned and we placed our order. She topped off Kerri's coffee, I waved her off on mine.

"Tell me about the apartment," I said.

"The apartment?"

"Yes." Was I detecting a chink in the armor, a crack in the wall, a slight stall tactic?

"Well, if you saw it, there's not much to tell. In some way she lived her life like a nun or something. I mean, one chair, nothing on the walls. Did you see the place? You were inside? If you were inside you must admit one would never feel comfortable, yes? I was there, inside, only once or twice. But I never got past the front door. You know that chair? The one sitting all alone in the front room? That's about all I ever saw of the place. I never even used the bathroom."

"Your sister's place, and you never used the bathroom?" That sounded like no woman I ever knew.

"Yes, can you believe it? I'm not kidding, Dev I never was beyond the front door."

So much for that crack in the wall.

"Wonder why? Was she a private person?"

"No more than anyone else. I mean, she could be fun, she loved a party, liked to laugh. It is not as though she stayed locked up in that place for a day or a week."

"Where'd she work?"

"Umm, like I told you before, some clubs. She was the nanny for a woman's children for a bit. She painted a house for some guy, cleaned for a couple of women. God, she hated the cleaning. I think she lasted about two weeks doing that."

"What about the photo?"

"The photo?" she asked.

I didn't want to pull out the eight and a half by eleven color copy that snooty Dr. Mallory Bendix had made for me when Aaron confiscated the photo. Evidence. He was probably leering at it right now.

"Yeah, did you know any of the other folks in that photo? The two guys on the beach or maybe that Asian woman?"

Kerri seemed to think for a brief moment then shook her head no. This struck me as a little amazing considering she was zipping around town in a sixty-thousand-plus little blue sports car owned by the two guys. Both dead.

"No idea? Not even a guess?"

"No!" she said adamantly.

I couldn't tell if she thought I knew about the car, or even suspected. In the end it didn't matter. I paid the bill and we walked outside and stood on the sidewalk. It was a warm day, sunny heading toward oppressive. We were on the south side, the shady side of the street. The sun was coming over the roof of the one-story brick building. I was thinking about how I intended to tell her that I was quitting.

I don't know the architectural term for the building design. I'd guess it was built back around 1920. A brick structure of eight, one-story retail fronts with large plate-glass windows. The brick was set in a geometric design above the windows then capped with some sort of blond stone. All the entrances were inset maybe four feet. At the corner there was a flower shop, then the restaurant, Bon Vie, a dance studio, bakery, a hairdresser, and a couple of nondescript offices at the far end.

The sky was cloudless. I really wasn't aware of much. Kerri was saying something, but I didn't hear her. I did hear that voice again, in my head, telling me *to shake hands like a gentleman and drop this case*. When will I learn to listen?

I think I heard the shot, but I'm not really sure. One minute I'm debating about dropping the case, the next I think I'm pushing Kerri out of the way. And then there was blood. Mine, unfortunately.

Chapter Twelve

It certainly wasn't the first time I woke up in a strange room with a woman next to me I didn't know.

"I'm sorry, did I wake you? Just gotta get this blood pressure checked. There," the nurse said after a moment. "Almost good as new." She patted me on the shoulder, wrote something on a clipboard, then looked beyond me across the room to the figure lounging in a chair.

"I think he'll live. Doctor will be by around noon or so. They'll probably release him sometime this afternoon," she said.

"Good thing they went for his head. With that thick skull the bullet just bounced off," Aaron said.

"What the fuck?" I groaned.

"That's a service not covered under your insurance." The nurse giggled at Aaron.

"He wouldn't be any good, anyway." Aaron laughed as she left the room.

"What the fuck?" I repeated, groggy.

"Uh-oh, you're repeating yourself. Maybe there is some brain damage. Of course that would mean you had a brain to begin with, so that's not it. You remember anything?"

"Huh?"

"The shooting, Dipshit, the reason I'm wasting my time in this hospital with you. You remember what happened? Remember anything at all?"

"Ahhh. I remember it was really sunny. I couldn't hear anything but there was all this blood, and I think I got Kerri out of the way. Pushed her. She okay?"

"Kerri? Oh, you mean the woman you were going to tell me the next time you got together with? That Kerri? Who knows? Missing in action. Waitress in the restaurant said she ran away. Can't say as I blame her. Lunch with you would do that to just about anyone."

"I was shot? Who? Why?"

"Well, we don't know why or by who. As to where you were shot? The bullet grazed your thick skull. Looks like it was probably a small caliber, maybe a .22 short. We couldn't find the round or any impact point for that matter. Doc last night said you'd have a hell of a headache for a while but you should be okay. You heard what nurse Sweet Cheeks said. They're kicking you out this afternoon. You're just in overnight for observation. Hell, if you're injured, the hospital is the worst place for you anyway. So it'll be good to just get your worthless ass home."

"Well, I mean do you have any leads? Any idea who it was?"

"Me? Hey look, pal, this deal is out of my hands. It's an attempted homicide. Nothing I can do to help. Well, except maybe offer to give the shooter some target practice so they don't miss next time."

Chapter Thirteen

Later that morning I spent the better part of an hour being interviewed by a homicide investigator. Aaron had left by this time. Not that I could tell the investigator anything. Aside from her name the only thing I could provide on Kerri was her apparent business phone number. I didn't even have an address. When he asked me what sort of business she was in, I got pretty vague.

"I'm not sure. It was some sort of service they provided."

"Service? You mean like cleaning or accounting?"

"Well, not exactly. I'm just not sure. I wasn't investigating Kerri Mathias, I was just trying to find her sister."

"And you didn't find this arrangement unusual?"

"No," I answered, beginning to sound a little defensive.

"Really bright," he said half to himself, making a quick note.

"She came into my office and we discussed her sister. She paid me for a few days in advance.

Nothing too unusual about that." I failed to mention her hundred-dollar "professional consideration".

"She find your name in the yellow pages?"

"I don't really advertise."

"Don't advertise? Interesting. Where's your office, Mr. Haskell?"

"Well, it's not really an office. I mean, I was sort of joking there. I was in The Spot bar, actually."

"The Spot? That joint down on Randolph?"

"Yeah, you know it?"

"Afraid so," he said, not elaborating.

For the last ten minutes he complained about the Twins pitching. I told him I was a St. Paul Saints fan.

"The Saints, interesting," he said, clearly not interested, then proceeded to repeat everything he'd complained about regarding the Twins. After I mentioned my splitting headache the third or fourth time, he closed his notebook, handed me his card, and left.

Chapter Fourteen

Later that afternoon driving home, Aaron stopped and got two takeout pizzas, then ran into a liquor store and picked up a twelve-pack of Leinenkugel's.

"I don't think I'm supposed to drink alcohol for a few days," I said.

"Exactly, but I'm not making a second trip, and as per usual I'm sure you won't have enough beer for me at your place."

"Define enough?" I said.

"How's the head?" he asked ignoring my question.

"Pounding."

"You better follow the doctor's orders then and stay away from the beer. They give you some pain pills?"

"Yeah, but you know I hate even taking aspirin. I'd just as soon not take any pain killers, if it's all the same."

"Fine with me. We'll see how you do."

Being trained to spot clues I had a suspicion someone had been in my place. I think the open front door as we pulled up was my first tipoff.

"Shit. Wait here, man," Aaron said hopping out of the car and pulling a very large, black, nine millimeter handgun from underneath his shirt. I followed him up the steps and across my front porch.

He wasn't kidding, with both arms extended, the pistol moving from side to side. He was moving forward, stepping ahead with his left foot, cautiously bringing his right foot along. He carefully poked his head into my living room, and looked around the corner. I shuffled up behind him.

"Police! Don't move!" he suddenly yelled.

"Oh, for Christ sake, Dev! You almost made me drop these damn flowers."

"Stay where you are!"

"What the hell's your problem?" a woman's voice replied. The tone was familiar.

"Put your hands up!" Aaron commanded.

"Oh for God's sake, where's Dev?"

I recognized the frizzy blonde hair and the lack of compliance.

"Heidi?"

"Dev? Hell of a way to treat a girl who brought you dinner and flowers? I see you finally got someone to keep you in line?" She nodded at Aaron.

"It's okay, Aaron. She's a friend."

"Oh, just a friend?" Heidi replied.

Aaron returned his pistol to the small of his back.

Depending on the week, Heidi was a blonde or brunette. She tried being a redhead once and vowed never again. She carried a few extra pounds extremely well and had the sexual appetite of a professional athlete. She was smarter than just about

68

everyone I knew, undergraduate degree from some big-name Ivy League school, a Masters in Finance from the University of Chicago, and she traded or sold bonds, stocks, derivatives, or some damn thing. To paraphrase Woody Guthrie, she stole more money with a fountain pen then any ten guys with a six shooter.

"Sorry, Heidi, we saw the door wide open. How'd you know?"

"You kidding? It's been all over the news. 'Course, once they said someone was shot in the head yesterday and going to be released today you came immediately to mind. I thought I'd bring you a little comfort food. I got in here and the joint reeked of stale perfume. You should try a different brand. I had to open the door just to air things out."

"Heidi, Aaron LaZelle, my bodyguard. Aaron, Heidi Bauer, great friend."

"Yeah and one of the few exes who still talks to him. Actually, I figured I should get over here so you can eliminate my name from the list of the dozens of women who want to kill you," Heidi said.

"I think the list is a lot longer than that," Aaron laughed.

"I think I'll take that pain medication," I said.

"Good idea. Did you really bring dinner?" Aaron asked, missing my worried look, about the only thing Heidi did in the kitchen was make coffee.

"Yeah, sort of, I got a tub of ice cream and a frozen pizza. Let me fire up the oven."

"No need, I got take out and beer in the car." Aaron turned and walked out the front door.

"Hey, your cop friend… he seeing anyone?" Heidi asked. I'd seen that spark in her eye before.

"At least wait until after dinner, okay?" I suddenly had a pounding headache and swallowed two of the pain pills I swore I wouldn't take.

I woke in the middle of the night and used the bathroom, then climbed back into bed. Heidi was there.

"You okay?" she asked, on the verge of awake if my answer was in the negative.

"Yeah fine, I think I'll live. Heidi, thanks for being here. You're a real friend."

"Yeah and real stupid, but glad you're all right. You had me worried." Then she snuggled closer, put her head on my shoulder and started to snore softly.

I woke with the sort of headache that felt like someone was driving a rusty ten-penny nail into my forehead, slowly. It increased in ferocity the second I opened my eyes. Something was pounding on the nail in perfect rhythm to my heartbeat. A glass of water and my brown plastic prescription bottle sat on the table next to my bed. I could hear Heidi talking to someone out in the kitchen.

"'Bout time you're up. How you feeling, fathead?" Heidi was sitting on a stool at my kitchen counter, writing what looked like a doctoral dissertation on a yellow legal pad.

"I'll live, I think."

"Okay, I gotta run," she said into her phone, then turned to me. "I was just gonna leave you a note. I made you some breakfast. Well, I mean there's a jug of Minute Maid in the fridge and some yogurt. I walked up to the bakery and got some caramel rolls, but I already ate mine. I did make some coffee. I think there's a little left. You want a cup?"

70

"No, you've done more than enough. Thanks, Heidi, really nice of you. I appreciate your help."

"Yeah, well I'm taking a rain check on last night, deal?"

"Deal."

"Okay," she said standing up and giving me a light kiss on the forehead. "You look a little worse for wear. Take it easy for the next couple of days. I'll call just to check in later on, okay?"

"Thanks. Yeah, I'd appreciate the call."

"Okay, bye-bye."

She threw her purse over her shoulder and headed for the front door.

She'd left me the better part of a cup of coffee, which I drank. I ate the caramel roll in about two bites and decided I could walk the block up to Bon Vie and see if my new favorite waitress was working today. Find out what she could tell me about other day's events.

Chapter Fifteen

Her nametag identified her as Madeline, like the little girl in Paris in the Ludwig Bemelmans books. At the moment I was the only customer in the place so I took a long moment to appraise her from head to toe. I didn't recall her looking as attractive as she did today. When she saw me she glanced frantically from side to side, as if my sudden appearance had somehow cut off any escape.

"I already told the police everything I know," she stammered, backing up slightly as she spoke.

"Yeah, I know. They told me. I just wanted to thank you and hope it wasn't too traumatic. I didn't mean to scare away any customers, that's all," I said, attempting to calm her down with a casual chuckle.

"Maddie, is everything all… oh, you, we don't want any trouble," the heavyset hostess said. She was wearing large glasses, and carried a stack of menus. She looked me up and down. The large black frames were severely pointed and emblazoned with rhinestones. The lenses were thick enough to magnify her eyes, which at the moment looked a decided icy-blue.

"Hello, I'm Devlin Haskell. I was in here the other day," I said extending my hand.

"Humph, you certainly were. You absolutely ruined our lunch-hour trade. Not to mention the fact a table of three just up and left without paying. Couldn't wait to get out of here. I doubt we'll ever see them again. Then there's the matter of the front sidewalk."

"The sidewalk?"

"How could you miss it?" She motioned me to the front window, a gigantic pane of glass about ten feet tall. She stood facing the street and gestured with her chins.

"We'll never get the stain completely out of the sidewalk. I've had Arturo out there scrubbing for hours. He even used straight bleach. Nothing worked." She frowned in my direction.

"You know, I'm terribly sorry about that. Next time I have someone shoot me in the head I'll make sure they do it on the lawn."

I thought I caught a smile from Madeline out of the corner of my eye.

"What? Well, you don't look the worse for wear. Cup of coffee? I'm Amy, by the way. I own this place," she said, still not smiling. I'd have to work my magic to win her over.

"Yeah, I'd love a coffee. Actually, I'm trying to piece together what happened. I really don't remember anything other than leaving the restaurant, squinting into the sun, and the next thing I know I'm in the hospital."

"Oh, for God's sake," Amy grunted, then took three steaming mugs in one hand and waddled back to a table close to the open kitchen. A large black man, sporting dreadlocks and dressed in kitchen whites was rapidly preparing items on a tray. The chair seemed to groan beneath her weight as she oozed into it.

"Did you see anything?" I asked, nodding thanks as she pushed a coffee mug in my direction.

Madeline sat down across from me. I noticed she had dark brown eyes and a nose that wasn't petite, but was somehow sexy with her high cheekbones. There was a tiny scar on the left side of her chin, maybe a stitch or two as a child. Her skin color was what could be called Mediterranean, with thick eyebrows and long eyelashes that...

"... down on the sidewalk. Hey, yoo-hoo, are you even listening to me?"

"Yeah, of course, but tell me that again," I said, back in reality.

Amy's frown was back, followed by a sigh of frustration. "As I just said, one of our customers screeched something like 'Oh God.' The next thing I know you're down on the sidewalk. That little honey of yours hightailed it up the street and around the corner. I haven't seen someone move that fast in a long time. Maddie, you saw everything, didn't you?"

Madeline nodded, then sipped her coffee so she wouldn't have to speak.

"Tell him," Amy grunted.

Madeline turned to face me, looked down at her hands a moment as if collecting her thoughts, then raised her head and focused her gorgeous brown eyes on me.

"Well, you were standing right out front, with your back to the street. Your girlfriend was..."

"She's a business associate, a client actually."

Amy harrumphed.

Madeline nodded then continued.

"Anyway, your back was sort of halfway to the street. I was clearing a table, actually that one up there." She pointed to a table set for four directly in front of the window overlooking the blood-stained sidewalk.

"I remember watching this car. It was going real slow, and I thought the person was on a cell phone, talking, not paying attention to their driving. Then you kinda turned toward the car. There's this sort of commotion, and all of a sudden you're on the sidewalk, not moving. Your, ahhh, client took off running up the block. I remember she held her purse like it was a football."

"Did you hear a shot?"

"No, nothing," Madeline said, then sipped some more coffee.

"Triple-pane window. Thank god it wasn't damaged, cost me a small fortune," Amy interjected.

"Which way was the car going?"

"This side of the street, toward downtown."

"Did you see the driver?"

"Sort of, I mean, just a person. I wasn't paying that kind of attention. I'm not even sure if it was a man or a woman."

"Was there a passenger?"

"I don't think so, but I really can't be sure."

"Do you remember what the car looked like?"

"Not really. I don't know cars. Maybe it was black, seemed nice, newer."

"Could it have been dark blue?" I asked.

"Well yeah, I guess, maybe, I can't say for sure. I just wasn't really watching. Don't you remember anything?"

"No, at least I don't remember much. I was squinting into the sun, and then I guess I was pushing Kerri out of the way or turning or something. As you're telling me this I sort of have a hazy vision of her going wide-eyed, I just can't remember. I honestly don't know except that all of a sudden there was blood everywhere. Next thing I know I'm waking up in the hospital."

"Pushing her out of the way? Well no, actually now that you mention it, she sort of jumped and pulled you. In fact for half a second I thought she maybe hit you or something but she pulled you, yeah definitely. She sort of pulled you in front of her."

"You mean I didn't push her out of the way? Save her?"

"Well, how could you? I mean your back was to the street, you had no idea anything was going to happen, then you turned around, right? Now, she's behind you. No, she sort of pulled you in front of her, maybe, sort of like a shield or something, you know?" She shrugged her shoulders as if she was sorry to give me the bad news. I wasn't a noble hero, just some dunce who essentially got thrown under the bus.

"Hey, I could be wrong, maybe, but it sure seemed that way. You should probably give her a call? Your client."

Chapter Sixteen

After leaving Bon Vie and promising Amy I wouldn't return for a while during their lunch hour, I phoned Kerri. Or at least I tried to.

The phone rang three times, then flipped into an official message center.

"The number you have reached, six five one, blah, blah, blah, has been disconnected. No further information is available at this time."

I phoned Aaron, and as usual left a message.

"Aaron, Dev. Hey I'm among the walking wounded today. I've got a couple of questions I thought you might be able to help me on. Give me a call when it's convenient. Thanks."

He phoned back right away. Right away for Aaron, meaning the same day.

"So let me guess, you've taken it upon yourself to find out who tried to put a bullet into your fat head, and you've run into a dead end or two."

"Thanks for returning my call. Yeah, sort of. How'd you know?"

"Well, for starters, the list of people who know you and don't want to shoot you would probably be a lot shorter than the ones who do. Then there's the matter of a brief, and I emphasize brief, conversation I had with Detective Crowley in homicide. He assured me in no uncertain terms that you were of no help. I think 'worthless fuck' was the actual description. I, of course, was unable to disagree."

"Crowley, that was his name?" I said making a mental note. "To tell you the truth that whole interview is just sort of a hazy blur."

"Why would it be different than the rest of your life? What do you need?"

"I'm not sure. I tried to phone my client earlier in the day…"

"Kerri Mathias?"

"Yeah, the number I have for her has been disconnected."

"And this is news?" Aaron said sounding genuinely surprised at my reaction.

"Ahhh, well, I don't know, I thought I could at least get in touch with her. She is my client after all."

"Yeah, well, you're the great super sleuth. Find her."

"Which is why I called you."

"I've already checked. Nothing. Not so much as a driver's license for a Kerri Mathias, at least in Minnesota."

"Property records, auto, nothing?"

"Oh Jesus, Dev, let me just drop everything and look for your client. Come on. You know if you'd spring for an office instead of conducting business out of a half dozen bars maybe you'd meet a better class of clientele, at least someone who was occasionally straight with you. The way you describe this deal, it almost sounds like she gave you a roll in the hay for a down payment."

"Well…" I paused.

"Oh, man. I knew it."

"Okay, okay I get it, Aaron. You've got a point. Look, let me just say you didn't see the woman, okay. And then there's the matter of a couple of adult beverages."

"You idiot."

"Point taken."

"So what do you want? Not that I'm agreeing to help." Aaron said.

"Well, for starters, I'd like to go through your photo books, see if I come across Kerri, or maybe the sister."

"Are you sure you'd recognize them? You know they still have their clothes on in all our mug shots."

"I'll do my best."

"I'm busy now. Look, come on down tomorrow morning around ten-thirty. It'll take a good two hours to go through our books, the Vice stuff. I'll round up what I can on your pals the Lee-Dee boys. Maybe we'll get lucky. By the way, bring your wallet. You're buying lunch."

Chapter Seventeen

The following morning Aaron popped his head out into the hallway where I was waiting.

"I'm on something right now. Take a seat for about fifteen minutes," he said then quickly ducked back into the office area. There was nowhere to sit in the hallway so I leaned against the wall for twenty-five minutes until I thought my head would explode from the blinking fluorescent light overhead. I fled back down to the main floor in search of the cafeteria or at least a machine with lousy coffee. My luck held. I found the cafeteria and the coffee was lousy. I sat by myself at a table and stared absently out the window at a nondescript brick wall across the street. Twenty minutes later Aaron called to me from the doorway.

"Didn't I tell you to wait for me upstairs?"

"You did, sort of. Actually you told me it would be about fifteen minutes and to take a seat. That was an hour ago. There was nowhere to sit, unless I used the floor, and I shouldn't have to remind you I'm still recovering from my wound. Besides, I always like to have some coffee here so that any cup I have, anywhere, for the rest of the week tastes better than this rotgut."

"Yeah, you're braver than I am," he said, shaking his head at my coffee cup.

We rode a crowded elevator up three floors in silence. Walked down the hallway toward the still-blinking fluorescent light, then turned and entered a large room of cubicles. Aaron's office was in a distant corner.

His desk was piled with files, his computer hidden beneath yellow and pink post-it notes. A family photo of his parents and siblings, two brothers and three sisters from about 1995 hung on the wall.

"Make yourself comfortable, toss those files on the floor," Aaron directed. He pointed to a government-issue gray vinyl and chrome steel chair opposite his desk that looked like it been there since the Korean War.

"I got three books of shots for you to go through. Take your time, see if anything clicks. You want a water or something instead of that battery acid you're drinking?" he asked, pushing three large albums across the desk toward me.

I'm aware that having a mug shot taken isn't quite like the photo portrait experience. That aside, I was examining the images of a lot of really rough-looking women. Most of them had been booked on prostitution or solicitation charges. The obvious question was who would be desperate enough to pay these women in the first place? The hand-in-glove combination of no education and poverty seemed a likely component in their background. A lot of health and life-style issues came across. Prime among them alcohol and chemical abuse. The occasional black eye, missing teeth, battered face. A number of identifying characteristics consisted of stabbing scars, bullet wounds, and homemade tattoos with misspelled words.

So much for the fairy tale of erotic escorts in million-dollar condos or making all sorts of money just lying on your back enjoying yourself. The vast majority of the women I was looking at were old before their time. If life hadn't already spit them out, they were certainly being chewed on.

I found no one remotely resembling redheaded Nikki Mathias, nor her sister, Kerri. After an hour and a half I closed the third and final album, then returned to the second album where I had marked a page.

I opened the album and stared at three images of the same black woman. Her skin seemed to be the color of coffee with the slightest bit of cream. Her physical description listed among other things, a silver front tooth and a heart-shaped, homemade tattoo on her left breast. The tattoo was described as "Homemade, of a bluish ink in the shape of a heart with the initials DB + DB". She sported what I assumed was a chemically induced grin, her silver tooth prominent along with an eighth-inch gap between her front teeth. Her name was listed as Da'nita Bell and I guessed she might hiss as she pronounced certain words and just maybe called me Devil the last two times I spoke with her on the phone.

"What about this woman?" I asked turning the album around so Aaron could see who I was talking about.

"That's Kerri, your client?" He looked at me more shocked than surprised.

"No, but I may have spoken to her when I phoned Kerri." I went on to explain.

"So based on her first name and the fact she's got a space between her teeth, you think she might have some sort of information?"

"Couldn't hurt to ask."

"Except, I could lose my job telling you her name was Da'nita Bell and that I happen to know she spends virtually all of her free time at Boxer's Bar on East Fourth Street. You know the place?"

I nodded.

"Good, 'cause it would be against the rules for me to give you that sort information."

"I've only driven past, never been in there," I clarified.

"It's memorable," Aaron said and slammed the album closed.

Chapter Eighteen

After buying Aaron lunch, I went home to nap. The combination of a splitting headache and a pain pill had wiped me out. I woke about 4:30 from a fitful, twitch-filled nap, the pain pills seemed to have that effect on me. I sorted through my mail. It consisted of an expired ten-dollar-off coupon for an oil change and a circular announcing a cosmetic sale. Both got dumped into recycling. I decided to try and find Da'nita Bell down at Boxer's.

Boxer's is located on the corner of East Fourth Street and Garfield. The building is a two-story red-brick from 1904, according to the iron plaque just below the roof line. I'm guessing it wasn't the best of buildings in 1904, and not much had changed over the ensuing hundred-plus years.

Two feet inside the door, just as my eyes began to adjust to the dim interior, a bouncer blocked my forward progress.

"Gonna have to wand y'alls," he said looking down at me. I pegged him at about six four.

"I can save you the trouble. I got a piece on my right hip, just under the jacket. I'm licensed," I said, almost under my breath, hoping not to cause a scene.

"Really?" He nodded, ran the wand over me anyway, smiled when it chirped loudly over my hip. He ran it over and over my hip. It chirped every time, loudly announcing my armed presence to the entire bar. Not that I needed any announcement. I was the only white face in the place other than the bartender.

"That's okay, officer. Don't you worry none, go get a drink at the bar."

I was going to tell him I wasn't a cop, but what was the point? Everyone in the place was watching and knew I was armed. Just in case someone had been asleep and missed my entrance, he called to the bartender as I stepped away.

"Charles, give the good officer a drink, on the house."

The wooden floor was worn, the room was dim, neon beer signs illuminated the back of the bar. The place had a musty smell and at barely five in the afternoon the clientele looked like they'd already been there for quite a while. Despite the statewide smoking ban there were more than a couple of cigarettes glowing. Something like hip hop or rap assaulted my ears and my headache returned with a vengeance.

People resumed talking, but the level of conversation was decidedly muted. Charles the bartender gave me as slight a nod as possible when I stepped in front of him. I placed both my hands on the bar.

"Charles, I think I'll have a Coke, please," attempting polite kindness.

"On duty," he said, not really asking.

"No, I'm not a cop, honest. Your doorman made a mistake."

"A mistake," he said, sounding not at all convinced.

"I'm just here to meet someone."

"Well, in that case, since you're not a cop, it's two-fifty for the Coke."

There, I'd made my point and I could relish in the fact I was deliberately overcharged for the soft drink poured into what I guessed was a fairly dirty glass.

When Charles returned with my change I worked at being polite.

"I'm supposed to meet Da'nita Bell here. Has she been in yet?"

"What you want with her ass?"

I felt myself beginning to harbor ill will toward Charles. I decided to smile and fake it.

"Look, Charlie, how'd you like it if the city inspector showed up in here tomorrow and shut you down for a week or two because of code violations? Then maybe someone might call the license inspector and have him look into reports of underage individuals being served in your fine establishment. Maybe some reports of controlled substances being sold on the premises could reach concerned ears. Would that make your day, Charlie?"

He seemed to think about that for a moment, looked me up and down, then came up with the right answer.

"That's her, at the end of the bar."

I looked down the bar but couldn't see anyone. The place was dim, but not dark.

"Where?"

"End of the bar, you can just see her head. Hey, Da'nita," he yelled. "Wave your hand for the nice officer."

A small hand slowly rose above the bar. I could just make out dark, curly hair an inch or two above the top of the bar.

I walked down the length of the bar, rounded the corner, and nearly knocked over a small woman in a motorized wheelchair. I spilled a little Coke on her.

"Watch where you're going, asshole. You're spilling on me, wasting good whiskey," she shrieked. As she did I caught the flash of her silver tooth, caught the subtle hiss when she called me asshole.

"Da'nita?"

"Maybe, maybe not, what's it to you?"

"I wanted to talk to you for a moment, I…"

"I haven't done anything. You get away, leave me alone," she shrieked again, then began hurriedly reversing the wheelchair, ramming into a table behind her, and knocking over a couple of beer bottles. I reached over her and righted the bottles, then apologized to the couple at the table.

"Oops, sorry about that. Here, let me get you a couple more. Ouch, damn it." Da'nita raced across my foot, gaining speed backing toward the ladies room. Fortunately, no one made a move to come to her aid.

"Hey, Da'nita, hold up will you? I just want to talk, it's me, Devil. Remember from the phone?"

That stopped her, although she kept her hand firmly on the throttle, just waiting for an excuse.

"Devil?"

"Yeah, that's me. I was always calling for Kerri, remember?"

She thought about that for a moment, then said, "I might. A drink might help me remember."

"Sure, sure thing. What'll it be?"

"Make it a Cosmopolitan, with a shot of Grand Marnier on the side." The way she said it made me think it wasn't the first time she placed that order.

Chapter Nineteen

I didn't believe Charles knew how to make a Cosmopolitan, and I was sure this dump didn't stock Grand Marnier. I was wrong on both counts. I returned with her drinks after dropping two beers off at the table she'd rammed. The couple at the table grabbed the beer bottles and never said thanks. I set her drinks on a back table, sat down and pulled a chair out so she could wheel in. She did so hesitantly. I wasn't sure what she expected me to do. Finally she reached for the Cosmopolitan, sucked down a goodly portion of the thing and didn't even blink.

"Da'nita. I'm hoping you can help me. I'm having trouble getting in touch with Kerri and I need to talk to her."

She downed the Grand Marnier without so much as a shudder.

"You see that bitch, you tell her she better not cross where I'm driving. I'll run her down."

She looked serious, hit and run with a wheel chair.

"You two have a little falling out?" I asked.

"Falling out? That's your term. Shit, more like getting pushed out. The bitch fired my ass, is what she did."

"Fired? When did this happen?"

"Just the other day. Middle of the afternoon she runs in all hot and bothered. Cleans out her desk in about one minute flat, literally pushes me out the door, and leaves me sitting in the damn hallway with my thumb up a hole. Then she locks the door, runs out to her car and drives off. Never looks back. I still got all my shit in there. Think she cares? Hell no. She don't give a damn bout little ole Da'nita," she said, then drained the last of the Cosmopolitan and quickly pushed both empty glasses toward me.

"Where was this office?"

"I might take a minute to try and remember," she said, glancing at the empty glasses.

"I'll be right back," I said.

"She didn't tell you why she locked up and ran off?" I asked, sitting back down with the next round.

"She didn't say a thing."

"Where'd you say this was, again?"

"You're slick, Devil, I didn't. Right next door to that Russian store. You know the one, on West Seventh?"

I nodded.

"Kerri was always eating that red cabbage, I couldn't touch it, lord save me, that shit did something to me nice people don't talk about."

I gathered she was growing a little more accustomed to me because she only downed a third of the Cosmopolitan.

"Bitch Kerri just ran in, mumbled something about closing the business. Them damn Russians, who can even tell?"

"Russian? She's French. Isn't she?" I asked.

"French? You fall for that too, dumb ass? She was always saying that and everyone always believed her, idiots."

"She's Russian?"

"That's what I said. Were you paying attention?"

"What about her sister?"

"Sister?"

"Yeah, Nikki. She said that…"

"That? God, Nikki ain't her sister. Nikki was the only smart one. She ran off after what happened to Mai. You ask me, she's probably long gone from this town."

"Mai?"

"Yeah, little Mai. She got connected, but they had her ass on the street. Had her turning a dozen tricks a day." She was back to draining the Cosmopolitan.

"This Mai, was she Asian, small, big boobs, with…"

"Those things are fake, Devil, bolt on's, and are you listening? Why do you think she's called 'Little'? It's not because she's tall."

"Did she have a tattoo, a sunburst around her navel?"

"Her bellybutton? Yeah. Gee, Kerri and now little Mai. Wow, you are a player, aren't you, Devil?" She looked at me slyly.

"No, not really. But I might have seen Mai just lying around. Has she got a last name, Mai?"

She pushed the empty glass in front of me, downed her shot, and set the empty next to her Cosmopolitan glass.

"You saw her and you want to see her again, right? You can tell me, Devil. I might know her name. I might know lots of what went on there. Maybe all sorts of things I'm not supposed to know. You said you saw her? Little Mai?"

"Yeah, but just for a minute."

"She good, she's that fast."

"No, I didn't mean it like that, and I don't really want to see her again."

Da'nita nodded at the empty glasses. When I returned with a new round I thought she was looking slightly glassy-eyed. Her head seemed to wobble for a brief moment.

"So, you were gonna help me get in touch with Kerri and tell me what went on there."

"You sure you're not a cop?"

"No, I'm not a cop, honest."

"It's against the law to lie about that. You tell me you're not a cop and you are, you're not gonna have a leg to stand on in court, Devil."

"I promise, Da'nita, cross my heart. Believe me the cops are very happy about the fact I'm not one of them." I traced a small cross over my heart as I took the oath.

She downed a good portion of her drink, slammed the glass harder than she meant to as she put it back down on the table.

"Kerri?"

"What about her? She's Russian, I know that. I had to sit there and listen to her talking all that yik yak on the phone enough times to know that much. Nikki, she's not her sister."

"What's Nikki's last name?"

"Nikki? I thought you said you knew? It's Mathias."

"So just the same as Kerri?"

"Kerri? Nah, not hardly. Her's was Vucavitch." She spit out the 'vitch' pronunciation. "First name's actually Karina, Karina Vucavitch, but she always goes by Kerri because it sounds more American."

"How'd you meet her, Kerri?"

"We danced together a few years back. You might not have guessed it to look at me now, but I was something. They all wanted little Da'nita."

"You mean stripping?"

"It was way more than that. A girl had to have real talent back then. I was dancing one night, some drunk son-of-a-bitch shoots at someone in the bar, misses, of course, and hits me. Next thing I know, when I wake up I can't walk and my ass in this damn thing for the rest of my days. Kerri comes outta nowhere, gives me a job answering the phones and all. She contacts the girls. I'm their voice to the public. Hell, most of those girls can barely speak English," she said, sitting up a little straighter in her wheelchair.

"So, it's an escort service?"

"Gee, really, you think?"

"How'd they get the girls?"

"They were all Russian as far as I know. Even Mai. Nikki too, her name was something like Nikolaevna. She told me once it meant 'On the side of God' I thought that was kind of funny, you know, she being a working girl and all."

"You ever meet a guy named Leo Tate, or a guy named Dennis Dundee?"

"Some guy named Leo used to come in. He and Kerri never really got on that well. They argued all the time. The arguments seemed to get worse as time went on. To tell you the truth, every time he came in I sort of made myself disappear. I really don't need any more trouble."

"What was the problem?"

"I can't be sure, but if I had to guess, I'd say money. They just seemed to argue more and more every time he came in. Then the last time I saw him he slapped Kerri around pretty good. I never saw him after that and then I heard he was killed."

"How'd you find out?"

"I've got my ways, Devil, I've got my ways."

I talked with Da'nita through another Cosmopolitan but didn't learn much more except that she was slurring her words. I thought I left knowing more than when I arrived but I had no idea what it was I knew. If Da'nita Bell was to be believed, I had Kerri and Nikki's names, knew they weren't sisters. I also learned that the heart tattoo, DB + DB stood for Da'nita Bell plus Darius Bell. Darius was her son, currently in the middle of doing eighteen months up in Lino Lakes.

I phoned Aaron, and as per usual left a message. I thought he should at least have Kerri's real name.

Chapter Twenty

I wasted the next day looking for Kerri and got absolutely nowhere. I would have had better luck checking under my living-room couch. In between times, I worked on not taking a pain pill. I placed two more calls to Aaron, figuring any more than that would put me into the pest category. He phoned the following day.

"Hey, I got your messages, quit being a pain in the ass. If I had something to tell you I would have called. God forbid I drop any of the fifty or sixty things I've got hanging fire to deal with your little bump on the head."

I wondered if pain in the ass ranked above or below pest, but decided not to pursue that line of questioning.

"Well, I just wanted to add some information, keep your investigation moving forward."

"Such as?"

"Kerri, real name, Karina Vucavitch, nationality believed to be Russian. Nikki Mathias, first name Nikolaevna, also believed to be Russian. Her name means…"

"Means close to God."

"Actually, on the side of God, I think," fudging, remembering my source. "How in the hell do you know that?"

"Whatever. Where'd you pick up all this new information, Holmes?"

"A little investigative effort at Boxer's bar on behalf of your boy. You were right, by the way, not a very nice place."

"You talk to Da'nita Bell there?"

"Yes, I did."

"You read the paper or listen to the news in the past twenty-four hours?"

"Huh?"

"Da'nita Bell's dead. Hit and run about a block away from Boxer's. Apparently she left the place shit-faced, nothing unusual there, got hit crossing the street. No witnesses, Pizza-delivery guy spotted her under a parked car sometime after midnight. Her wheelchair was all smashed up about twenty feet further down the street. When did you last see her?"

"I think it must have been around six thirty or so. Actually, when I phoned you I was on my way home after talking with her. Whatever time that call came in, I had left her maybe five or ten minutes before that."

"You shouldn't phone while you're driving."

Aaron's joke was lost on me. I was working the odds in my head of a hit and run not being related to my conversation with Da'nita, not having something to do with Kerri and Nikki. The odds seemed about one in a million.

"You there?" Aaron asked.

"What? Yeah. No idea who hit her?"

96

"Does the term hit and run mean anything? No, no idea. They got some paint chips off her wheelchair. They'll analyze them, maybe get a color if not a vehicle type. That should only take about twelve months before the results get back to us."

"You working it?"

"No, thank God. I got enough stuff not going anywhere. I don't need that headache."

"Aaron, I'll bet you lunch it was a dark blue vehicle, and if you could find Nikki Mathias you'd have a good chance of getting your hands on the driver."

"I'll pass it on. We should probably talk, but I'm up to my ass in alligators right now. Stay in touch, okay?"

"Yeah, hey can you run Karina Vucavitch through your computer see what comes up. I, hello, Aaron, you there? Hello?" He'd already hung up.

I thought about Da'nita Bell. Was she killed because she talked to me? Because she worked with Kerri? Did she know more than she'd told me? I thought maybe I could start to get some answers at the deli Da'nita mentioned, and check the escort office while I was there. Who knew, maybe Kerri might even be there, sitting back with her feet up on the desk, just waiting for me to show up so she could help get all these nagging questions off my chest.

Chapter Twenty-One

The Moscow Deli was located in a fifties-era strip mall constructed of singularly unmemorable beige brick. Despite the fact it was a bright, sunny afternoon, the neon sign outside the door was on. The "M" in the sign was out and the red letters read "oscow Deli". All the storefronts opened on to a cracked sidewalk beneath a rusty sheet-metal canopy. The view from inside the deli was of a sparsely-filled parking lot, with just a hint of faded white lines and more than a few potholes. The traffic on the street raced past constantly. Rarely did a vehicle risk venturing into the parking lot.

Inside there was virtually nothing I recognized on the shelves. All the shelf labels and canned goods were in Russian. There was a pungent smell of fish, cooked cabbage with maybe some body odor thrown in the mix. The man behind the meat counter looked like he could have been a distant cousin of Leonid Brezhnev. Stocky, ruddy cheeks, a day-old beard, salt-and-pepper hair combed straight back accenting his prominent widow's peak. He sized me up through bloodshot eyes set beneath heavy eyebrows and a forehead that looked about a half inch high and six inches thick. His plastic nametag read Tibor.

"How's it going?" I smiled, hoping to thaw some of the icy greeting.

"Mrumph," he grunted in my general direction, then sniffled.

My attempt at charm didn't seem to work. He just blinked his bloodshot eyes at me, expression unreadable.

"You're Tibor, yes?" I said, reading his nametag and using my best "I'm a good guy" smile.

I watched him process my question. You could almost hear the rusty wheels beginning to turn inside his thick skull. Eventually, he gave a slight nod, probably wondering how I knew.

"Karina Vucavitch said you'd help me if I needed to get in touch with her. I'm trying to return some things of hers. Can you tell me where I can find her?"

That got a reaction, but not the one I'd hoped for.

"I no know Kerri," he said, then folded fairly heavy arms across his chest, sniffling again. He had a blurry blue tattoo on his right forearm, an anchor, three lines of Russian scrawled beneath, all in Cyrillic script. His hands were chapped pink, with scarred knuckles, the right hand missing most of the ring finger. The hands looked like they'd be able to form pretty solid fists, not for the first time.

"Well, you know she goes by Kerri, so you must know her. Where can I find her? I've been doing some work for her. I found someone she was looking for."

Another blink and vague look.

"Okay, look, have her give me a call. I've got information for her. Get it, information?" I raised my eyebrows and nodded, wishing I knew the Russian for asshole.

He waved me off with his three-fingered right hand, shaking his head like he couldn't be bothered anymore then began to shovel ground rat or something into a section of the refrigerated counter, mumbling in Russian all the while.

"When you talk to her, pal, give her this card and have her call me." I pulled a business card out of my wallet, wrote "call me" on the back with my pen and left it on the meat counter. "Nice chatting with you," I said and headed for the door.

Once outside I looked around for the escort office Da'nita had said it was right next door. I found it, actually two doors down. There was a grimy hallway with a series of fairly solid office doors numbered 1-9. No name on the doors, but a roster of tenants just inside the entrance listed number 5 as the office for Lee-Dee. That seemed close enough.

Number 5 was locked and from what I could tell there was no noise coming from the other side. The hallway had a drop ceiling and I was sure the wall rose just a few inches above the ceiling, not that I intended to climb. I walked out to my car, made a show of driving off for my new pal Tibor, then parked around the corner. I grabbed my pick set out of the glove compartment and strolled back. I was inside the office in under three minutes.

Chapter Twenty-Two

The room was dark, windowless, and smelled of Kerri's perfume. I hit the light switch and an overhead fluorescent above a plastic ceiling panel flickered on. I relocked the door then headed to the gray desk four feet inside the office. A laptop with a screen saver of fireworks bouncing around sat on the desk. I moved the mouse, and the screen came to life. It looked like an appointment calendar, numerical codes in date blocks. I printed the page.

My thought was to navigate around the computer and find out where Kerri was, where Nikki was hiding, who took a shot at me, and who ran over Da'nita Bell? I learned I wasn't going to get very far without passwords. There was a Rolodex on the desktop, next to that a coffee mug with maybe an inch of coffee and an oily slick on the top. Nuclear red lipstick lined the edge of the coffee mug. Two semi-clean mugs sat in a desk drawer along with a box of Tampax, a pack of cigarettes and seventy-five cents. I pocketed the three quarters.

There were no file cabinets, no files, no checks, nothing. Which I guessed meant just about everything was done electronically. I noticed there wasn't an office chair, and I remember Da'nita complaining that Kerri rolled her out into the hall and left her to sit there. It made sense that this was Da'nita's desk. There were two other doors off the room.

The first door I opened was a small walk-in closet, nothing of interest unless you were looking for the coffeepot, which I turned off. A metal shelf held four reams of paper for a printer. I turned the light off in the front office and opened the second door.

I entered a slightly larger, windowless office. Kerri's, I guessed. There wasn't a thing to suggest the office had actually been occupied by anyone with a personality in the last year. A couple of cords ran across the desk where a computer used to sit. There was a printer on the corner of the desk, still plugged in and on. It meshed with Da'nita's version of things. Kerri running in, taking about a minute to unplug her computer, push Da'nita out the door, and drive off. The desk revealed nothing of interest as I went through the drawers. I was looking around the room, hoping something might jump out at me, but nothing did. I was probably frowning when I heard the hallway doorknob jiggle. I could see the shadow of two feet through the crack at the bottom of the door. I quickly turned the office light off, then stood there in total darkness with my hand on my right hip, taking a little comfort from my pistol. The handle jiggled again, then the shadows beneath the door disappeared, and a muttered voice faded down the hallway.

I remained still for what seemed like four or five hours, probably five minutes in reality. Heart pounding in my ears, willing myself to take normal breaths. I eventually made my way in the dark to Da'nita's desk. I shut down her computer, unplugged it, and walked out the door. I scanned the dismal parking lot for a long minute, but didn't spot anyone sitting in a car and watching. As a matter of fact I didn't see a living soul. I walked back to my car, checking the reflection in the storefront windows for signs of anyone behind me. I didn't spot anyone.

I took a roundabout route home, but didn't notice a tail. Just to play it safe I drove into a pay parking ramp downtown, circled up to the top floor, then drove back out on a side-street exit. Still no one behind me.

Chapter Twenty-Three

I can do a lot of things on the computer: write letters, invoice clients, email, download iTunes, and watch porn. I had no business thinking I could get into the files on Da'nita's laptop so I took the thing over to Sunnie Einer.

Sunnie had done some projects for me over the years. If she had been a guy she had a great name for a gangster, maybe someone who ran with Tony Soprano. Sunnie wasn't a gangster. She had a doctorate in Education and another one in Computer Science. She was a tenured professor at the University of St. Catherine's and had a sixteen-year-old son, named Josh, who was driving her nuts. I phoned her enroute.

"Hey, Sunnie, Dev Haskell. You interested in a little project?"

"Possibly. Is it legal?"

"Sort of," I hedged. "I can be over in about ten minutes."

She gave an audible sigh.

"Yeah sure, okay. We'll talk about it when you get here. Can you stay for dinner?"

"What are you serving?"

"Like you care, I'll see you in ten," she said and hung up.

I was there in closer to twenty once I stopped and picked up a bottle of wine. As I pulled in I couldn't help but notice her car, a black Prius, her pride and joy, sporting a broken headlight and smashed right front-quarter panel.

"Hey, Dev, come on in," she said, opening the door and sounding genuinely glad to see me. She gave me a slight kiss on the check. She wasn't good looking, she was beautiful and a friend. Oddly, given my history, the friendship was really important and I'd never attempted to try and work the sexual end of things.

"Gorgeous as always, Sunnie. How are you?"

The home smelled delicious. There was a bell ringing somewhere.

"Come on back to the kitchen, my timer's going off. Lasagna, I'm just taking it out. We'll eat in about ten minutes, which should give me time for a glass of your wine and you can tell me about this opportunity." She stressed the word opportunity like it was anything but as she nodded at the laptop under my arm.

"Now be positive," I encouraged. "Hey, what happened to your Prius?"

"Oh God, Mr. Grounded-For-The-Rest-of-His-Life, did that, the little idiot. Only one friend in the car is my rule. Of course five of the little deadbeats are driving out to the Mall of America, Josh doing everything but paying attention. He rammed someone in the parking ramp."

"The parking ramp? How'd he do that?"

"Exactly! You have that wine opened up yet? I could sure use it."

Ten minutes later we were at the dining-room table, a contrite Josh seated across from me rolling his eyes as Sunnie carried the pan of lasagna into the room and said,

"Dev, will you lead us in grace, please?" Not really a request, more of a directive.

Josh rolled his eyes again.

I winked back.

After dinner Josh dutifully cleared the table and loaded the dishwasher. As he headed upstairs to his room, Sunnie gave a final instruction.

"No computer, no TV."

He gave an exasperated sigh, similar to his mother's earlier on the phone with me, but had enough sense not to offer further protest. After he'd gone upstairs she said,

"God, I really want to kill him right now. Is that bad? Do you think they'd catch me?"

"I think it's normal. Look, at least no one was hurt, were they?"

She shook her head no, then changed the subject.

"So, tell me what you have there?"

"Oh, this," I said reaching for the laptop resting on her coffee table.

"Yes, the reason you came in the first place." She smiled coldly, then sipped some wine. She was curled up in the corner of the couch, her legs tucked beneath her. The gas fireplace was on even though the evening wasn't cold. She brushed her blonde hair off her shoulders, looked me in the eye, and raised her eyebrows as if to say get to the point.

I took out the page I had printed off, handed it to her and told her most of what I knew, which wasn't a lot. I couldn't see much point in worrying her about the murders of Leo Tate, Dennis Dundee, or little Mai. I didn't bring up being grazed by a bullet. I neglected to mention what I assumed was Da'nita's hit-and-run murder. Skipped the part about Tibor or actually breaking into the Lee Dee office. Then wound up my request by saying,

"So anyway, I'm just trying to figure out what was going on. I'm guessing based on that page." I nodded at the page I printed off, now resting on her lap. "All this is coded. I don't have passwords to get in there, and if I did, I probably wouldn't know what I was looking at anyway. I'm trying to find out how to contact Kerri, or her sister, Nikki. If there's anything obviously illegal, I'll take it to the police. I'll most likely do that anyway, but I just want to see if you can find anything out."

She poured herself another glass of wine, sat back, and thought for a moment.

"Okay, it might take a bit. I've got some programs and algorithms I can work. You know what might help. The woman you mentioned, what's her name?"

"Da'nita Bell?"

"Yes, if you could get her date of birth, her son's full name, his date of birth. Those are standard password sources. It's at least a starting point," she said.

"I think I can get that for you."

"You didn't happen to see a Rolodex or Post-it notes around the desk in the office, did you?"

"No, there wasn't. Well, actually there was a Rolodex. Why?"

"Amazingly, it's not uncommon for people to put their passwords in their Rolodex or tape it right to their computer. If you could ask to borrow that Rolodex it might help."

"I'll ask them," I said not even blinking.

"All right then. I'll get started tomorrow."

Chapter Twenty-Four

My phone rang before eight the following morning. Although I was awake I had to crawl out of bed to answer it.

"Hello." I couldn't read the phone number displayed on the cell-phone screen.

"You called," Aaron said.

"Huh?" I was crawling back into bed.

"I had a message from you, said to give you a call. What, don't tell me you were still in bed?"

"Okay," I said.

"Okay what?"

"Okay I won't tell you I'm still in bed."

"God, you are so worthless."

"I was wondering if you could run Karina Vucavitch and Nikolaevna Mathias through your system, let me know what comes up."

"Let you know?" he asked, emphasizing the "you" in his question.

"Yeah, look, I got you the names, Kerri Vucavitch and Nikki Mathias. If you get a hit on anything it'd be nice to know. I think I got something else that might at least be connected."

"Like what?"

"You gonna run the names?"

"Already did. Once you get out of bed you might drift down this way and maybe learn a thing or two."

"I'm there within the hour," I said jumping out of bed.

"I can hardly wait," Aaron said and hung up.

Chapter Twenty-Five

Actually he wasn't kidding. He was waiting for me in the hallway when I got off the elevator.

"Did you sense my magical presence as I ascended in the elevator?" I asked.

"No, I glanced out the window and watched as you pulled that piece-of-shit car of yours into a no-parking zone. You'll probably get ticketed."

"Good thing I know you, then."

"I'm not fixing a ticket for you. I only do that for friends and gorgeous women."

We were passing a series of blue and burgundy cubicles, walking back to his office as we spoke. I saw two figures seated in his office. Even a hundred feet away one looked to be in a pressed suit, starched shirt, trendy tie, blond crew-cut hair. He screamed FBI. The other guy was a little more casual. Striped shirt, slacks, dark hair, and more of it. He was cracking a piece of gum, working it.

"Feds?" I asked Aaron.

He ignored me. As we approached his office he broke into his good-cop routine.

"Hey, Dev, come on in. Let me introduce you. Gentlemen, here is the man with all the answers, the guy I've been telling you all about, Mister Devlin Haskell."

I smiled grimly, feeling like I was being delivered to the lions and wondered exactly how much Aaron may have told them as I extended my hand.

"Agent Peters, FBI," Aaron introduced the suit.

"Kimball Peters," he said, springing out of his chair like a jack-in-the-box, giving me the rock solid, vice grip Bureau handshake. He wore a dark suit with just the slightest hint of a pattern in a not quite as dark blue. Black wingtips shined to a high gloss.

"Agent Hale, I.C.E." Aaron directed me to the dark-haired guy in the striped shirt.

"Billy Hale," he said not getting up, but nodding in my direction. "Nice to meet you, man."

"I wonder if you wouldn't mind telling us in your own words what you know about this Vucavitch business," Agent Peters said as he sat down. He pulled at his trousers just above the knee so he wouldn't ruin the crease.

"I was thinking of some coffee first," I joked.

Peters looked at me deadpan and didn't crack a smile.

"Lieutenant LaZelle has been filling us in, but we'd be interested in your take on things," Hale said. He'd smiled at my coffee request.

"What's I.C.E.?" I asked.

"Everyone asks that. Sounds sort of sinister, doesn't it? We were in the old INS up until 9/11. Now we're rolled into Homeland Security. It stands for Immigration and Customs Enforcement. But I.C.E. sounds so cool, I can't resist, you know?"

"The Vucavitch woman?" Peters asked, giving an exasperated glance in Hale's direction before he brushed imaginary lint from his immaculate trousers.

"Not much to tell you," I said and then reiterated most of what I knew. I forgot to mention my drunken, sexual romp with Kerri the night she hired me and I skipped the part about my visit to the Moscow Deli and grabbing Da'nita's laptop. I'd be turning that over to Aaron soon enough, anyway.

"And you didn't think to contact the authorities about any of this?" Peters asked.

"Contact them about what? A woman can't find her sister? That was the information I had and operated under. It turns out that was incorrect, but I had no way to know it at the time."

"Russian gangs shooting up the place, trafficking illegals for sex between here and Chicago. We've got a number of homicides. Tate, Dundee, and the Asian Jane Doe to name just three. A probable fourth with the Bell woman just the other night. You seem to have at least a tangent relationship in all four instances," Peters suggested, reminding me why I so disliked Federal agents.

"Hey, I didn't know Kerri was Russian. She told me she was French, not that it makes a difference. This is the first I heard about any illegals. Over the years I've been with a couple of women who've had accents. I think it's kind of sexy. But it's never really crossed my mind to call the FBI. I get into a tangent relationship every time I watch the St. Paul Saints win or lose, doesn't mean I had shit to do with the outcome of the game."

Peters gave me a very practiced FBI glare.

113

"By the way, Dev, I checked those paint-chip samples from Da'nita Bell's hit and run. You owe me lunch. They were red, not dark blue," Aaron added, getting the discussion back on course.

I nodded.

"We'll be moving on those samples. I don't want to wait," Peters said, then looked from Hale to Aaron. "Does anyone have any more questions for Mr. Haskell?" He asked, apparently concluding my portion of the meeting before I could ask anything.

I.C.E. Agent Hale shook his head, pulled a business card out of his pocket, and handed it to me.

"Please give me a call if anything else comes up, or if you want to catch a Saints game." He smiled.

"You can reach me through Lieutenant LaZelle, here," Peters said as he stood, dismissing me.

"Can't thank you enough for the time," I said looking around the room. Aaron sported a crafty grin. They knew something and I wasn't going to be a part of it.

Chapter Twenty-Six

I was still pissed off thirty minutes later, not because I was cut out of the information line. That was fine. But the superior act, the "we'll let you know if and when it suits us", that frosted me. After all, I was the one who had the bullet bounced off his thick skull.

I parked in the shadeless, mostly empty parking lot about forty feet away from the Moscow Deli. I thought if I could grab Da'nita's Rolodex, get it to Sunnie, I'd be able to point to accomplishing something productive over the course of the day.

The Lee-Dee office door was unlocked and the lights were on. The Rolodex was still sitting undisturbed on the desk, but the rest of office had been tossed. The larger office, the one I assumed was Kerri's, had sheets of paper scattered all over the floor. The seats and cushions on the couch had all been sliced open and the stuffing scattered around the room. The printer lay smashed in a distant corner looking as if someone had lifted it over their head and tossed it fifteen feet. Bits of plastic from the shattered paper tray were all over the floor, toner sprayed across the wall.

I came to the quick conclusion this maybe wasn't the best place to be. I picked up the Rolodex and made for my car. I was just climbing in behind the wheel when a shout came from the direction of the Moscow Deli. I glanced at three large individuals funneling out the door and quickly decided nothing positive would result from my meeting them. So I did what any red-blooded male would do. I fired up the engine and fled the scene.

I was two stoplights farther down the street when I caught a red Lexus in my rearview mirror. They were swerving in and out of traffic in an effort to catch up to me. I didn't know if they had seen me yet. If they hadn't, it was only a matter of a minute, possibly two. I placed my pistol on the passenger seat.

The light ahead turned yellow, then red when I was maybe fifteen feet from the intersection. I leaned on the horn, pushed the accelerator down, then cringed as I sailed through the intersection. A high-pitched screech followed by an angry horn blast almost shattered my passenger side.

I checked in the rearview mirror, but didn't see the Lexus. So I raced on for three more blocks then dropped down to the posted speed and checked the mirror again. This time I saw them, coming up fast in the oncoming traffic lane.

I took a half right at the next light, shot onto St. Clair Ave and dodged a thin, elderly woman in some unflattering tweed outfit. She was wearing sensible shoes and just stepping off the curb to cross the street as I shot past. She had to jump back, then gave me the finger, and shouted a string of obscenities.

St. Clair followed the edge of the river bluff here and curved back around. I swerved into the oncoming lane to avoid two kids on bicycles and then swerved back into the right lane after almost hitting a car head-on. The driver hit the brakes and leaned on her horn as I streaked past. Unfortunately my actions were not lost on the police squad just behind her. I heard the siren, then watched as the squad made a U-turn and roared after me. I immediately pulled over figuring at least I'd be safe with the police.

The squad car pulled up behind me, two officers climbed out. One stood at the ready about five feet off to the rear of my passenger door. The other officer approached cautiously and called to me, none too gently.

"Place your hands where I can see them."

I put my hands on the dashboard. They studied me for a very long minute.

"Exit the vehicle. Keep your hands where I can see them."

"I'm gonna have to open my car door," I called to him.

"Do it carefully," he cautioned.

I opened the door, pushed it all the way open with my foot.

"I'm getting out," I said, holding my hands in front of me.

"Move back here to the rear of the vehicle," he instructed.

I did as I was told, moved to the back of my car, and had just placed my hands on the trunk and spread my feet in anticipation of what would come next. I guessed wrong.

My feet were suddenly kicked out from under me. My forehead bounced off the trunk of the car with a decidedly hollow-sounding thump.

"Oh, cool! Did you see that?" It was one of the two kids on bikes, they had pedaled up and stood watching my predicament.

One of the officers knelt on my head while the other pulled my right arm back and cuffed my wrist, then attempted to twist off my left arm. When that didn't work he bent it back and cuffed it. Once they'd ground enough sand and pavement into my face they lifted me up and slammed me onto the car trunk.

"What the fuck? You guys having a bad day?"

"Going a little fast there, sir. You been drinking?"

"Me? No, I mean, not recently."

"When was the last time…"

"Weapon in the front seat," his partner called. Ever the sleuth he'd seen my pistol sitting in the passenger seat.

"I've got a license to carry that weapon."

"May I see some identification, sir?"

"Yeah, sure, just undo these cuffs for me and I'll get it out of my wallet,"

"That your wallet, in your back pocket?"

"Yeah, help yourself, but be gentle, my pet." I gave him my sexy smile with a little wink.

He reached for my back pocket and tore it almost completely off. My wallet tumbled to the ground.

"Gentle enough for you?" he asked, then winked back.

118

I read the name Jorgensen, V. stitched in gold above his pocket.

"Look, Officer Jorgensen, I don't know what your problem is, but if you'll check with Lieutenant LaZelle, Aaron LaZelle in Vice, he'll vouch for me. My name's Devlin Haskell. I'm a private investigator. I'm licensed in the state of Minnesota, and I'm licensed to carry a firearm."

He nodded to his partner who went back into the squad car. That's probably where they kept the doughnuts. A few minutes later the partner returned, and whispered something into his ear.

"Really? No kidding, okay." Jorgensen chuckled.

"You getting it straightened out?" I asked, figuring Aaron had read them the riot act and I was eager for the cuffs to be taken off before I gave him a piece of my mind.

"Yeah, Lieutenant LaZelle cleared everything up, sir. In fact, you're under arrest. You have the right to remain silent, anything you say can and will be held against you…"

"You gotta be kidding. You're fucking arresting me? Did LaZelle tell you to do this?"

"Wow, cool," said the kid.

"Taser him," cried his sadistic little pal.

"You have the right to speak to an attorney. If you cannot afford…"

Chapter Twenty-Seven

I learned on the way down to the station that somehow the FBI had gotten involved. Jorgensen's partner, Officer Elling, never even talked to Aaron. Friendly FBI agent Kimball Peters intercepted the call and told them to arrest me. I was pretty sure he would approve of them tearing my back pocket and kneeling on my head just as long as he didn't get his hands dirty. I was having a tough time seeing any humor in the situation. I decided it might not be the safest move to call Aaron if that douche bag Peters was hanging around.

I called Heidi instead, figuring she'd understand.

"What?" she answered.

"Heidi, I need a little favor."

"Not now, please."

"Yeah now. Why?"

"I'm kind of in the middle of something here," she half whispered. "Can it keep until tomorrow?"

"I'm in fucking jail!"

"No kidding? God, now what'd you do?"

"I didn't do anything. Look, it's kind of a long story but I need you to get down here and post bail for me so I can get out of this hell hole."

"Bail? That's the little favor?"

"Okay, okay, a big favor. I'll consider it a big favor, honest, but I need you to come down here and spring me, please."

"Now?"

"No, next week. Of course now."

I could tell she had put her hand over the phone and was discussing my options with someone. The voices went back and forth for a bit.

"Okay, I suppose. I'll be down in a while."

"Heidi, I need you here right away, not hours from now. More like thirty minutes ago, okay?"

"God, okay, as soon as I can. I have to get dressed," she whispered.

"Just hurry up. This place is not conducive to my well being," but she'd already hung up.

It wasn't thirty minutes… more like two hours and thirty minutes. It was evening and the moon was up when I walked out with Heidi and Harold, the boy toy she had in tow.

Surprise, surprise, Heidi looked like she just rolled out of bed.

Harold was fairly good looking in that too skinny, lounge-lizard sort of way. Dirty blond hair, longish and parted in the middle, with a carefully trimmed three-day growth of beard. Sandals, loose-fitting jeans topped by an untucked grayed T-shirt touting Insane Clown Posse, a band I despise. A line of pizza or taco sauce was dribbled down the front of his T-shirt. I guessed him to be a day or two past his eighteenth birthday, barely legal.

"Dude, that was way cool. I've never been inside a cop shop before," Harold said, brushing his hair back behind his ear. It fell forward almost immediately.

"Stick with me, Harold, you ain't seen nothing yet," I said.

"Okay, Dev, I got you out, so don't screw up this time. I'm on the hook for five grand here," Heidi snarled, seeing even less humor in the situation than I did.

"Screw up this time? What do you mean? You've never had to bail me out before."

"What about the Allman Brothers concert?" she said.

"That doesn't count."

"The Allman Brothers, oh man, gnarly." Harold laughed.

Heidi wrapped her arm around his waist and glared at me.

"Come on, let's get some takeout and go back home. I've worked up an appetite," she said, looking up at Harold. Harold smiled and placed his youthful pink hand on her shapely firm rear.

"I could go for Thai," I said.

"You're so not invited," she growled, eyes glaring.

"Okay, just drop me off at home."

"Drop you off? Where's your car?"

"Those fascists impounded it."

"So we're supposed to drop you off? It's not enough you've already royally screwed up the entire evening. Now I'm supposed to drive you home? Maybe I should just tuck you in."

Harold gave me a brief smirk as if a thought might have fluttered close to the surface, but then disappeared.

I had a joke on the tip of my tongue about getting tucked in, but thought better of it since I really needed the lift.

"It's on the way," I groveled.

"It's in the opposite Goddamn direction. Jesus! Okay, but you owe me big time, Dev. I mean it, big time."

"Thanks, Heidi."

She bitched the entire way to my place. Okay, she'd interrupted her scandal-filled evening to bail me out. Now she was driving me home instead of climbing back into the sack with her personal scrawny sex pistol, Harold, and his one-watt brain. The ten-minute drive seemed to last an eternity and I attempted, unsuccessfully, to just tune her out.

"… not that you'd even care! Honest to God, Dev, I mean it. I'm really tired of the same old shit. It just never ends. Either I'm worried sick about some horrible thing you're involved in or I want to kill you myself. Like now!" Her eyes flashed at me in the rearview mirror.

"So Dude, like, do you do a lot of that random shit they're always screwing with on <u>CSI</u>? Ever cap anyone?" Harold asked, half turning toward me from the front seat.

"Don't even speak to him," Heidi said, then rubbed his thigh and smiled.

I'd barely climbed out of the backseat and was actually in the process of closing the door, bending over to thank her for coming down and bailing me out when she roared off, causing the door to slam shut.

"Later, Dude," Harold yelled back at me then waved, hanging out the window as they raced up the street.

Chapter Twenty-Eight

The main impound lot for the St. Paul Police is located on Barge Channel Road. The perfect location for one of the most depressing experiences a person can have. The following morning I thought it probably wasn't the best idea to call Heidi for a ride to spring my car, and so I took a taxi instead. My driver didn't speak English and I had to point, nod, and shake my head as I gave directions. A few times we came to a complete stop in the middle of an intersection, until eventually we arrived. But he knew exactly what he was doing when it came time for me to pay my fare and understood perfectly my directive to keep the change.

Over the course of the past thirty or forty years, St. Paul, like most municipalities, had put at least some effort to make dealing with city employees a quasi-pleasant experience for the taxpayer. Such was not the case with the impound lot. On the other hand, I assumed most people arriving here would, right from the get-go, not be in the most positive frame of mind.

The lot itself was surrounded by a ten-foot-high cyclone fence crowned with miles of concertina wire. You walked a fifty-foot corridor of fencing with razor wire strung across the top to get to the front door. Just beyond the front door a narrow staircase with worn carpet rose between grimy walls. At the top of the staircase, a large window made up of a half dozen layers of bulletproof glass protected employees from taxpayers.

It was mid-morning, already hot and humid. I quickly concluded the heavyset woman ahead of me on the staircase hadn't showered for the better part of a week. Including her, there were eight people in front of me. Amazingly, none of them could understand why their car had been towed, not that it mattered to the attendant behind the glass. Over the course of forty minutes, I inched my way up the staircase until I confronted the pale, humorless clerk behind the glass.

He was actually more sallow looking than pale, about one hundred and twenty pounds soaking wet, and in need of a shave. He wore rumpled jeans and a stained, wrinkled T-shirt with a hole in it that he had probably pulled on a week ago. He had the look of someone who'd slept in his clothes, regularly. I guessed he hated his job. Who could blame him? Although he'd probably stick with it for forty years. The place seemed to have leached all humanity from his soul.

"License number," he mumbled, not looking up at me.

"Minnesota, IAB 114."

He typed my plate number into the computer. I saw a screen flash in the reflection of his glasses, and a moment later he wheeled around on his desk chair to grab a sheet coming out of a printer.

"Three twenty-five," he said, still not looking at me.

"Huh?"

"Three hundred twenty-five dollars," he replied, looking down at his desktop.

"But it just got here yesterday."

"Ticket, tow charge, two days in the lot, processing, and tax," he said in an expressionless, practiced manner as his head sunk a little lower.

Arguing would only waste more of my time, and they'd probably charge me by the minute so I nodded, slid my debit card into the metal tray and prayed.

He retracted the tray beneath the thick glass panel and ran my card.

"Access denied, sorry," he mumbled, sounding like he wasn't, looking straight ahead at his computer screen.

"Oh, shit," a disgruntled voice from somewhere back in line wafted up the staircase.

"I just came from the damn bank," I lied.

"Might want to get it checked out then. You got a credit card we can run?" he asked, still completely disinterested and now focused on the wall behind me.

I handed him my credit card, then prayed I wasn't already over my limit.

"I'll need proof of insurance before I can release the vehicle."

"It's in the car."

He nodded. Maybe he'd heard some of this before.

"Show the attendant this, along with proof of insurance," he said returning my credit card with the invoice stamped paid in the metal tray. He never looked up at me.

Chapter Twenty-Nine

The Rolodex was still in the front seat. I phoned Sunnie as I exited the impound lot.

"Sunnie, I've got that Rolodex you wanted."

"Oh, when can you get it to me?"

"I can be there in fifteen minutes."

"No later, Dev, I've got a lecture at eleven I have to review for."

"Any idea how long this might take?"

"The lecture?"

"No, finding the password."

"No, I ran some programs yesterday, without much luck. We'll just have to see. It's a little like asking what the weather is going to be like in three weeks. Who really knows?"

Twelve minutes later I handed the Rolodex to Sunnie at her front door as she said,

"Look, sorry, don't take it personal, but this is my crazy day. I've got a lecture at eleven and then I'm working labs all afternoon. You interested in a late dinner, say seven tonight?"

"Yeah, I can do that, what are …"

"Don't ask what I'm serving."

"I was going to ask what can I bring?" I lied.

"Just your good company. See you at seven, I gotta run," she said and closed the door.

Chapter Thirty

I phoned Aaron from in front of Sunnie's house and left a message.

He phoned me back about fifteen minutes later just as I was driving past my house. I noticed a red Lexus across the street, the right front end looked mangled and scraped, like it had hit something. Maybe a wheelchair?

"Where are you?" Aaron asked.

"You know those red paint chips taken from Da'nita Bell's wheelchair?"

"Yeah?" Aaron sounded curious.

"Well, I was chased yesterday by three thugs in a red Lexus, an SUV. There's one parked across the street from my place right now, and it's got a damaged front end."

I heard some paper rattle before he answered.

"That's not red, it's Nobel Spinel, and the vehicle isn't an SUV it's a Lexus LX11."

"Oh, that's just great. And the three thugs?" I asked.

"They in it now?"

"No, it's empty actually. I'm going around the block. Hell, as far as I know they could be waiting inside my place for me."

"They chased you yesterday, you said?"

"Yeah, fortunately I fell into the gentle caring hands of a couple of your guys, with the help of that jackass Peters."

"Peters? The Fed?"

"The same. Look, I'll tell you about it later. How soon can you get here?"

"Okay, I'm there in six minutes, pull over. I'm sending a squad to meet you. Don't let them do anything until I arrive, clear?"

"I'm not going anywhere. See you in six," I said and pulled to the curb.

The police squad arrived about five minutes after Aaron. I was finishing up telling him about my previous day and the interaction with officers Jorgensen and Elling.

"And they told you they spoke to Peters?"

"Yeah, said they contacted you, or tried to, Peters answers tells them about a task force and that they might be saving the city a lot of money by getting me in custody so soon. They were thinking they made a big score."

"With you?"

"Yes, me, that's beside the point. From the way they talked, could that jerk have answered your phone? I mean how else would they even know about the guy?"

"Possible, I was going over some stuff in homicide with Hale for ten or fifteen minutes. Call could have come through then, I guess."

"Hale, the I.C.E. guy?"

Aaron nodded, deep in thought.

"Here's your squad, pulling up behind us," I said, watching in my mirror as a squad car came around the corner.

We used our three vehicles to box in the Lexus against the curb, then approached my house. The two uniformed officers went into the backyard. Aaron and I went up onto the front porch.

"I feel like I may have done this once or twice before," he said, pulling his pistol and jiggling my front-door handle. It was locked.

"You wouldn't happen to have your key, would you?"

I unlocked the door, pushed it wide open, then quickly stepped back behind Aaron.

"Police," Aaron called.

No one answered.

"Police," he called again, this time much louder.

We went through the place cautiously, room by room, and found nothing except my breakfast dishes. He called the officers out of my backyard, then walked with them over to the Lexus.

"Run the plates on this damn thing," he said to one of them, then turned to me. "I think this is an unfortunate coincidence. I said LX11, right?"

"Yeah."

He pointed to the chrome model number on the rear of the vehicle.

"This is a GX 460, the lower-priced version. Goes for something like fifty-five grand, about twenty less than the LX."

"So, you're saying this is the wrong car? In front of my house and with the damage to the right front?"

"I think so. Hell of a coincidence, but I'm guessing it's not your pals."

"Well, it sure as hell got my attention."

"Never hurts to play it safe," he replied.

"Oh Officer, did the insurance company send you?"

A small woman carrying a dozen different shopping bags called from about fifty feet away.

"I ran into my daughter's bicycle, didn't even see the thing in the driveway. Of course she left it where it wasn't supposed to be. I have to say, all of you here to investigate the damage, I'm really impressed."

Chapter Thirty-One

Since Sunnie wouldn't tell me what she was serving I picked up two bottles of wine. One red, one white.

"Oh, gee Dev, you didn't have to do that. It almost makes up for all the headaches you've given me over the past few days," she said when she opened her front door. She wore cutoffs and a T-shirt, "I heart St. Paul" emblazoned down the front. I followed her back into her kitchen waiting for the headache explanation that never came. The house smelled wonderful, garlicky.

"I don't know what you're cooking, but it smells absolutely delicious."

"Garlic chicken."

"Any luck on that password?"

"Well, I thought of a half dozen different programs I could try on the thing. They could take up to a week, maybe longer. It's hard to say. And, it's not like I don't have other things to do."

"More than a week?"

"Yeah at least, and even then there's no guarantee. So instead, I just checked the Rolodex you dropped off, under "P" for password. Any idea who DB + DB is?"

"That's the password?"

"Yep, took about ninety seconds. I suppose I shouldn't have told you and just hung on to the laptop for a week, then sent you my exorbitant bill."

"DB + DB was a heart-shaped tattoo on her left breast, Da'nita Bell plus Darius Bell. It's Da'nita's laptop you've been working on."

"Was a heart-shaped tattoo? Did she have it removed?"

"She passed away and we couldn't, my client that is, couldn't access the computer files."

"Dead with tattooed boobs, how charming. I'm not sure I want to know much more."

"Okay. So could you get into the files?"

"Well yes, such as they are. There aren't too many of them on there. It looks like some sort of appointment calendar. A phone directory and a couple of dreadful homemade pornographic videos."

"You watched them?"

"Only long enough to know they were dreadful. Honestly, how can anyone find that sort of thing even remotely appealing?" She took the pan with the garlic chicken out of the oven and then set it on a cooling rack. She looked really sexy in the cutoffs and probably didn't even know it.

"Did you open any wine or did you just stand there and stare at my butt?"

"I could tell you I was looking for an opener, but your butt took priority."

"Opener's right next to the wine glasses, on the counter in front of you. God..." She shook her head, but then she laughed so I knew I was safe.

136

Her son Josh wasn't around, probably confined to a dark corner in the basement. I didn't bring up her car. We talked about everything and nothing over a candlelight dinner. After we finished eating she gave me a quick tutorial on how to access Da'nita's laptop files. She was right, there were only a handful of files. I decided I could spend most of tomorrow going through them, not that I knew what exactly I'd be looking for.

Chapter Thirty-Two

I woke the following morning still tasting the garlic from the night before. I was going through Da'nita's files while still on my first cup of coffee. I felt pretty sure the numeric code next to each phone number represented a client name. Probably guys who'd paid for an escort in the past. That didn't mean they knew or had even met Kerri or Nikki. On the other hand I guessed that at least one of them might have information that could help me, whether they knew it or not. Now, if I could just get them to talk to me.

In order to talk to me they had to accept my call. Of the first seven phone calls I placed, three were disconnected, one was busy, two never answered and had no message center and one simply hung up. All of which was probably fine because I was still attempting to figure out exactly what I was going to say if someone did answer.

A polite male answered call number 8.

"This is Wayne Lentz."

"Mr. Lentz, my name is Devlin Haskell. Your name came up in an ongoing investigation of a woman by the name of Nikki Mathias. I'd like to meet with you, privately, see if you could be of any help."

"Investigation?" he said sounding concerned.

"Yes, let me stress, you're not being investigated. We're just attempting to get some general background information on Miss Mathias."

"What'd she do?"

"She didn't actually do anything that we're concerned with. She's been missing and we're trying to locate her." I was a little surprised I'd gotten this far and expected him to ask me if I was the police.

He didn't. Instead he said, "Yeah, okay, but not here. How about later this evening?"

"That'll work, you just tell me where and I'll meet you."

We agreed on the Depot bar, I knew the place, about as out of the way as you can get. The next dozen calls I made resorted to pattern, no answer or a hang up once I'd stated my purpose. I decided to wait awhile, and not make any more calls until I spoke to Wayne Lentz.

Chapter Thirty-Three

The Depot bar sits on a busy corner across the street from one of the uglier parking ramps in St. Paul. A little one-story brick hovel, forgettable from the moment it was built back in 1953. On an average day close to ten thousand people probably walk or drive past. Which is what people do all day, every day, none of them ever giving a second thought to entering.

I guessed it was a pretty busy night once I walked in the side door. There were two people sitting at opposite ends of the bar. One was a disheveled older woman with frizzy gray hair who appeared to have been drinking since breakfast. The other resident was a lean bald guy in some sort of green work uniform, the name Gene sewn above his shirt pocket in white letters. Gene continued to stare down at his half empty beer, looking neither left nor right.

A guy occupied a booth against the wall, alone. I guessed his age at maybe forty-five. He was big, but not fat, heavy in a labor sort of way, solid. He had a crew cut, light brown hair going a little gray at the temples, oxford blue shirt with a button-down collar. His tie had been pulled off, but a gold tie clasp was still attached to his shirt. I figured him for a tradesman, maybe a cabinet-maker, a plumber or electrician all dressed up to meet a police detective. As I approached I noticed the large hand wrapped around his beer mug wore a wedding ring.

"Wayne?"

He nodded, then indicated the other side of the booth.

"I'm Devlin Haskell. Get you another while I'm up?" I asked.

"Leinne's," he said.

I returned with two mugs and slid into the booth across from him.

"Wayne, I appreciate you taking the time to see me. Like I said, we're just trying to get some background information on Nikki Mathias."

"You're not gonna arrest me or anything?" he only half joked. His voice just a little shaky, I could tell he was worried.

"No, I can assure you I will not arrest you. Look, neither one of us needs that headache. I'm really just trying to get some background information, that's all. Anything you could tell us would help." I didn't see any point in telling him I wasn't a cop. He'd made that assumption on his own, and I figured it could only help once I put him at ease.

We chatted for a few sips about the weather, the Twins, vacation. Wayne wasn't too eager to give up a lot of information, but I had the feeling he was resigned to a certain fate and was answering me truthfully, hoping this could just all stay nice and private in the back booth at the Depot bar.

"So Nikki Mathias, how long have you known her?"

"Maybe a year and a half. I haven't seen her in probably three or four months. I really don't actually know her that well, except on a sort of business level."

"See her often?"

"I suppose a few times."

I gave him a look and was about to ask him to define "a few."

"Okay, about every three or four weeks," he quickly added in response to my look.

"This isn't going to get out, is it? Should I have a lawyer present?" he asked, looking more than a little worried.

"No, you don't need a lawyer, Wayne, honest. You're not under investigation here, nor will you be. I'm not going to pass your name on to anyone else investigating this." I didn't add because there is no one else. I don't think any of what I said offered much in the way of relief. I noticed beads of perspiration dotting his pink forehead.

"Look, I know this was a business arrangement, but she was really nice to me. Tell you the truth I would have seen her more often, it's just that on an assistant librarian's salary it's pretty tough. Well, and of course my wife."

"I guess I can understand that. How did you first meet her, Nikki?"

"I answered one of her ads, on-line. She emailed back, then sent a picture for my picture, that sort of thing. Then sent her phone number and I called her."

"This was about a year and a half back, you said?"

"Yeah."

"So then what? You got together for a night?"

"No, not really. Tell you the truth that's what impressed me. She met me in a public place, a bar out at the Mall of America. We had a couple glasses of wine, chatted, then she said she figured I was okay and I could call her and we'd set something up."

"Did you ever have a sense there was anyone else around, watching you or anything?"

"No. In fact she left and I paid the tab. Then I followed her out, from a distance you know, so she wouldn't see me."

"And?"

"And she did just what she said she would do. She got on the light rail and left. Took her time in a couple of stores along the way, not in a hurry. Never met up with anyone else or anything. You always hear about guys getting together with some woman only to get set up. She arrives with three or four friends who empty the guy's bank accounts or something. I didn't need that."

"So you eventually got together with her?"

"Yeah, she met me in the lobby of a hotel, over in Minneapolis actually. I gave her a lift to a high-rise downtown afterwards. She said she lived there. I always picked her up and dropped her off there, but I never actually went inside. I never saw her apartment or anything."

"She ever go to your place?"

"No, you kidding? She was never even curious about where I lived, beyond making casual conversation."

"She have an accent?"

"Yeah, that was kind of funny. It was Russian, possibly from the Baltic region. You know, Estonia, Latvia, Lithuania. Up there."

I nodded like I was following where this was going.

"Funny thing, she told me she was German. I happen to speak German, fluently. I asked her something in German a couple of times that first night. She answered, but she had an accent."

"You mean her German?"

"Yeah, right. And her grammar was okay, but not always correct. See, I also speak Russian. I'm not fluent, but I can get around okay."

"She know this?"

"No, I never mentioned it. I spoke German to her a few more times and always the same result, but to tell you the truth, I wasn't seeing her to practice German, you know. Then a few times, in what you might call the throws of passion, she would blurt something out in Russian, nothing specific like 'I'm from St. Petersburg' or 'I like Vladimir Putin,' but, well, you get the idea, right?"

I nodded.

"We didn't stray into each other's personal life. We kept things strictly business. Anyway, the last couple of times I tried to phone her there was no answer. Then, like I said earlier, three or four months ago I phoned and the line had been disconnected. End of story."

"When you phoned her, did you ever go through an answering service?"

"Answering service? No, never. I'd always leave a message, but it was her voice, on the recording. I still remember it, 'Hi this is Nikki, leave your message, thanks.' Doesn't sound as good when I say it, but it was cute, sexy. Then she'd phone back, sometimes in a few minutes, sometime in a few days."

"You ever pick up on anything with her? You know like something was wrong or she might be frightened? Anything?"

"You know, I've been thinking about that as we're talking. Maybe the last two times we were together, she was almost clingy, wanted to be held, cuddled. Not a complaint from me, at the time I was thinking, man, this hot chick is falling for me big time."

"And she wasn't?"

"Let's just say when some gorgeous woman is lying next to you, naked, and she can't seem to get enough of you, wants to stay with you awhile longer, who cares why? It's not that far a leap to delusional."

"You recognize anyone in this besides Nikki?" I asked, taking out my printed copy of the photo, Nikki on the beach with Mai and the Lee-Dee boys.

"Yeah, that's her all right. Damn, I miss her. Don't know any of the others." Wayne shook his head and sounded wistful.

"You know, the last time I dropped her off..."
"Downtown?"
"Yeah, she always wanted to be let off near a side door of the building. I figured she wanted to

avoid the lobby, maybe prying eyes or something. Anyway, that time she wanted me to drop her off in front of the building. She made a point of saying she wanted to get out of the car where it wasn't dark, somewhere there were a lot of lights. Then said there had been some purse snatching in the area or something. Think maybe it might have been something else besides purse snatchings?"

"Could be, I just don't know," I said, shaking my head.

We chatted a few minutes longer. I was reasonably sure Wayne wasn't going to add anything and I didn't need to know specifics of their sexual preferences. He gave me the name of the building where he'd dropped her off, the Baltimore. I handed him my card.

"Wayne, will you call me if you think of anything else?"

"Haskell Investigations?" he said looking up at me, back at the card then back up at me, blinking wide blue eyes.

"That's me."

"I thought you said you were with the police?"

"No, I think that may have been an assumption on your part, Wayne. But I am investigating the disappearance of Nikki Mathias. What you've told me will remain in strictest confidence. And I'm sure it will help," I said, although in truth I really couldn't see how.

Chapter Thirty-Four

I went back to working the phone numbers from Da'nita's computer. Actually talked to four different guys, none of whom were of any real help, other than they more or less corroborated what I already knew. Nikki Mathias was an escort. Her contacts either originated online or from when she was entertaining at a party. She had an accent, was a gorgeous redhead, hadn't been heard from for a couple of months, and apparently was rather memorable since two of the guys asked me to pass their names and numbers along if and when I did find her. The name Lee-Dee meant nothing to the gentlemen I spoke with. I saw no point in meeting with any of them personally.

Chapter Thirty-Five

I could say all roads led back to Kerri, but I had no idea where she was, so I guess they led back to the Moscow Deli and my friend Tibor. Except that it wasn't really a road, more like a footpath, and not well traveled at that.

After creeping past and spotting my Neanderthal pal Tibor, I parked at the far end of the desolate parking lot outside the Moscow Deli a good hour before it closed. Not that there was anything in the way of last-minute customers. I thought it might be best not to confront Tibor in his place of business, knives and cutting blades being a staple of his skilled trade.

For all I knew he'd locked the door an hour before closing just so he wouldn't have to deal with pesky customers wanting him to dirty a knife. Fifteen minutes after his posted closing, the lights went off and Tibor exited the front door, locked it, then looked cautiously left and right before walking toward a sprawling, dated apartment complex across the street.

The complex, known as the Sibley Apartments, consisted of thirty or forty three-story stucco and brick structures built just after the Second World War. They'd served as home to returning GI couples in the early fifties. Then refugees from Castro's Cuba, the Hungarian revolution, Vietnamese boat people, Cambodians fleeing the Khmer Rouge, and now Eastern Europeans and Russians, just a stop on the road to the American Dream.

I attempted to shuffle aimlessly, hands in my pockets, walking a parallel path across the street from Tibor. He had a noticeable limp, maybe arthritic, and although he was glancing around constantly, he seemed not to notice me. Two blocks into the complex he made a B-line for a buff-colored building with painted orange trim.

There was no point in running. I was just far enough away to not be able to reach him before he ducked inside the security door. I watched from across the street and a minute later the lights came on in an apartment on the third floor, just to the left of the stairwell window. Tibor appeared for a brief moment as he lowered a window shade.

I walked around the rear and checked things out, then drifted back to the front door. The door lock didn't look all that difficult, and I was about to retrieve the pick set from my car when two boys approached. They looked to be about ten. One pulled out a key and unlocked the door, never stopping his conversation, which wasn't in English and sounded decidedly Slavic. I smiled, held the door as they entered, and then followed. They couldn't have cared less although I suspected they'd been lectured a good portion of their young lives about the danger of strangers.

Names had been taped onto aluminum mailbox doors set in the entryway wall. Last names with a first initial. Apartment 302 was listed as Crvek, T. T for Tibor I guessed. I quietly climbed the stairs. The hallways were a little too warm, a bit stuffy and smelled of heavy cooking. Fried things, bacon, pork, cabbage. I heard the hum of conversations in the hallway, but couldn't discern any words.

Tibor's unit was at the top of stairwell, one of four units on the third floor, and if my bearings were correct the same unit where I'd seen Tibor drawing the window shade barely fifteen minutes before. Black plastic numbers on the door, just above the peephole identified it as 302. I felt fairly confident that if Tibor knew it was me knocking, I wouldn't be welcome with open arms.

There was music playing inside the apartment, classical, possibly a cello solo. Who would have guessed Tibor for a culture vulture? I knocked softly, then stooped down so just the top of my hair would show through the peephole, hoping he would think it was a woman knocking and open.

Amazingly, the music stopped a note or two later. Had he actually been playing? I could just make out padded footsteps approaching the door, so the floor would most likely be carpeted. A muffled voice was calling something, then repeating the phrase. Whatever it was, it wasn't English. I heard a body brush against the door, looking through the peephole. I pressed my head closer against the door, just below the peephole so my hair was visible. The voice repeated the phrase, a little louder this time, paused, muttered something crossly, and then I heard the sound of a chain being unhooked.

The door opened widely, two or three angry words spilled out before they stopped, and Tibor, wide-eyed, wearing boxer shorts, white socks, and a strappy T-shirt attempted to slam the door closed.

I exploded from my crouch and burst through the door. The door flew open with a bang, knocking over a lamp that had rested on a small table just behind it. There was a slight pop and an audible fizzle as the light bulb broke when the lamp hit the floor. Tibor stumbled back. I wrapped him in a bear hug and tripped him to the floor. Fortunately I landed on top of him. Full force.

"Uff!" He gasped, then groaned.

I seemed to have knocked the wind out of him and though he struggled it was half-hearted. I was able to get on top of him, my weight pinning his shoulders and arms. He hissed and glared but that was about all he could do. A slight electrical burn smell came from the broken lamp behind us.

I pulled his ears back to the carpet between my thumbs and forefingers. They were slick, greasy, and slipped from my grasp as I attempted to keep his head still. Thankfully, he didn't scream out. I could feel his coarse beard bristle through my jeans, very unpleasant.

"Tibor, Tibor, I just want to ask you some questions," I half growled through clenched teeth, squeezing his ears as hard as I could.

He seemed oblivious and began to struggle again, this time a bit more forcefully, moving my weight slightly. I didn't have control of this by any stretch. I grabbed a handful of hair in both my hands. It was even greasier than his ears, but I hung on, lifted his head, and slammed it down hard into the floor. It seemed to have no effect, nor the second time when I slammed harder. The third time he blinked strangely and let loose with a low, throaty groan. But he didn't struggle.

"Tibor, Tibor, listen to me. Now listen. I need to find Kerri. You know Kerri?"

He glared back at me.

I slammed his head into the floor, then did it again, as hard as I could.

"I'm going to ask again. Where is Kerri, Karina Vucavitch, Kerri, where is she?"

He focused on my face, glared again, as I grabbed a bigger handful of greasy hair, lifted his head to slam it.

"No, do not, no!" he said.

Thank God.

"Tibor, I need to find Karina Vucavitch, where is she? I just want to talk to her. She's in danger."

He refocused on me, strangely. He seemed to be thinking, although one could never be sure.

I tightened my grip in his hair.

"With Braco, lives with Braco."

"Who's Braco?"

He looked at me like I was from another planet, studying me for a moment.

"Braco Alekseeva. She is his woman."

"Braco Alekseeva?"

He actually smiled. At least that's what I think he was doing. Lips curled, teeth exposed, or was he planning to bite me?

"Braco Alekseeva, he would like you to meet," he half snarled.

"This Braco, he wouldn't drive an LX11 would he? He drive a big red car, Tibor?"

152

He nodded, eyes glaring.

"You tell Braco I'd like to talk with him. I'm going to find him and…"

"Braco find you." He gasped.

"Good, it'll save me time. Now, Tibor, I'm going to get off you. I want you to stay on the floor. Understand? Nod your head yes."

He did.

I climbed off carefully, but quickly. Tibor lay on the floor, glaring at me in his strappy T-shirt, striped boxer shorts and white socks. I noticed the tip of a big toe poking through one of his socks and hairy shoulders, arms and legs with a beer belly beneath the T-shirt that was rising and falling from his heavy breathing.

"You just stay there, Tibor. I'll let myself out. Sorry about the lamp. Nice music by the way," I nodded in the direction of a cello, leaning against a wooden chair in the far corner. I backed to the door and began to pull it. Bits of broken lamp and shards of glass clinked and tinkled as I closed the door.

Tibor lay still, smiling strangely, like he was the only one in on the joke.

In the hallway I left the opposite way I came, going down the back stairs and out, if only to avoid Tibor tracking me from his window or worse, following. I walked quickly past two buildings, turned a corner, then jogged to my car. I didn't believe anyone was following, but why wait to find out?

I thought about Braco Alekseeva all the way home.

Chapter Thirty-Six

"What do you mean, how did I get that name? I'm an investigator, remember? I came across it as part of my investigation. So what can you tell me about my friend Mr. Alekseeva?"

"Braco Alekseeva, Braco the Whacko, believe me, you want to stay as far away as possible from that guy," Aaron said.

We were having dinner at Geno's, which might sound casual, but was very trendy. I had once dated a waitress from Geno's for a torrid three and a half weeks a couple of years back, then broke it off when her ex-husband entered our relationship. He was a professional arm wrestler. Well that, and the fact that she went off her meds. Our parting had been unpleasant, public, and memorable when she attacked me with a steak knife on the outdoor patio of a restaurant I've never revisited since. I figured given the mobility of servers in the restaurant biz and her craziness, I had a pretty good chance she wasn't still employed here. Wrong again.

"Good evening, gentlemen, may I get you something from the bar or perhaps you'd like to see our wine… Dev, Devlin Haskell?"

"Oh, hey, Renee. How you doing? I'm here with officer LaZelle. So, you're still working here? Going well, I hope." I was praying the idea of police protection might fend her off for the evening.

Aaron nodded, smiled, then turned to the page marked "prohibitively expensive" in the wine list, while Renee glared at me and never blinked.

"Well, yeah, I guess it's going okay. You know, the handicap and all, tough to get work, so I'm just thankful I've got a job to go to. You know me, soldiering on, uncomplaining," she said, sounding serious. I guessed it must be whatever meds she was on at the present.

"Gee, that's great, you look fabulous," I said, and she did.

"I think we'll have the Sangiovese, bin nineteen." Aaron smiled.

"Oh, very nice selection, sir. I'll be right back with that." She smiled, then flashed her eyes at me as she left.

"Is this place okay or would you prefer somewhere else?"

"The table?" Aaron asked looking at me like I was crazy.

"No, the restaurant. Look, I have some history with our waitress and…"

"No Kidding? Not bad, man, you may have just gone up a notch in my estimation."

"Oh. God, don't even go there. Bottom line is she wigged out, tried to kill me with a steak knife out on a patio."

"I'd like to hear her side of it. Were there witnesses?"

"Witnesses? God, it was at a restaurant, she went absolutely crazy. Look, I don't want to get into it tonight, okay? But I'm more than a little uncomfortable with the whole thing right now. How about you just watch my back here, will you?"

"Jesus, will you relax? Someone that good-looking, believe me, she's glad to have you out of her life."

"Thanks for the…"

"Gentlemen, would either of you care to sample before I pour?" Renee smiled sweetly at Aaron.

"Yes, I'd love to," he said, pushing a wine glass ever so slightly in her direction.

She poured.

Aaron made a production of swirling, inhaling, swishing around in his mouth, eventually swallowing before deeming it acceptable.

"Delightfully fruity," he said, as if he'd know.

She poured us both a glass, delivered menus, and told us about the specials. One was a steak I immediately vetoed for reasons of cutlery safety.

"So what can you tell me about Braco Alekseeva?" I asked, sticking my nose in the wine and checking for arsenic.

"How'd you get that name?" Aaron asked. There was no humor in his voice, about as deadly serious as I've ever seen him.

"What do you mean, how did I get that name?"

The night continued, mercifully uneventful. I relaxed a bit more as our conversation turned to other things besides Braco Alekseeva and Kerri Vucavitch. Or maybe it was the second bottle of wine Aaron ordered. Or the fact that Renee seemed reasonably stable for the moment. We ordered dessert, after-dinner drinks, a second round of after-dinner drinks. I paid the bill, feeling no pain, left a generous tip as a safety precaution, told Renee she was beautiful, and wished her all the best. Aaron bought us a nightcap in the bar.

It was about three in the morning when I woke with that particular lower intestinal discomfort. A friend described it best when he said "your body tells you it's about to do something awful. Your choice where, you've got ninety seconds to decide." Fortunately the master bath adjoins my room.

Without going into specifics I was still there at six in the morning, only I'd added a metal bowl on my lap. I was losing it from both ends, hell of way to make your goal weight. I collapsed into an exhausted sleep sometime after nine, only to leap out of bed and run into the bathroom forty-five minutes later. Eventually, I showered, slept on and off for three fitful hours, and was back in the bathroom. There was nothing left. I dozed off and on through the afternoon and early evening, then snapped back into action by excruciating intestinal cramps. I sipped a bottle of spring water, hoping it would stay down and phoned Aaron. Amazingly he answered and sounded happy.

"Hey, thanks for last night, man. I should bet against you more often."

"You okay?"

"Oh, a little slow moving this morning, but nothing that an order of hash browns, ground sausage, and fried eggs smothered with hollandaise sauce couldn't handle."

I felt my stomach lurch at the description.

"You?" he asked.

157

"God, don't even ask," I said, then proceeded to give him the details.

"Really, I can't believe it. You sure you didn't just get some weird bug, maybe some twenty-four hour thing?"

"It's that damn Renee. She couldn't kill me with that knife. Now she's poisoned me."

"Well, I'm sure you were a jerk and most likely you deserve it, but I don't think she poisoned you. I mean I'm not sick. Like I said, I was a little hung over, but nothing that an order of..."

"Don't go there," I groaned, struggling out of bed. The mere mention of Renee crossing my lips restarted my cramps, and I crawled back into the bathroom.

"I'll talk to you later," I groaned and hung up.

I phoned Heidi from the bathroom.

"I need you," I pleaded once she answered.

"Now what?" she snapped back.

"Look, ditch the boy toy, please. I'm in real trouble here."

"If you're in jail again, you can just stay there because I'm not bailing you out this time. You can call..."

"Heidi, I'm not in jail. I'm in real trouble here."

"What's wrong?" she sounded genuinely concerned.

"I'm sicker than a dog. I think I've been poisoned."

"Oh, God, more of your neurosis. What? Baby has a little tummy ache?"

"Tummy ache! I've been cramping for close to twenty-four hours. I'm dehydrating, I can't keep anything down, let alone in."

"You see a doctor?"

"I'm too sick to get there. I can't get more than about ten feet away from porcelain."

"No kidding? What have you had since you've been ill?"

"To drink? Just some bottled spring water, but it didn't stay with me. I think I've probably got a fever. I'm exhausted."

She gave a long sigh.

"Okay, I'll be over. Let me stop and pick up some things that will probably help. I'll be there in an hour or so."

"Promise?" I sounded desperate, even to myself.

"God yes, I promise I'll be over. Get back to bed if you're not there already."

Getting back to bed wasn't an option at the moment, and I remained in the bathroom.

Chapter Thirty-Seven

I had drifted off to sleep for probably fifteen minutes. I heard Heidi call to me as she entered.

"In here," I groaned from bed.

She took her sweet time. I could hear the rustle of paper grocery bags, the occasional kitchen-cabinet door closing. Eventually she appeared in the doorway.

"What the hell happened to you?" I asked, beginning to sit up until the cramps kicked in again. Her hair was an Easter Egg pink.

"Oh, Harold thought it would be really radical," she said, tossing her head, seemingly not too convinced.

"The boy toy?"

"Yeah, he's a hairdresser, too."

"He does your hair?"

"Oh, please don't go there. I never want to see that disgusting little piglet ever again in my life."

"Gee, who would ever imagine gnarly old Harold might come up with a bad idea?"

"Arghhh. On a happier note I've got some Imodium and a glass of Pedialyte for you."

"Pedialyte?"

"It's for babies, so they don't get dehydrated, which you certainly are. A baby and getting dehydrated. God, you look like shit, pardon the pun."

"I don't know…"

"That's right, stop right there. You don't know. You called me for help so that's what I'm doing. Take these and just shut up." She thrust a glass and two small pills at me.

I swallowed the pills, then chased them down with a couple of swallows of something that tasted like bubble gum. I felt the cool liquid run all the way into my empty stomach, begin to splash up only to eventually settle. I must have had a cautionary look on my face.

"Staying down?" Heidi asked, ready to jump aside if necessary.

"Yeah, I think so. Look, I just wanted you to…"

"I know what you wanted, Dev. Wouldn't it be nice if I could just sit around and waste my time rubbing your back and attending to your every need for about forty-eight hours? Then clean your bathroom on my way out the door? Forget it. Listen, under the circumstances I brought you a twelve-pack of extra gentle Charmin and a container of baby wipes with aloe. You got any white wine in your fridge?"

"I'm not ready for white wine," I groaned.

"I wasn't thinking of you."

I pulled some sweats on and exited my bedroom for the first time in about thirty hours. It was just after seven in the morning. My pink-haired Nurse Ratchet was asleep on the living-room couch under a faux leopard-skin throw, snoring softly. An empty bottle of my white wine had rolled halfway under the couch. The remnants of a devoured package of Oreo cookies rested on the coffee table next to a wine glass with barely a swallow left. From what I could ascertain, she'd downloaded <u>Sex in the City 2</u> from Netflix the night before. I decided not to wake her.

Just to play it safe, I had another Imodium and a Pedialyte over ice for breakfast. I sipped as I looked out the window and thought about Braco Alekseeva.

Chapter Thirty-Eight

It was another twenty-four hours before I felt strong enough to venture outside. Even then, I was subsisting on dried toast, Chamomile tea, and the dreaded Pedialyte. I carried the Imodium in my pocket just in case.

According to what I could find out, which wasn't much, Braco Alekseeva resided in a penthouse suite on the thirty-sixth floor of St. Paul's Twin Towers, a condo saddled with an unfortunate name choice made in 1999. Actually, Alekseeva didn't reside in a penthouse suite, he resided in the only penthouse suite making it virtually impossible to get anywhere near the thirty-sixth floor. Amazingly, there was a heliport up there, which might make it rather difficult to follow Mr. Alekseeva should he travel by that method. The Twin Towers made it downright impossible to closely watch who came and went, since you'd have to watch the common lobby servicing both towers. In the interest of sanity, I took up a position at the rear of the building, on Robert Street. Down half a block from where the entrance and exit to the underground parking garage was situated. It was a

163

monitored entrance, with a twenty-four hour manned security desk, which eliminated any option of casually ducking in and wandering through underground parking looking for a blue BMW Z4 that smelled like Kerri's perfume.

I sat in my car armed with thirty dollars worth of quarters to stuff the parking meter and a six pack of Pedialyte, which I was beginning to acquire a taste for. On day three, with about a dollar seventy-five worth of quarters remaining, a blue BMW drove up the exit ramp from underground parking and headed north. I followed.

The car wove a circuitous route through downtown, eventually turning one hundred and eighty degrees before traveling west following the Mississippi river along Sheppard Road. The road is eight miles of four-lane and then just beyond a cloverleaf interchange Sheppard Road becomes the River Boulevard, a wooded city street riding along the edge of the river bluff. There are scenic overlooks all along the route where cars can pull into a tailored parking area and view the sights. The BMW pulled into one of these and Kerri climbed out of the car, leaned against the trunk smoking a cigarette with her arms crossed, looking like she was waiting for someone. She held the cigarette between her thumb and middle finger, like a French movie star, or someone smoking dope, come to think of it.

I pulled into the parking lot, circled around, then stopped just opposite her, perpendicular to her BMW. I lowered the window, but kept the car in gear, not sure what was going to happen. I had my .45 resting on my lap, just to feel comfortable.

"God, it is about time," she said, taking a final drag from her cigarette, then dropping it to the ground, crushing it with her toe and exhaling a cloud of smoke. She took a step or two toward my car and crossed her arms. Not in a sense of inflexibility as much as she seemed to be hugging herself, making things safe. She glanced quickly over the roof of my car and looked up and down the road.

"So, Dev, what is new, have you found out anything for me?" she asked, sort of shrugged her shoulders, and smiled innocently. She was anything but.

What's new? I thought. Aside from you not answering my phone calls? How about I've been shot, chased, arrested, poisoned, I've still got whisker burn on my inner thighs, my beverage of choice is now Pedialyte and the last woman I spoke with for more than twenty minutes was run over by a red Lexus LX11. Which, I was willing to bet, belonged to your boyfriend. And all of that was connected to you, in some way. Instead I said, "Oh, you know, not much, same old same old," trying to act coy.

"Have you learned anything of my sister, Nikki?"

"Your sister? Would she have been born in France, too?"

"What? That really is not the point, is it, Dev? Have you learned where she is?"

"Not really, Kerri. Other things keep popping up, you know."

"We're all busy, but when I hired you..."

"Like your boyfriend, old Braco, there. What can you tell me about him?"

"I don't think Mr. Alekseeva is the point, Dev. I hired you to find Nikki, for me."

"Your sister."

"Yes."

"Was she born in France?" I asked again.

"I don't think that has anything to do with what I hired you to learn."

"Look, Kerri, I'm walking. I'm off the case, I quit."

"Quit. You mean you're not going to find Nikki for me?"

"Not exactly what I said. I said I quit. I'm not working for you anymore. I am going to find Nikki. While I'm at it, I'm going to find out who ran over Da'nita Bell. Make sure someone gets held accountable for that. Then, I'm probably going to press my luck and introduce myself to your little fuck buddy Braco."

"I wouldn't advise you bothering Mr. Alekseeva," she said, looking over the roof of my car, checking up and down the road again.

"I've never been one to heed advice, Kerri, even if it's good."

"Are you doing this because of the shooting? Did the bullet make you cuckoo or something?"

"Me? No, I've always been like this. We call it pig headed, you familiar with the term?"

"I'm familiar with pigs," she scoffed.

"I'll bet you are."

"Look, Dev, I'm sorry about the shooting. I didn't mean for it to happen like that."

"Not entirely your fault, darling."

"But it is, if I'd been more careful, I should have…"

166

"Look, you can't be watching over me all the time. How were you to know Nikki, or whoever, was going to attempt a drive-by at high noon on a busy commercial street?"

"Nikki?" she asked, looking at me strangely.

"Or whoever it was."

"Dev, don't you remember? My God, it was me!" she said.

"Huh?"

"Don't you remem... Dev, it was my gun. I saw her car and thought she was going to shoot me so I, well, that is... Well, you were in front of me and I pulled the pistol from my purse. I meant to shoot at her but it was so rushed it just went off, you know. I was so frightened, I didn't think to aim, sort of...... maybe."

"Wait a minute. You mean it was you that shot me?"

She nodded and batted her eyes like that might make it okay.

"And you shot me when you were pulling me in front of you. The pistol just sort of went off, and my head just happened to be in the way."

"Yes, exactly." She seemed to be relieved now that I got it.

"Well, of course, now it all makes sense," I joked.

"Okay, so now you will come back to work for me and find Nikki, no?"

"Exactly right, no. No, I won't, Kerri. I got a loose idea of what you and Braco are into here and no, I'm not going to work for you. You can tell old Braco I'm going to be on his ass, and yours too, although I'm sure in your case it's just part of an average day."

"We always used to meet right here, to talk. Nikki and I, just the two of us. We called this our private place."

She casually slipped her right hand into her jacket pocket, the jacket hanging just a bit to the right.

"Oh, please don't. It would make everything so easy," I said picking up the .45 from my lap, laying the barrel on the door, and pointing it in her direction. She took a step backwards.

"Dev, I'm beginning to think you really are crazy. I was only going to reach for a cigarette," she said, then ran both hands through her hair.

"Just keep your hands where I can see them. Kerri, tell Mr. Alekseeva, Braco, that I'm beginning to take all of this very personally."

"Typical American. This is real life, Dev. It isn't some movie where you say your silly lines. You think we didn't see you sitting out there in the street waiting day after day, for what? We could have taken you anytime we wanted, with no problem. At the end of the day you are just a fool, Dev, a fool."

"Probably. But I may be watching, and from now on you'll never be sure, will you, Kerri?" I bluffed.

"I think you better go, Dev." She looked over the roof of my car. "Unless you want that meeting with Mr. Alekseeva now."

I turned and saw a large red vehicle entering the parking lot. The odds were pretty good it was the same Lexus LX11 that hit Da'nita Bell. The right front bumper was scraped and dented.

Four very large, neckless heads were silhouetted through the tinted front windshield. I waited until they'd cleared the entrance, then quickly exited across the park lawn, over the curb, rolled into the street and accelerated. When she brushed her hair back it must have been some sort of a sign. They'd either tailed us all the way here or they'd been waiting all along. Either way it was a set-up.

I watched them in my rearview mirror. Everyone suddenly flew out of the car and ducked behind the LX11. One of them actually tripped and just lay there. What a bunch of idiots. Kerri must have fallen for my 'may be watching' line and those dumb heads thought I meant it. Now, who was the fool? I didn't race, but I didn't hang around either. I drove away as fast as prudently possible.

Chapter Thirty-Nine

The next day I was still pondering Kerri's confession that she was the one who shot me. Wondering at the same time how I got myself into these things. The phone interrupted.

"How you feeling?" Aaron asked when I answered. No hello, no introduction, just the question.

"Thanks for asking, I'm back to about ninety percent, but I'm able to be out and about."

"Ninety percent, I guess that's a lot better than the half-assed way you usually conducted yourself before you got sick."

"You mean poisoned."

"You weren't driving around on the River Boulevard yesterday afternoon, were you?" he asked, ignoring my poisoned comment.

"Possibly. I was all over town, running errands after being confined to the bathroom for the last three days. Why? What's up?" I said, attempting to sound nonchalant.

"Oh, nothing much. Just wondering is all. You know a guy named, well actually we don't know what his name is, his real name. The driver's license said Andrew Quinn."

"No, I don't think I know anyone by that name. What am I missing here?"

"I'm not sure. Hard to figure why a guy named Andrew Quinn might have Russian naval tattoos. I suppose he could be a wanna-be Russian sailor or maybe he vacationed once on the Black Sea or something and fell in love with the place. Of course, the more we're digging into him the less we seem to know. No apparent next of kin. The address we have for him is a Holiday station, so that would seem to be bogus. No record of this guy anywhere, yet he has a Minnesota license."

"And Mr. Quinn would concern me how?"

"I don't know that it does. Just that someone took the back of his head off with a high-caliber rifle shot over on the River Boulevard yesterday. You may have seen the news reports in between cartoon shows. We have an eyewitness report of a couple of vehicles racing out of there, one a red SUV, the other a blue sports car. Ring any bells?"

Yeah, alarm bells. I remembered the guy tumbling out of the car, thinking he'd fallen. Had he been shot? Who shot him? A shot to the head might be Kerri's style, but she didn't seem likely.

"Are you suggesting I had something to do with this?"

"No, not really. I know you're not that good a shot, for starters. But suddenly you never seem to be too far from the action when our Russian friends are involved."

"Maybe you should check with your pal special agent Kimball Peters, if he can break away from

171

answering phones and whoever's ass he's kissing. I'm sure he'd have lots of answers."

"Yeah, right. Okay, just checking on you. Word to the wise, you might want to keep a close watch on your back."

"Appreciate the advice."

"Okay, catch you later, man. Be careful."

I may not be the brightest bulb on the tree, but experience had taught me that if Aaron was concerned, panic on my part would not be out of line. I didn't panic. But I wondered who had fired that shot, and I thought it might be wise to limit my exposure.

Chapter Forty

I was just pulling out of the grocery-store parking lot when I phoned Heidi.

"Hey, thought I'd check up on you for a change. Thanks for your help yesterday," I said.

"Well, gee, not a problem, glad I could help. You feeling any better?" Heidi asked.

"Feeling great, thanks to you. Look, I'm thinking I've been sort of a pain in the ass lately and wondered if I could maybe make it up to you. Doing anything for dinner?"

"Dinner? Tonight?"

"Yeah, well, that is unless you've already got something planned."

"No, nothing planned. It's just so out of character for you to be so nice. You're not thinking of sticking me with the tab or something, are you?" She was only half joking.

"No. In fact, I tell you what, I'll pick up some steaks and be at your place in ten minutes. I mean, if that's okay."

"Here? Well, yeah. I suppose."

"It's not Harold, is it?"

"I told you never to mention that worthless jerk to me ever again."

"Okay. How about this, I'm going to stop and pick up some wine, get the steaks, give you time to get organized. We'll just have a relaxing night. Let me pamper you for a change."

"Give me thirty minutes. Gosh, Dev, this is really nice of you," she said sounding genuinely surprised.

I already had the wine and steaks in the car, right next to my overnight bag with Da'nita's laptop, and now I had thirty minutes to kill. I decided to swing by The Spot, and pop in for just a minute.

The stools at the bar were barely half full, but then again it was just a little after five on a weeknight. Jimmy was tending bar.

"Dev," he called, then by way of greeting, poured a Leinenkugel's for me. He had it waiting by the time I'd given a couple of perfunctory hellos making my way down the bar.

"Good to see you, been awhile," Jimmy said.

I nodded as I sipped.

"Yeah, been a crazy week."

"Man you must have some sort of special power. Last time you were in here you ended up leaving with that gorgeous blonde, remember?"

"I'm trying not to, that didn't exactly work out for me," I said shaking my head.

"Well, you must have done something right, she was in here asking for you last night, and then again this afternoon. Man, looks like she can't get enough of you. No accounting for some people's taste, right?" he laughed again.

174

"She was in here? Looking for me?"

"Yup."

"Anyone with her?" I asked, suddenly not that intent on finishing my beer.

"You mean, like those three weight-lifter guys and her husband?" He chuckled at his own joke for a moment, "Oh, God, you should see your face. Naw, no one was with her."

"What'd you tell her?"

Jimmy looked at me for a long moment, serious.

"You know how many homicides and domestic disputes I'd be responsible for if I gave any sort of information out? Come on, Dev, I'm a professional. If you're gonna get some action, all I ask is that you take pictures and share 'em with me." He laughed.

I didn't want to waste the beer, but I wasn't going to hang there any longer than necessary, so I quickly gulped down half of it.

"What's the deal, she some sort of nutcase or something? God, it figures, the good-looking ones are always crazy."

"She's okay, I guess. Just a little more baggage than I need right now."

Jimmy nodded in agreement.

"I hear ya. Kids in the way, a jealous ex-husband lurking around, upside down mortgage, and nowadays you gotta buy them dinner before they'll climb in bed. Who needs it? Remember that chick I used to date from Minneapolis? I thought, great, a kinky, sexually repressed Lutheran babe and she just…"

I drained the remainder of my beer, and tossed a five-dollar bill on the bar. I didn't want to wait for the end of the story or my change.

"Jimmy, you working tonight?"

"Yeah, you coming back to link up with that sweetie?"

"No, I got something else I gotta deal with. Look, if she comes in again, tell her I was here and I'll be back tomorrow night. Tell her I'm usually here around nine."

"Not a problem, Dev. Hot one tonight?"

"Hopefully. Sorry Jim, but I gotta run. See you."

"You're a player, Dev, an honest-to-God player, man. Don't forget to mention my name when you get back together with her," he called as I ran out the side door.

I took a roundabout way to Heidi's, driving past the scenic overlook where I spoke to Kerri yesterday and apparently some guy lost his head, literally. You wouldn't know it to look at it now, although there were remnants of yellow-plastic crime-scene tape still tied around some trees that had roped the area off from curious onlookers.

I pulled into the lot, then stopped approximately where I had spoken with Kerri yesterday. I could still see the telltale indentations where I'd driven across the grass and jumped the curb to get out of there. Just looking around, there were easily a thousand different places where a shooter could have hidden. Someone who really knew what they were doing, make it a million hiding places.

Whoever it was and wherever they had been, they must have been in position when I was talking

176

to Kerri and had an easy shot at me. What did that mean? Why shoot someone in Braco's LX11? They'd only just arrived. Just more questions I didn't have answers for.

Chapter Forty-One

Heidi answered the door barefoot, in cutoffs, a T-shirt and no bra. No complaint on my part. I guessed she was just out of the shower. The pink hair was gone, replaced by a blonde so white it was almost see-through. Based on the stains cupping across the front of her T-shirt, I guessed she was just reaching for the towel to dry off when I rang her doorbell.

"Well, what do you think?" she asked, raising her eyes up toward her hair.

"They're fantastic. I think you should toss out all your bras."

"Not my boobs you perv, my hair," she said hitting me in the shoulder.

"Hair, oh, it's not pink anymore. Harold do that?"

"It wasn't pink, it was Atomic Magenta, and not my idea. That creep Harold, the big dope. Don't even mention his name in this house."

"Hey, it looks great. What's the new color?"

"Albino snow blonde. Like it?"

"Different. But in a good way," I quickly added. She looked at me like she wasn't sure.

"Here," I said, lifting the grocery bag. "Let me get these steaks marinating and pour you a glass of wine. Not in that order."

I poured her a glass of wine, opened a beer for me, set the steaks to marinate in red wine with some rosemary, then started the grill. Once the coals went down I put the steaks on the grill, and cooked them just the way she liked them. I had the makings for a salad, buttered carrots and baked potatoes, plus another bottle of wine for Heidi. It was maybe 10:30 before we finished dinner. I cleared the table and refilled her wine, not that she needed more.

"God, I just can't get over how nice you've been tonight. Nice to be with you when you're not you're usual asshole self," she said, then followed that faint praise with a major slosh of wine.

"Gee, thanks for the compliment," I said, opening another beer, my second of the night.

"Not a problem, thanks for the dinner. You know, maybe I should bail you out more often."

"Let's hope you don't have to do that."

"Can I ask you something, Dev?" She was slurring her words at this point.

"Yeah, sure," I was loading her dishwasher, cleaning up the kitchen.

"Do you really like my hair color?" she asked, then absently shook her hair.

"Well, I like it a lot better than the pink that Har.. that you had before. You're far too beautiful to have to stoop to that sort of thing to get anyone's attention."

"Do you really think I'm beautiful?" Her head was weaving back and forth ever so slightly, eyes getting glassier by the minute. She reached for the

179

wine bottle and filled her glass almost to the rim, slopping some across the kitchen counter.

"Oops!" she said, smearing the wine across the granite countertop with the palm of her hand. I knew where this was going. I'd been here uncountable times before with her. I'm the master when it comes to giving women that one drink too many that pushes them out of the throes of nymphomania and into alcohol-induced sleep or nausea. Take your pick.

We chatted for another fifteen or twenty minutes. Heidi suddenly lurched off her kitchen stool, took an unstable step or two, then steadied herself against the counter, she grabbed her glass of wine and said, "I'll be right back. No peeking, mister." She waved the wine glass back and forth, sloshing red wine onto the floor.

"I promise."

I straightened up the rest of the kitchen. Mopped up the wine on the floor. Got the coffeemaker ready for the following morning. I shut down her iPod, carried the trash bag out, wheeled the trash bin to the curb, then grabbed my overnight bag from my car.

I plugged in Da'nita's laptop and turned it on, then went back to Heidi's bedroom to check on her. She was asleep on the edge of the bed, feet on the floor. Passed out might have been a more accurate description. Snoring. She'd taken her T-shirt off and pulled on a neon blue, see through nightie, although she still wore her cutoffs. She'd left the faucet running in the bathroom.

I was tempted to do something to her like draw a mustache on her face or autograph her butt. Cooler heads prevailed and I lifted her feet onto the bed, hopefully made her comfortable, covered her with an afghan, and turned out the light. Then I went back into the kitchen, pulled a stool in front of the laptop, and punched in the password DB+DB to see if I could learn anything. After two hours I was just as stupid as when I started.

Sometime well after midnight, I grabbed a blanket from Heidi's hall closet and ever the gentleman, settled in for the night on her couch.

Heidi's cursing coming from the kitchen woke me about 7:15 the following morning.

"God, I hate these god damned things," she growled. She was fully dressed, groomed, and shaking an aspirin bottle.

"What is the problem?"

"I just want to open this damn thing. Why do they have to make them so fucking difficult?"

"Are you referring to the childproof cap?" I asked, taking the white plastic container from her hand.

She stormed over to the sink and ran tap water into a glass.

"Oh please, spare me the superior attitude and just open the damn thing."

Heidi with a hangover was not a fun experience, for anyone.

"Two or four?" I asked, shaking two into my hand.

"God, the whole bottle. Oh, why did you do that to me? I've got an 8:45 conference call and then follow-up meetings all day. I'll never be able to make it."

"Okay, first of all, I didn't do anything to you. Believe me, nothing happened."

"Oh sorry," she said, looking beyond pitiful.

"Second, I admit I was out of line sitting on you and forcing you to drink the better part of two bottles of red wine."

"Okay, okay, that's not helping just now."

"If it's any consolation, you look beautiful."

"Do I?"

"Yes. I've got the coffee ready to turn on. Can you wait two minutes and I'll pour you a travel mug?"

"No, I need to run. I'll grab some at work, and…"

"Okay, but make sure you do, and grab a couple of pastries just to get something in your stomach, promise?"

"Yeah, okay. Thanks, Dev. Sorry about the lack of… well you know, catch you later?"

"Not a problem, Heidi. Now go on and get to that conference call," I gave her a kiss on the forehead.

"Yeah, sorry, but I better run. Let yourself out."

Chapter Forty-Two

I was standing in the dark, in a two-car garage across the street and kitty-corner from The Spot bar. It was half past eight in the evening. I was looking out a grimy window to see if Kerri would show up, and if she did was she alone? Jimmy had talked with her the night before when she came looking for me, and bought her a double vodka martini.

"God, I could have watched her drink those things all night long, on the house. She is one great-looking woman, Dev. How'd she ever end up with you?" he asked, sounding like she'd somehow had to settle for second prize.

Kerri didn't show at nine, or nine thirty. About ten minutes to ten I saw her car creep past and park fifty feet farther down the street. As she parked, a dark-colored SUV flicked its lights at her from across the street. She walked into The Spot alone, exited a minute later, and had a short, but animated conversation on her cell. When that was finished she stuffed the cell in her purse and went back inside.

I figured Jimmy must have enticed her to wait with the offer of another free double martini while her friends across the street just cooled their heels.

There's a front and a side door to The Spot. The SUV was parked in such a way that it could watch both doors. The nice thing about being a regular at a place is that you learn the pattern of how things operate, or at least how they're supposed to operate. There's a back door, too, used for the occasional picnic in the parking lot and taking out the trash after closing.

I left the garage, walked in the opposite direction, then around the block, crossed the street a block farther down, and went up the alley to the back door. I peeked around the corner; and noticed that the SUV was still parked across the street. I tried the door. It was locked so I phoned the bar.

"The Spot and we're open," Jimmy said.

"Jimmy, Dev. Don't say my name."

"Hey, Dev, that lady is here waiting for you."

"Are you fucking listening? I said don't say my name."

"Oh, yeah sorry 'bout that."

"Did she hear you?"

"No, she's picking a couple of songs over at the jukebox. Want me to put her on?"

"No, no, Jesus don't do that. I don't want her to know we're talking." I peeked around the corner again, the SUV was still in the same place.

"You coming in or you want me to tell her to take off?" Jimmy was finally getting on board.

"I'm at the back door. Can you slip back here and let me in?"

"The back door?" He paused and I could almost hear him thinking on the phone. "Okay, yeah I can be there in just a minute, hang on." He'd obviously set the phone down on the bar, 'cause I was still listening to background noise when the door clicked open.

"What the hell is it with all the secret stuff? You trying to surprise this chick or something?" Jimmy asked.

"Look, Jim, we're going to leave out this door in just a half minute or so. Can you leave it unlocked."

"You're going back out this door? You must have a husband or boyfriend on your ass."

"Yeah, that's it."

"Well, she might be worth the risk. Like I said before, I wanna see the pictures, man."

We walked across the nondescript little back room that used to serve as a kitchen and into the barroom. Kerri had returned to her stool at the far end of the bar and sat sipping her free martini. She was staring at the front door, looking bored. Jimmy stepped behind the bar. I walked the length of it and came up behind her.

"Kerri?"

She turned and stared at me with a shocked look on her face., then looked over my shoulder like she expected something to happen. Maybe the side door was supposed to burst open.

It didn't.

"Kerri?" I asked again.

"Oh, Dev, what a surprise. I was hoping I might run into you here. Sorry you had to leave so quickly the other day." She said it like I'd had to make a meeting instead of fleeing a carload of her thug pals, one of whom was promptly drilled between the eyes.

"Yeah, that was unfortunate. Hey let's you and I take a walk, okay?"

"I would like that. Can I buy you a drink first? I guess I wanted to tell you how sorry I am if I caused you any trouble. You know, with shooting you in the head and all. Of course, I feel bad about doing that."

Trouble? I thought, lady, you have no idea what I got planned for you. But then again, neither did I. So I said,

"No problem. Look, leave the drink and let's go outside for a minute." I looked to either side then raised my shirt, showing her the pistol shoved into my belt. I took her by the arm, not too forcefully.

She didn't protest, and she didn't appear to be very concerned about the pistol, for that matter. She just smiled and led us toward the side door.

"Oh, not that door. Come on, there's another one back here," I said, directing her by the elbow again. There was some slight hesitation and she looked up at me, unsure.

"Relax, if I was going to do something like hurt you, you think I'd want all these witnesses around who can place us leaving together?"

"I suppose you are right. Mind if I just phone a friend? I'll tell her I might be a little late." She smiled nastily, slowly licked her lip, then produced the cell phone in her hand, ready to call.

"Yeah, actually I do mind. Let's go." I took the cell out of her hand, and steered her into the back room and out the door.

We stepped outside and she looked furtively from side to side.

"I promise I won't hurt you, Kerri. I just have a couple of questions to ask and then you can go." We were walking back down the alley, retracing the route I'd taken a few minutes before.

At the end of the alley I directed us left instead of right. My car was parked fifteen feet from the alley. I opened the passenger door for her, and she slid in after the slightest hesitation. I went around the front of the car, then climbed in the driver's side. Kerri looked at me with large eyes, shoulders hunched, hands stuck in her coat pockets. She shivered slightly.

"To tell you the truth, Kerri, I've got so many questions I don't even know where to begin."

"Questions about what?"

"Well, for starters, who in the hell is Nikki?"

"I told you she is my sis…"

"Nikolaevna Mathias is your sister?"

"Who told you that name?"

"Same person that told me your name is Karina Vucavitch."

Her eyes widened, but she didn't say anything. Eventually she just shrugged her shoulders, answered,

"So."

"So, what's going on? I start looking for your sister, and the next thing I know people are getting shot. Like me for instance and the …"

"I already told you I was sorry."

"Gee, thanks. And, the guy with the drivers license that said his name was Andrew Quinn. Who the hell was he?"

I caught the slightest hint of surprise cross her face.

"He's called Sergie."

"Sergie?"

"Sergie Alekseeva."

"Any relation to your main squeeze Braco?"

"His son."

"And yours? Your son?"

"Don't be a stupid," she said then mumbled something in Russian. Given the tone I didn't really need a translation, but then she switched back to English.

"He was a pig. He raped me. Braco would give us to him. They all thought it was funny."

"Funny? I thought you were Braco's I don't know, what... partner?"

"I'm whatever Braco wants me to be. I'm soulless, a ghost, his whore of the moment."

"Well, don't sugarcoat it, Kerri. Gee, you make it sound really healthy. Why not just leave?"

"You would not understand."

"Try me?"

"It is all very simple. If I do not do what Braco wants he will kill my family back in Russia. My mother, my father, my two brothers, and my little sister. I know this. He will do it. Then he will show me pictures of their bodies. Then he will make me a five-dollar whore. And then, just before I die, he will turn me into your police because I have no passport and I stay here not legal. There is no one who can help me, and I am the only one who can save my family."

"But there must be something you can do?"

"When Braco wants something, there is nothing you can do."

I almost couldn't hear her, she said it so softly.

"That's bullshit."

"Bullshit, is that what you would call it? Really? You will see, because Braco wants you now."

"Me? What the hell does he want with me?"

"Now he blames you for Sergie. He thinks you tricked him."

"Tricked Sergie? I didn't even know he existed until a moment ago when you told me. Now what's going to happen?"

She looked at me out of the corner of her eye, then slowly pulled a pistol from her jacket pocket.

"I wish it was someone else, Dev," she said.

"Jesus, don't point that thing…" I slapped the pistol off to the side, just as it went off. I grabbed her wrist and forearm in my hands and slammed them hard against the dashboard. She gasped each time I slammed her arm into the dash. I held onto her wrist, but let go of her forearm and punched her on the chin, punched a second time, and she dropped the gun. I let go of her wrist.

"I'm so sorry, Dev," she said as she rolled out the passenger door, and sort of landed on all fours. She began crawling, then quickly picked up speed and was on her feet running back up the alley. I could have chased her, but there was that SUV at the other end of the block, and in all honesty, I just sat there. My ears were still ringing, the inside of my car smelled like cordite, and I had a bullet hole in my windshield with a spider web pattern running around it the size of a dinner plate.

It would only be a matter of thirty seconds before she made it to the SUV and told whoever was in there where I was. I thought the prudent thing might be to just calmly get the hell out of there.

"I wish it was someone else, Dev." Did she mean someone else she was going to shoot or someone else who was going to shoot me?

Chapter Forty-Three

I drove a zigzag route over to Jefferson Avenue, then headed west in the general direction of Heidi's, driving on side streets to make sure I wasn't being followed. My first call was to 911.

"Nine-one-one, Ramsey County Dispatch."

"Yeah, I want to report an SUV with some guys in it parked on Randolph Avenue. They had a gun."

"A gun, sir?"

"Yeah, I was just walking past. I was in The Spot bar across the street. I came out, walked past their car, and they had a gun."

"Were they pointing it at you?"

"No, they were yelling at this woman in a blue sports car, a BMW, I think. I just got out of there."

The dispatcher asked my name, the number I was calling from, a call back number. I didn't expect anything to happen, but it would be nice to have a police cruiser or two driving up and down the street just to keep those clowns out of the area.

My next call was to Aaron. I got dumped into the usual message center.

"Aaron, Dev. Hey look, it's about 10:15. I might have a name for you on that Andrew Quinn body. The guy who lost his head, it may be Sergie Alekseeva. That would be the son of 'Braco the Whacko.' Give my regards to your close pal Kimball Peters. Later, man."

Chapter Forty-Four

I drove over to Heidi's. Although the street was nearly empty, I parked up on the next block, just in case I was unlucky enough to have some hapless Russian stumble across my car. I phoned Heidi from her front door.

"Hey, you feeling any better?" I said once she answered her phone.

"Oh, Dev, that's so sweet of you to check on me. Yeah, long day but I think I'll live."

"Listen, I was thinking if you're not too busy and it isn't too late, I might swing by just to…"

"Why, what's wrong?"

"Why does something have to be wrong? I'm on your end of town is all and I was thinking you could maybe use a backrub. Look, if it's a problem, just say so."

"Backrub?" she sounded skeptical, then said, "Well, I guess it's okay. You can come over."

I rang the doorbell, heard it echo back in my phone.

"Oh, God, hang on. There's someone at the door. What idiot is ringing my doorbell at this hour of…" She opened the door and stared at me, then shook her head.

"You idiot," she said and hung up.

"Thanks for inviting me over," I said, stepping in and closing the door behind me.

Heidi looked out at the empty street.

"Where's your car? You didn't walk here did you?"

"Car? Oh, I parked a couple of houses away, just in case you looked out the window. I didn't want to ruin my joke."

She seemed to buy that.

"Get you a glass of wine or a beer?" she asked, walking back into the kitchen. She was barefoot, wearing a T-shirt and gray sweatpants. Across the rear of her sweatpants the word PINK was spelled out in pink letters. As if her perfectly firm ass needed anything to draw attention to it.

"You having anything?"

"I'm having a glass of wine," she said, opening her refrigerator.

"Little hair of the dog?"

"No, it's white wine." She was serious.

"Beer for me, no glass is fine."

We chatted in her living room about everything and anything. I really do enjoy her company. I also noticed she was in one of those guarded drinking modes. She would raise the glass and then begin to set it down just as the wine touched her lips. I was opening my third beer.

"I like your hair," I lied.

"No you don't. I've got an appointment the day after tomorrow, so save it. It's going back to normal." She got up and walked into the kitchen. I could see her set her mostly full wine glass in the sink. She walked back out into the living room, turned off the light on the end table, then picked up my nearly full beer bottle.

"Come on, let's go to bed," she said. She put her free hand in mine and led me through the kitchen. She set the bottle on the counter as we walked past, but never slowed.

Chapter Forty-Five

I woke to Heidi kissing me good-bye. She was dressed, smelled of perfume and hair conditioner, and was out the bedroom door after telling me to lock up when I left. I drifted back to sleep until Aaron's phone call rudely interrupted my dream recounting the previous night.

"Sergie Alekseeva? Where'd you get that information?"

"Fine thanks, how are you?" I answered.

"Sergie."

"Someone who would know. You can check it with his old man if you want. Might be a way to get on his good side, you know, giving him his son's body. On the other hand it…"

"I don't really need to be on Braco Alekseeva's good side, should he have one. You know anything else on this, like maybe who pulled the trigger?"

"Believe me, if I did I would give them a medal and then tell you who it was. From what my source told me, old Sergie was a bit of a jerk."

"To put it mildly," Aaron said.

"So you knew him?"

"I knew of him. The old man's the power. Sergie was just the idiot son in line to take the reins someday. This is the logical result. It's just ahead of schedule. Something ever happened to the old man Sergie wasn't going to last the day. The list of jackasses who could do a better job of ruining the social fabric of the saintly city is long."

"Gee, he sounds like a real charmer."

"Aren't they all?" Aaron said. He added his good-bye and hung up.

Chapter Forty-Six

Given the state of Heidi's pantry, I felt fortunate to find coffee and some mint crème Oreos for breakfast. I wondered how someone could look so good on such a constant diet of crap. Following her parting instructions, I locked up on my way out the door.

I'd barely left Heidi's front steps when I spotted two guys sitting in the front seat of a nondescript car. It was a Ford or Chevrolet, maybe a Buick. I wasn't sure, but American made, burgundy, with no white walls on the tires. They were parked across the street from my car, maybe two houses farther down the block. They seemed to be talking, sipping coffee. I didn't think they'd seen me yet.

All they needed was a rack of flashing lights across the top of their car. City cops would have been a little more discreet, maybe parked around the corner. Bad guys probably would be under a front porch or up in a tree with a high-powered rifle. I was half a block away and these two screamed Feds. I could only hope it was FBI agent Kimball "Dickhead" Peters because I wanted to make him run in his shiny wingtips.

As I walked toward my car I could see them looking back and forth discussing something. Then the guy behind the steering wheel passed something to his partner. He glanced up and down, from me to whatever he was holding, and then back up to me. I guessed it was probably a copy of my driver's license photo. Maybe they couldn't recognize me because I was wearing my St. Paul Saints baseball cap or because my license photo looked like I should be arrested for war crimes.

I was maybe ten feet from my car when they opened their car doors simultaneously. I took an immediate right, climbed three steps toward the front door of a house, then followed the sidewalk around toward the back.

That stopped them for a moment. I could see them look at each other out of the corner of my eye, not sure what to do. They wore dark suits, ties, and although neither one looked like Kimball Peters I could tell from here their shoes were shined.

"Haskell?" one of them called to me.

I kept walking around the side of the house and disappeared from their view.

"Haskell, wait, FBI. Stay right where you are," they yelled, like that was supposed to work.

I hopped a picket fence, ran across the backyard, hopped the far side of the fence then up along the side of the house, and peeked around the front corner. They were just charging across the front yard of the house next door, heavy on their feet. I could hear one of them gasping and either pocket change or car keys jiggling. I waited a moment until they'd cleared the corner and headed toward the backyard. I figured they'd probably run at least to the alley and look up and down. I jogged to my car, shaking my head at the bullet hole in the windshield as I started it and drove up to their vehicle.

I was right, it was a Ford. Sections of newspaper were spread across the front seat and an enlarged copy of my driver's license photo rested on top of the dashboard. There was a takeout cup from Starbucks on the street with a sizeable puddle of coffee slowly running across the asphalt. What a waste. I grabbed a screwdriver from the floor of my backseat, and jammed it into their front tire, then pulled it out to the sound of an audible hiss, and jammed it in again. After that I got behind the wheel and drove off. I still didn't see them in the rearview mirror as I turned the corner.

It occurred to me that driving to my house may not be the best of ideas. So I headed down to The Spot.

Linda was there, working the lunch-hour trade. Not that The Spot served lunch. Still, it was reasonably busy with the liquid-diet crowd.

"Hi, Linda. Anyone been looking for me?"

"You mean like that blonde with the big ones."

"Big eyes?"

"Shut up. No, no one. Who needs the kind of headache or heartbreak that follows you around?"

"I'm just misunderstood. Look, do me a favor, if someone comes looking, let me know." I pulled a ten out of my pocket and put it on the bar.

"Everything okay?"

"Yeah, just sort of dodging some possible trouble, you know."

She rolled her eyes.

"Which one this time, husband or boyfriend?"

"Would it make a difference?"

"Not really," she said, pocketing the ten. "Anyone asks, I'll give you a call."

"Thanks."

"Get you something?" she asked, pulling a beer tap for the couple two stools down.

"Nah, I just finished breakfast."

"What do you think this is?" she said and pushed the fresh beers across the bar, then picked up two empty glasses.

Chapter Forty-Seven

I didn't know what I was looking for or who I should talk to even if I did know. I needed a friend. No one sprang to mind, so I decided to go to the Moscow Deli and see Tibor. When I walked in he was leaning against a chopping block behind the meat counter, arms folded across his chest, looking pissed off and disgusted with the world in general. Some things never change. He didn't seem overjoyed to see me. As I approached the counter he didn't move, which I guess was good. As far as I could tell, we were the only two in the place.

"Tibor, how's it going?"

He grunted, at least I thought it was a grunt.

"Look, Tibor, I want to thank you for introducing me to your friend Braco, that's worked out real well for me. Too bad about little Sergie. Who knew?"

"Braco not forget." Then he reached behind him and picked up a wicked-looking cleaver, grasped it in his right, three-fingered paw, recrossed his arms and proceeded to stare at me without blinking.

"I'll be honest, Tibor. I found Kerri but I guess she's over me. I'm still looking for Nikki Mathias, though. Any ideas?"

He actually sort of smiled, sort of, I think.

"Everyone look for Nikki. They not find her."

"Why's that, they won't find her?"

"Huh," he scoffed. "She from the Urals, father a hunter. Only find her when she wants. Not before."

I felt like congratulating him for growing a brain, such as it was. Instead I said, "Can I give you a message for Nikki? Tell her I just want to talk with her. Could you let her know?"

He seemed to ponder that within his thick skull for a brief moment, then shook his head, and said, "Fuck you." Then he smiled and settled back against his chopping block in self-satisfaction.

Chapter Forty-Eight

My phone rang. I was training myself not to attempt to read the incoming number.

"Haskell Investigations."

"I have it on good authority you are responsible for the destruction of government property," Aaron said.

"What?"

"You slit a tire on a couple of Feds?"

"You gotta be kidding. Talk about needing a little more street time. I thought I was helping. What? Did my close personal friend Kimball call you and complain?"

"Yeah, he was pretty steamed."

"Steamed? About the tire? It doesn't bother him they were spotted almost a block away. That they went after me like a couple of Keystone Kops? He's lucky I didn't take the damn car. The tire, God, I wish that was my biggest problem. Things are so screwed up on this end I don't know how screwed up they are."

"That's pretty screwed up."

"I suppose now he wants me to go back over there and show those two clowns how to change a tire, or did they just call AAA on the Bureau plan?"

"Actually, he wants you to come down here and talk."

"About what?"

"You know, I gotta tell you, I have to work with these people. I don't like it sometimes, but it comes with the territory, and despite what you read in your comic books, we do work together. Now, we are in the process of concluding a long-term investigation. I'm hopeful we'll be able to bring it to a successful conclusion. There's a lot of man hours, including mine, a lot of money, including the city's, and maybe you could find time to climb off your high horse and at least listen to the man. Instead of being the pain-in-the-ass distraction you've become."

I thought about that.

"Dev?"

"I'm thinking."

"Well, think while you're driving. You can do two things at once, can't you?"

"You know…"

"What I know is Peters wants to meet with you at five. He's going to be down here in my office at four this afternoon for a Task Force meeting. I'm hoping you'll be here too, you know, just to sort of lend support, to me. You might find it interesting to sit in on the meeting."

"Sit in? That gonna be all right with special agent Tight-Ass?"

"Let's just say it might be educational for everyone involved."

"Educational? Yeah okay, I'll be there."

"Good, I'll let him know you're going to join us. See you then," Aaron said and hung up.

I hated it when Aaron played the loyalty card.

Chapter Forty-Nine

I was tempted to be stylishly late, maybe fifteen minutes or so, but I didn't need Aaron pissed off at me. I was issued my visitor's badge at exactly eight minutes before four and a blond detective from Vice came down to escort me up to Aaron's office.

My luck held when it came to the blond. He was about five foot six, needed a shave, and wasn't too happy about interrupting his day to escort me up on the elevator. If that doesn't paint a picture his last name was Griswald, which seemed to fit.

"How's it going?" I asked.

"Shit," he half growled. That was the beginning and end of our conversation.

When we entered the office area he jerked his stubbled chin in the general direction of Aaron's office, turned and walked away.

"Thanks," I called after him, ever the gracious guest then made my way to Aaron's corner office. It was empty, but there was a handwritten sign taped to the doorframe that read "Conference Room" and an arrow pointing the direction. I found the place in about twenty paces.

The room had a long rectangular table with some sort of light gray Formica top and lots of comfortable looking chairs. Certainly more upscale than the outdated government-issue stuff dumped in Aaron's office. Aaron sat on the far side of the conference table. Next to him was Hale, the I.C.E. guy that I sort of liked. There were a couple more faces I didn't recognize and some that I did. Peters sat at the head of the table, behind two neat stacks of stapled handouts. He had a brand-new yellow legal pad and a freshly sharpened pencil set in front of him. I pulled out a chair across the table from Aaron, then nodded at the few faces I recognized, including Hale, who smiled and winked back.

"All right, now that we're all finally here, we can begin," Peters said just as my butt hit the chair.

I glanced at my watch, it read two minutes before four.

"Agent Dziedzic, if you'd do the honors," Peters said to a woman sitting against the wall behind him. He slid one of the two stacks of handouts to the corner of the table.

Agent Dziedzic had dark curly hair and brown eyes that seemed overly pronounced behind her large round frames. She wore the female version of a dark FBI suit, pressed and starched, although it looked better on her than Peters.

She picked up the stack of handouts and began working her way around the table distributing one to every individual. She worked her way down the opposite side, around the far end of the table then back up toward me. When she came to me she glanced quickly at Peters, skipped me, then handed copies to the three guys between Peters and me.

Peters gave her a perfunctory smile, pushed the second stack of handouts toward her, and she began the distribution process again. The recipients were flipping through the pages as Peters began to drone.

"I'd like to thank you all for coming." He made a point of giving perfunctory nods around the table, skipped over me, and continued.

"What you have before you is a flowchart of the task force, identifying various local, state, and federal authorities providing a clear and concise chain of command. Please reference this schematic in future reports so that the information you provide can be accessed by everyone with the need to know in a timely manner. This second handout Agent Dziedzic is passing around is the most up-to-date flowchart of the Alekseeva organization up here in Minneapolis and how it interacts with the Kumarin organization down in Chicago."

Pretty Agent Dziedzic passed me by again, so I looked over at the copy of the fellow next to me. Not only did he not seem to mind, he moved the copy of the Russian organizations toward me. I noticed there was a Vlad Vucavitch listed as a player down in Chicago. The image was grainy and I couldn't tell if he looked anything like Kerri. For that matter I didn't know, maybe it was a common name, like the Russian version of Smith or Jones. Peters was still droning on about how fantastic and up to date the information was. I noticed that Sergie Alekseeva, late of this world, was listed as the number two in Braco's chain of command. I didn't see Tibor listed anywhere.

"… armed with this information we are now able to…"

"Excuse me, Agent Peters."

Peters gave a brief grimace in my direction, suggesting maybe he had some momentary intestinal discomfort, then cleared his throat ever so slightly.

"Mr. Haskell, you are here out of respect for our hosts, and my understanding is you are only here as an observer." Then he nodded in Aaron's direction. "I would ask that you refrain from interrupting these procedures so that the rest of us might continue with the business at hand. As I was saying, we will now be able to proceed..."

I think the fuse had been lit when I saw him sitting smugly at the head of the table, wearing another neatly pressed subtle patterned suit, nicely starched shirt, tie complementing everything perfectly. I'm sure he'd taken his wingtips out of some poor bastard's ass just long enough to polish them. Or maybe it was his ill-advised reference to being in Minneapolis instead of St. Paul. Either way, I smiled back gracefully, then said,

"Before you get down too far, I think you've missed an organizational adjustment here."

"Oh really? An organizational adjustment, that you just happen to know about," sigh.

I smiled innocently, wondering why some people have to be such insufferable pricks? then said, "Yes, sir. The number two man in the Alekseeva organization, Sergie Alekseeva. I believe he was killed about forty-eight hours ago."

I glanced over at Aaron. His eyes were trained, target-like, on Peters, which told me to go for it.

"We're aware of those reports but there hasn't been any confirmation. There has really been nothing of a concrete nature to indicate the victim in that particular incident was indeed Sergie Alekseeva."

"You think he was Andrew Quinn? The name on the guy's driver's license? He had Russian navy tattoos. Does that suggest his last name was Quinn?"

"We deal in facts here, Haskell. Not speculation or innuendo. We can't rush to a conclusion simply because it might be convenient. As I said, we are waiting for corroborating evidence. Now if there are no more…"

"So, if someone from inside the Alekseeva organization confirmed it was little Sergie who is lying on a block of ice down at the morgue, that would help?"

"What do you intend to do, ask them?" Peters said tossing his pencil on the table.

I thought Aaron gave me the slightest of nods I wasn't sure, but I went with it.

"I've already done that. It's been confirmed, twice."

"By who?"

"A woman named Karina Vucavitch, she goes by Kerri. I'm sure you're aware of her, she's Braco's main squeeze, or one of them." That got pages shuffling as people sought out Kerri's name on the Alekseeva flow chart.

Someone at the end of the table muttered, "Like Vlad Vucavitch."

"The other is Tibor Crvek, the butcher."

"You know who 'The Butcher' is?" Some guy I didn't know asked across the table. I thought I might have picked up on a little south side Chicago in his accent.

"Where in God's name do you come up with this fiction?" Peters asked, shaking his head.

"Fiction? I got a bullet hole in my windshield that adds some credibility to my claims. I had a bullet graze my head about a week ago compliments of the charming Ms. Vucavitch. And as for Tibor Crvek, I was up close and personal with him the other night." I looked at the guy across from me, "you know he plays the cello, pretty well actually. He is 'The Butcher.'" I neglected to add "at the Moscow Deli."

Peters looked like he had a put down ready to go on the tip of his tongue but the guy I'd guessed was from Chicago spoke first.

"Back up a minute here, son. Are you saying you know Karina Vucavitch. You've talked with her recently? And that you spoke with 'The Butcher' as well?"

"Yeah, I was with her last night. Actually she had been looking for me. Fortunately I was able to dodge the carload of thugs she brought along for company."

"We have no idea if it's the same individual. For all we know you're making all this up, Haskell," Peters said.

"How well did you get to know Karina Vucavitch?" I was sure he was from Chicago, now.

"How well?" I asked, not following.

"Any identifying characteristics you might remember?"

"Oh yeah, well, she's very attractive and speaks at least three languages, Russian, English and some German. She can drink vodka like a fish, and she's trimmed, not shaved, a real blonde if that's what you mean."

"Jesus Christ, how many people do you have on your surveillance teams?" The Chicago guy asked.

"Just me."

"And you've infiltrated these people?" a voice asked from the end of the table.

Aaron looked at me wide eyed. I shrugged my shoulders, suggesting I couldn't help myself.

"Anything else, any markings on the Vucavitch woman?" A voice asked from somewhere down the table.

"Markings? You mean the tattoo on her ass? It's a little angel sort of sitting on a cloud, looking off to the side like it was thinking or something. It had wings, sort of old fashioned looking, like a Victorian valentine or something. And it had writing, but I couldn't read it."

"Agent Dziedzic?" he said to the woman sitting behind Peters.

She cleared her throat, spoke a short phrase in what I assumed was Russian, then said,

"Lord forgive me for bringing tears to my mother."

"Thank you, that's Karina Vucavitch all right. If she said the body was Sergie, I think we can take that as gospel," my new best friend from Chicago said.

"I'm not at all convinced," Peters scowled. "I'll take it under advisement. Thank you for sharing your conquests, Mr. Haskell."

"I'm not sure who was doing the conquering," I said.

There were chuckles around the table, except for Peters who just stared at me. Dziedzic smiled behind his back. Aaron gave me a look that suggested "are you kidding!"

"If we can get back to where I left off," Peters said red-faced, looking at the papers in his hand. He then proceeded to drone on about all the good things that were going to happen because he'd taken the time to put together the two charts. Ever the corporate type he gave a short Power Point presentation, basically regurgitating all the information included in the handouts.

Eventually, the meeting wound up. Peters couldn't seem to get out of there fast enough. He had two other Federal toads traveling with him. It looked like it was left to pretty Agent Dziedzic to clean up the conference room.

Chapter Fifty

"Agent Peters," I called to him out in the hallway. A couple of people were leaving, others hanging around in groups of two or three. The mood didn't suggest a lot of business.

"Did you want to meet with me at five?" It was already five forty-five.

"I think I've heard enough from you for one day, Haskell."

"So we're cool, on the tire I mean. I don't want to get a surprise AAA bill in the mail."

"You know, Haskell, you might find destruction of government property funny. I don't. My agents have a lot better things to attend to than chasing you all over town. You might think it cute, maybe even funny to hop in and out of bed with known prostitutes. I find it reprehensible and not at all the sort of conduct I deem appropriate in this or any other investigation."

"I came across your kind of appropriate conduct this morning. Those two stiffs you had watching me. If that's your idea of undercover surveillance we are all in trouble."

"The trouble with people like you, Haskell, is that for some unknown reason you think you matter."

I just smiled at him, which got him even madder.

"Gentleman," he said as he turned and headed for the elevators. Tweedle dumb and tweedle dumber followed like little lap-dogs.

"Way to smooth things over for me," Aaron said from behind.

"You think that guy is gonna really do anything with Braco the Whacko Alekseeva and his gang of merry men? You'd be better off going after them with pea shooters instead of having that guy on your team."

"There might be some manpower and budgetary considerations you're glossing over there," Aaron said.

"Quite possibly," I agreed.

We spoke for a few minutes more. Aaron directed a couple attendees into his office, two of them Chicago guys. I noticed agent Dziedzic still back in the conference room packing up, so I poked my head in. She looked tired.

"Long day?"

"You can say that again." She smiled.

"Where'd you learn Russian?" I asked.

"Home, my family's from Kiev. I was actually born there, but we came to the US before I was one. It was my major in university, grad school," she said, then closed her briefcase, picked up another case, which I presumed held the Power Point stuff.

"Let me help you," I said and grabbed the larger of the two cases.

"Oh, not necessary, but thanks. Hey, I hope you didn't take it personal, not giving you the handouts. That was Peters. He instructed me not to give you either of them at the meeting. I have to follow orders." She shrugged her shoulders.

"Not a problem. I can't imagine working for that guy. I don't know what I did but I really rub that guy the wrong way."

"It's because you're you." We were walking toward the elevators now.

"I don't know how to be anyone else."

"No, I mean you're sort of snaky, in a neat way, sometimes, I would guess. But he can't come up with a box to put you in."

"You mean like a coffin?"

"Not exactly, but I'm sure that's crossing his mind right about now. No, I mean he prepped all of us on your being here. One of the problems when dealing with the locals, unable to see the big picture, blah, blah, blah. We've heard it all before. He basically said the same thing about the team in Chicago, so don't feel like the Lone Ranger. Then you come in and in about two minutes, not only do you confirm Sergie Alekseeva's death, from two sources, you use two sources we've wasted months trying to get close to. Maybe you don't know it, but you blew him right out of the water."

"I really didn't mean to. I just thought it might help to work with current information."

"You actually slept with Karina Vucavitch?"

"We didn't sleep much," I said as the elevator door opened. She shot me a quick glance, but didn't respond. We continued talking as we walked across the small ground-floor lobby and out the door. I carried the Power Point case to her car.

"Thanks for your help," she said when we got to her car. She popped open the trunk and I laid the case I was carrying inside.

"My pleasure," I said. "Hey, you wouldn't have time for dinner, would you?"

"Oh gee, thanks, but I don't think that would be the best career move for me, under the circumstances. But wait, here." She opened her briefcase, and gave me the two handouts.

"Disobeying orders?" I asked.

"Orders were not to give you the handouts at the meeting. We're in the parking lot. I'd classify that as still obeying orders."

"It's been a pleasure to meet you, Agent Dziedzic."

Chapter Fifty-One

I went home to study the handouts. I drove around my block three or four times in different directions just to be sure no one was lurking in the dark. I parked on the next street over, then stuck a business card in the steering wheel, reminding me to check the engine before I turned on the ignition in the morning. Then I cut through the backyard of the house directly behind mine and went in my back door. I left the lights off and quietly went through the house. Thankfully, it was empty. I placed a trunk in front of the kitchen door and an upholstered chair against my front door, just in case someone decided to forgo sneaky and just kicked the door in during the middle of the night.

I pulled the shades before I turned on a light then fired up my computer and Googled Russian mafia. Two hours of reading and watching five-minute videos later, I knew more than I wanted to, none of which was good. Reviewing Peters' handouts I learned absolutely nothing about Kerri Vucavitch or Nikki Mathias. I learned even less about Braco the Whacko. But Agent Dziedzic had managed to slip her card in there and I placed it in my wallet. Her first name was Valentina.

I phoned Aaron the next morning, leaving my daily message.

"Just checking in, anything I can help with, just let me know."

I phoned The Spot next. Linda answered after a half dozen rings.

"Spot Bar and we're open."

"Linda."

"Yes," she said cautiously.

"Dev Haskell, just checking in. Anyone been looking for me?"

"Are you kidding,? Who needs to ruin things this early in the day?"

"I'll take that as a no."

"Wow, I don't know if it's a wife or girlfriend this time but they really got you spooked."

"Just trying to be careful is all. Don't want anyone to get hurt, especially me."

"No one's been asking. You wanna describe the guy to me? Maybe if I see him I could give you a call?"

"Not sure who it'd be. They might have an accent, maybe a muscular guy or a good-looking blonde woman."

"Now you're dreaming. An accent, like what? In Fargo or something?"

"No, more like Russian."

"Yeah right," she said, but didn't elaborate. "I'll give you a jingle if anything comes up. Look, I gotta run. We got a breakfast special, shot and a beer with a second shot for free," she said, then hung up.

I decided to drive over to the world's most depressing parking lot and see who came in and out of the Moscow Deli. Not because it was necessarily a good idea but because I didn't know what else to do.

Chapter Fifty-Two

It was raining the following morning, not hard, but a steady drizzle. A flat gray sky that gave all the indication the rain would continue for at least the next month. I left the chair pushed up against the front door and ducked out the back, cut through my neighbors' backyard to my car parked on the street. My card was stuck in the steering wheel, reminding me to check the engine. I debated for a moment, looked at the drizzle, and debated a moment longer. Water dripped slowly but steadily through the bullet hole in my windshield. It had pooled up on the dash before it dripped into one of the defrost vents. I decided my luck had not been the best of late, climbed out of the car back into the rain and popped the hood.

Other than filling the gas tank and bringing my car somewhere to have the oil changed on a quasi-regular basis, I know nothing about cars. I do know enough that a plastic bag with what I assumed might be C-4 explosive wrapped around a series of wires with black electrical tape was not part of some manufacturer's upgrade.

I called Aaron, twice, just so he'd know it was urgent. Left the hood up and climbed back inside out of the rain. Aaron phoned back shortly.

"What?"

"I've got a situation," I said.

"What kind of situation?" Aaron asked calmly. He rarely, if ever, showed strain in his voice.

"A bag of what looks like C-4 is wrapped around what I'm guessing is the starter coil of my car."

"Where are you now?"

"In the car," I said, realizing how stupid that sounded.

"Take the key out of the ignition and get the fuck out of the car."

"The key isn't in the ignition," I said, climbing out from behind the wheel.

"Get out of the car, Dev, and get far away from it, now. Move!"

"Will you dial down, I didn't…"

"Don't argue, just get the hell away from there."

"I don't think the thing is gonna blow, Aaron. I haven't started the engine. I'll probably…"

"Get away from that car, fast. That device could be on a timer, or a mercury switch activated by your weight behind the wheel or maybe there's someone watching with a remote-control device."

I glanced around as I began to walk away, but didn't see anyone watching. To be honest, Aaron's hyper cop rant wasn't really helping just now.

"Look, how about you have the bomb-disposal guys quietly come out and…"

The explosion was so loud I didn't hear it. The force of the blast bounced me off the back of a parked van. I had probably walked about thirty feet down the street as I was talking to Aaron before the bomb detonated. I was in shock, dazed, and had no recollection of anything until after the surgery.

Chapter Fifty-Three

I woke, sort of. I was groggy, confused and in a beige recovery room. There was a blue curtain drawn around me, and I was on my stomach lying on pillows or something that seemed to lift my entire backside up in the air. I had IV's taped to my right hand. I could move my head, but it hurt to do so.

"Can you hear me?"

I attempted to look up. I moved my head to the right and there was a vicious stabbing pain from the back of my head. I heard a groan I didn't recognize, then slowly realized it was coming from me.

"We have you on a pain killer for now, just lay still. Do you mind if I have a few of our students come in?"

I didn't recognize the voice. It sounded distant and seemed to echo in a weird sort of way. I murmured something and closed my eyes again. When next I opened them, I was looking down at four pairs of shoes, three round toes and shined black. The fourth pair was sort of a pearl gray with a pointed toe and a small heel. From somewhere behind me a voice droned on about buttock contusions and anal laceration, then said,

"Miss Shipley, if you'd clean up here, please. Gentlemen, follow me."

The three pairs of black shoes disappeared and the pointed toe, pearl gray pair moved closer.

"Three years of med school and I'm wiping your ass. Have a nice day, asshole," she whispered.

Chapter Fifty-Four

Eventually I came to, but still felt a little foggy. I was in a different beige room, still on my stomach with pillows propping my butt in the air at what felt like a forty-five degree angle.

"You waking up?" I recognized Heidi's voice.

"Ughhh," I groaned.

"Here," she said, holding some sort of container at an angle and directing a straw into my mouth.

"Ughhh."

"The nurse said to get plenty of liquids in you. You've been out for the better part of the day. It's a little after eight."

I sipped what I guessed was water.

"Oh God."

"You're telling me! You're lucky to be alive, Dev. If you'd been any closer to that explosion..." Her voiced cracked.

I took another sip. If it was water it was some of the best I'd ever tasted.

"My car, is it okay?" I asked, exhausted with the effort.

"Your car? You can forget about that. I think it was scattered all over the street. Don't worry about it, just rest now."

I did, or attempted to. I had frightening dreams. Faces exploding, wolves or something chasing me, a lot of fire all around. I was aware of being woken by nurses at least twice, and both times they had me sip liquids. I thought it was water but I couldn't be sure. Someone gave me a hypo in the butt.

When next I woke it was daylight, and I felt ravenous. Aaron and Heidi were arguing over a blueberry muffin from my breakfast tray.

"See what you did, he's awake. Now neither one of us will get any. He's not any good at sharing," Aaron said.

"Hey, Dev, how you feeling?" Heidi asked as she gently laid a hand on my head.

"I feel like I've been run over by a bus."

"Not far from the truth. Someone seems to have a real hard-on for you, buddy," Aaron said.

"My pal Braco the Whacko?"

"Who's that?" Heidi asked.

"I would guess," Aaron replied. "Braco the Whacko is an individual we have an interest in and Dev was, well, doing some investigation."

"Well, he's crazy, obviously. Have you arrested him?"

"We're working on it."

"Working on it, God."

"Look, if it's any consolation, Dev, the docs in surgery worked long and hard and have made you a perfect asshole," Aaron said.

I couldn't quite see it, but I sensed Heidi gave him one of her patented disgusted looks then said to me,

"They had all sorts of metal and plastic and stuff to dig out of your butt and head and back. It's why you're in this kind of goofy position, you know, with your butt up in the air and all."

"I suppose I could have brought a flower, you know stick it…"

"That's not even funny," Heidi said, half giggling at my expense.

"God, when can I get out of here?"

"We'll have to wait until they say it's okay for you to go home. You're going to be doing some physical therapy and…"

"Physical therapy, on my ass! I don't think so."

"Well gee, nice to know you're prepared to be the model patient. I can hardly wait," Heidi said.

"Hey, I'm the one who's lying here with his ass up in the air."

"See how you like it for a change," Heidi said.

Neither Aaron nor I had a response to that.

Chapter Fifty-Five

I was in the hospital for another night, then Aaron gave me a lift home. I was sitting on this sort of donut-hole foam thing as he drove, with my back at an angle to the seat. I was, to say the least, uncomfortable.

"Gee, me bringing you home from the hospital, just like old times, darling."

"Kiss my ass," I said in no mood for humor.

"Touchy, are we?"

"It's just such a pain in the ass, pardon the pun. Hey, in case I didn't mention it, thanks for your help. If it wasn't for you I might have gone up with my car."

"Yeah, no problem. For what it's worth there was a switch that activated some sort of a timing device. Either your weight in the seat or possibly opening or closing the car door set the thing in motion. The idea is to make sure you're in transit, stuck behind the wheel, then boom. I guess the good news is there wasn't someone watching you who set it off with a remote. Small consolation."

"I'm here to tell the story, right now that's good enough for me. Any ideas who?" as if I needed to ask.

"You mean besides any woman you've had a relationship with in say the past twenty years? Probably Braco Alekseeva or one of his thugs spring to mind. Maybe your girlfriend Kerri? I'd say either one is a pretty safe guess. Am I missing anyone?" Aaron asked.

"No, but I'm missing the 'why' part of all this. I mean it's not like I'm the only one investigating these creeps. In fact, I was just looking for one woman, Nikki Mathias, barely on the radar screen. If Kerri Vucavitch hadn't hired me, then gotten me drunk so I'd hop in the sack with her, I wouldn't even be on their radar screen."

"There you go, maybe we could get her for date rape."

I looked at him disbelieving.

"Look, I'm serious. What jury would possibly have trouble believing a drop-dead gorgeous woman forced you to drink yourself silly so she could take advantage of you in your incapacitated state?"

"Yeah, yeah, but I still don't get what the big deal is, from their standpoint that is. And, who shot that sleaze ball Sergie Alekseeva? I mean they pull up and he gets nailed just as he's coming out of the SUV."

Aaron glared at me then put his eyes back on the road.

"I knew it. I knew you were fucking there. I just knew it," he said.

Oops.

"Actually I was leaving, had left in fact. I just saw it out of my rearview mirror." I went on to tell Aaron the rest of the tale. Waiting outside Braco's condo building for three days, following Kerri, chatting with her. He asked a couple of questions about who had been in the SUV with Sergie. I had no answers.

"And that brings us to "The Butcher". So, tell me what you know about that guy. What's his name?"

"Tibor Crvek. Not much actually," I said foolishly thinking I had a chance at dodging his question.

"How did you find out about him?"

"I went to the Deli and he was working."

"What?"

"I went to the Moscow Deli, Da'nita Bell told me about the place. They have a meat counter and Tibor Crvek was working, he's the butcher there."

"You mean he's a butcher, for real, at a deli? And that's who you told Peters about in the Task Force meeting?"

"Well, yeah."

"Jesus, you idiot."

"What do you know about "The Butcher" the real guy?" I asked.

"About just what you'd guess from the name. These clowns got a habit of enforcement. They have someone, who based on what we can determine, has a knowledge of butchering, lays out his victims like dressed beef. Tongue, kidneys, heart, hams."

"Hams?"

"You get the idea. We're not sure who it is. Could be anyone of these idiots."

232

"Could also be someone with the simple knowledge of how to field dress a deer, which covers about every third guy in Minnesota," I added.

"Yeah, although, how can I say it, there's an apparent efficiency of effort in his work. The guy's experienced."

"Charming."

"Hey, don't blame me. You're the one sleeping with them."

"God, if only I'd known."

"I think we're back to you being taken advantage of."

Aaron pulled up in front of my place then walked me to the front door, slowly. I could move but only gingerly. I unlocked the door but it wouldn't open.

"Oh God, I forgot I got a chair pushed in front of the door."

"A chair?"

"Yeah, little extra security."

"Wow, high tech. I suppose an alarm system would just be too run of the mill for a super sleuth like you."

We walked around to the back, I unlocked the door and stepped in. Aaron glanced at the trunk in the middle of the floor I'd shoved against the door a couple of nights back.

"Amazing."

I didn't comment.

"You feeling okay?"

"Yeah, all things considered. I'm thinking of lying down, on my stomach."

"Want me to do a walk through, just in case?"

"Thanks, but not necessary."

"Sure?"

"Very."

"Okay, I'll leave you to your own devices. Keep your outside lights on all night. I'll have district run a squad car past from time to time. You know my number if you need anything, but nine-one-one will be a lot faster if it gets hot. Might want to carry some protection with you, just in case."

"A condom?"

"If you think you'll have a use for it."

"Aaron, I just want to say thanks. Like I said, if it wasn't for you I might be splattered all over the street."

"Yeah well, you know how the city is about litter."

Chapter Fifty-Six

I was home no more than twenty minutes and getting a little more paranoid with every passing minute. A bomb blast will do that to you. At the half-hour mark I phoned Heidi.

"Can I come to your house?"

"You okay?"

"Yeah, I think so, just wigging out a little, sitting around over here alone. I need a place to camp for three or four days until I get a little more mobile. Would it be too much of an imposition?"

"I'm on my way," she said without the slightest bit of hesitation.

"Call me when you're two minutes away. I want you to pick me up on the next street over."

Heidi called, amazingly, just as I instructed. I left via the back door, through the neighbor's yard, and out to the street. I was moving slowly and was just walking to the sidewalk as she pulled up.

"Hop in, Lover Boy." She smiled.

"God, I don't think I'd even be able, the 'Lover Boy' part, I mean," I said tossing an overnight bag in the back before positioning my foam donut cushion and carefully climbing in. It was going to be a few days before I got to the hop-in-and-out stage.

"Wow, you are banged up. Oh, pardon the pun." She giggled.

"Well, maybe I could, bang that is."

"That's better. See, you're already coming around."

She pulled away from the curb. About fifteen feet farther on there was a large blackened area on the asphalt. Bits of chromed plastic and glass twinkled in the gutter as we drove past, remnants of my car. It was very uncomfortable to look at.

"You okay?" she asked after we'd gone a few blocks.

"Yeah, but I'm beginning to take this seriously. I'm gonna get the bastard that did this to me."

"Let's get you better first. You up for a trip to the grocery store to get a few things?"

"I think we better, I'm not gonna get back to normal on a diet of Oreos."

"Especially since I don't intend to share my Oreos with you."

Heidi's idea of a few things and my idea of necessities seemed to be at opposite ends of the spectrum. She tossed necessities like three packs of Oreos, eight ounces of maple syrup, and cherry-flavored ice cream into the cart. I, according to her, got boring things like flour, fruit, olive oil, and pasta. We left the store with six bags' worth of a few things.

"Man," she said as we exited the parking lot. "I don't think I've ever bought that many groceries in my life."

236

"I'm not surprised. Both of us are going to be eating well and eating healthy. I'll have dinner ready for you when you come home the next couple of days. It'll give me something to do, okay? Say, as long as we're in this mode, stop at the wine store. We might as well stock up."

I was a little slow getting dinner ready. I was in a strange kitchen for one thing and well, I was moving a little slow. I served up two salmon fillets in a brown sugar chipotle glaze with a side of angel hair pasta, just after our fresh green salad with a light balsamic vinaigrette.

"Mmm-mmm, this is really good. Where did you learn to cook like this?"

"I've slept with a lot of women who worked in restaurants."

"No, seriously?"

"Seriously."

"Can I ask you something?"

"Yeah, sure."

"Do you think it's really necessary to wear that gun? You know when you're cooking or just hanging around the house."

"Let's hope not. But I've been shot, blown up, chased, and assaulted in the past couple of weeks and I'd just as soon hedge my bets. Besides, I'd never forgive myself if something happened to you."

"Really?"

"No, not really, I was just kidding on that one. I'm just worried about me."

She poured herself another glass of wine, leaned over, gave me a kiss on the forehead then dashed out of the kitchen saying, "Thanks for doing the dishes and cleaning up."

Chapter Fifty-Seven

It was perhaps indicative of my physical state that I slept in Heidi's guest room. Secure with extra pillows propping my butt into the air in my new favorite position. Heidi didn't wake me whenever it was she left for her office. I dressed in loose-fitting jeans and a T-shirt. I left the shirt untucked covering the .45 on my right hip. I was cleaning up the kitchen after breakfast, doing everything I could to avoid the series of stretching exercises that were floating out there in my not-too-distant future when the doorbell rang.

I thought about not answering it. Then decided it would be best to at least see who it was. If it was a neighbor I could ignore them. If it was Braco Alekseeva, I'd just shoot the bastard.

It was I.C.E. agent Billy Hale.

I opened the door, Hale smiled.

"Agent Hale."

"Hey, heard about your big bang. How you doing?"

"Getting better, come on in," I said.

He carried a waxy white paper bag, the kind from a bakery. I could only hope.

"Picked up a couple of rolls for you, hope that's okay."

It was. There were four of them, with more cinnamon caramel than roll.

"You got time for coffee?"

"I was hoping you'd ask," he said.

"So, tell me what happened," he said, a cinnamon caramel roll crammed in his mouth, and I did.

"What I can't seem to figure out is why," I said, finishing up my story.

"Well, I'd say you touched a nerve somewhere. Question is where? What? Maybe even who? Your buddy LaZelle filled me in a little. Right, wrong, or indifferent you've bumbled into more action than we've been able to generate on that snail-paced Task Force over the past eighteen months."

"I don't know. Was your intent to generate car bombs? If it was, yeah, I'm way ahead of you, but otherwise, I don't know. Despite whatever friction I seem to generate between Peters and myself, from what I saw you got a hell of a list of bad actors up here and down in Chicago."

"Yeah, great. We had that list twelve months ago. You hear any talk about actually doing anything? Arresting or charging anyone?"

"Well, no, not really."

"Exactly. We just continue to gather more and more information. Whoever took out that moron Sergie, they should get a medal. These guys, the rest of them, Braco, 'The Butcher,' God, we arrest any of them they'll be lawyered up so fast, it'll be a decade just to get the legal right to charge the bastards, let alone prosecute."

"Well, yeah, about that butcher comment I made at your Task Force meeting, I…"

"Relax, LaZelle told me about it. The fact is, I think that's the guy, your buddy Tibor Crvek. He runs under the radar but we've been aware of him for quite some time. 'By the Book' Peters won't believe it, but I think he's our boy. Might just be dumb luck but it seems you stumbled onto him. You had any close up dealing with that psycho, you're lucky you're in one piece."

I felt myself beginning to sweat noticeably.

"But the thing is, I'm still an innocent, essentially. If Karina Vucavitch, Kerri, hadn't contacted me, and paid me, I wouldn't be involved in any of this. I was just trying to find one missing person. Not too successfully, I might add. Why me?"

"You wanna know what I think?"

"Yeah."

"Okay, no offense, but you're a bit of a known fuckup. Look, I like you, but I think she probably got you involved because she, well, they, figured you wouldn't ask too many questions. You'd do the grunt work, take some money, and go away. You had a better chance of finding this Mathias woman."

"Nikki," I interjected.

"Yeah Nikki, you had a better chance of finding her than they did because, well, she's hiding from them. If you did find her it's probably a fair comment you would have told them where she was, taken the money, gone off, and pissed it all away in about a week. Right?"

"Your point?" I sounded a little more defensive than I meant to.

"Not a criticism, just a probable fact, okay? Look, you got lucky, if that's the right word. Either way, you've stumbled into something and until you see it through, you are gonna have to hide."

"Me?"

"Yeah, you. That car bomb, Peters didn't set that. You got something, whether we know what it is or not is another question, but you got something and they're gonna come looking for you."

"But I don't know shit."

"But they think you do, and that's all that counts. I'd say the key for you is Nikki Mathias. You find her, your answer, whatever it is, is probably nearby."

"Well, I'm lying low here for the time being."

"Hey, look, with all due respect, I found you, with one phone call. I didn't even have to get out of bed."

"Yeah, but Aaron wouldn't tell…"

"I don't know, where was he when he told me? Can they tap his cell? Didn't you say Peters had two guys out there in the street just the other day?"

"Yeah, but I figure they just saw my car and…"

"Jesus, they might be Feds, but do you think they got the resources to cruise up and down city streets just so they can locate your vehicle? Even the Feds can't waste money like that, too often."

"You got any ideas?"

"Matter of fact I do. May not come with some of the fringe benefits your little friend can offer you around here, but no one will find you and she might be a bit safer, too with you gone. We could pool our resources."

"What resources you got?"

"The best," Hale laughed. "Me!"

I packed my gear, such as it was, couple of shirts, underwear, two boxes of .45 rounds, and my donut hole, cushion. Then I wrote Heidi a note and left with Hale.

Chapter Fifty-Eight

On the way over he told me a little bit more about his role in the task force.

"Our hot button is illegal aliens. What do you think of when you hear that term?"

I was on my donut-hole cushion, sitting at an angle against the back of the passenger seat.

"I guess I think of people crossing the border in the dark of night down in Arizona. Hot, dusty. If they get picked up they're sent back down to Mexico, and they maybe try it again a couple of nights later."

"Yeah, well, that's part of it. I mean that's the one that makes the news. The stuff I'm involved with is young women coming here, usually under the guise of schooling or a job waiting for them. Instead of sneaking across the border they arrive perfectly legal in an airport. Someone meets them, picks them up, gets hold of their passport, then gets them drunk, drugged or both. A team breaks them in, rapes them for maybe a week or two straight. Then they're working the Internet brothel scene, hookers on call, delivered right to your door, like your little girlfriend running that escort service.

That's one of about half a dozen connected with old Braco, by the way," he glanced over at me.

"The girls complain or screw up, they're out on the streets, strung out, hooking for a couple of bucks. They go to the authorities, they've been told their families back in Russia or wherever will be murdered. That part may or may not happen, but after what these girls have been through, they'd be stupid not to take it as gospel. They've got no passport, they're in an illegal industry, not to be too unpleasant, but they are literally fucked."

"That's the scenario Kerri laid out for me the other night in my car."

"Yeah, well take whatever that broad says with a grain of salt. She's management. She likes to play the part of the victim, but she's Braco's front person in a lot of deals."

"Were the Lee-Dee guys part of this?"

"Not in so many ways. Yeah, they had an escort service. Braco put your gal Kerri in there, then he just took the whole thing over. Pretty safe guess he murdered Leo Tate and Dennis Dundee, made some adjustment, and built off the Lee-Dee model. Essentially, what they've got is a cyber-brothel. They take credit cards, advertise a full GFE."

"GFE?"

"Girl Friend Experience. Nice way of saying a hooker. You read anything about the economies in Eastern Europe and you know Braco's got a constant supply of new eye candy available. One of the girls burns out here and he can have two more flown over within the week. They show up thinking they scored some dream job or school course. It's a dream all right, a real nightmare."

244

Hale's narrative didn't get any more cheerful as we drove. Eventually, we pulled into a large garage attached to an industrial building, took a freight elevator to the fourth floor and then went down a short hallway to a metal fire door. Hale took out a key and unlocked the door. We stepped into a fairly large room, a kitchen area to one side, about a dozen computers going. Three guys looked up, nodded, and went back to what they were doing.

Along the far wall stood five bunk beds. A couple of couches were arranged next to the beds. A flat-screen TV sat on a card table. There were red, black, blue, and white cables bundled together and strung across the open ceiling. Behind the fire door we had just come through was an overflowing trashcan and standing next to that, a three-foot stack of pizza-delivery boxes. The place needed some airing out.

"Home sweet home," Hale said.

"Charming."

"I'll give you the formal introduction at lunch time. Gang, meet Devlin Haskell, guy I told you about." That elicited two slight nods and a grunt.

"Look, why don't you throw your stuff on an open bunk? Top and bottom on the far right are reasonably clean, I think. You want anything? A Coke or root beer? I don't have any hard stuff or beer 'cause we're operational. Help yourself and let me check in with these guys for a bit. Then we'll all sit down and get to know one another over lunch. Bathroom is behind the kitchen area. You on any meds or anything?"

"They gave me some pain killers after my surgery, but I've been off them for close to twenty-four hours and I'd like to keep it that way. Damn things gave me horrible nightmares."

Hale nodded, but didn't say anything.

I hung my shirts on the corner post of a bunk bed, dropped my overnight bag on the floor, then put my donut cushion on a couch, settled in and watched for the next hour.

Chapter Fifty-Nine

Lunch consisted of hot dogs and nacho cheese Doritos from a bag that was constantly passed around the table. No one bothered to just take a handful and pile them on the "Happy Birthday" paper plates in front of us. I was famished and had three hot dogs. I met Gary, Mike and Mike.

"So, you're the guy got his ass blown off the street." One of them chuckled. I'd already forgotten who was who.

"Yeah, not my best day."

"Man, I don't know… sounds pretty lucky to me," another one of them added.

"What we do here," Hale said, cramming half a hot dog into the right side of his mouth. "…is monitor traffic on a little over a dozen websites. We're building documentation, coupled with sworn statements from customers after the fact."

"Sworn statements?"

"Yeah, we pay them a visit, gently confront them, and suggest they can either go to jail or sign a statement that basically says they responded to a particular Internet ad that led them to engage in sex for payment."

"You get guys to sign?"

Hale looked around the table. They were all smiling.

"We got something like an 85 percent close rate. What would you do? Sign and we promise to keep it quiet, not prosecute them, or they can go to jail and sort it out."

"You arrest them?"

"Nah, we just tell them we will. I doubt it would hold up in court anyway. Besides, I don't want to screw with the paperwork. But, these guys are so freaked, they gladly sign, promise never to do it again, and then thank their lucky stars once we leave."

"We can nail the ground troops, the working girls, anytime… today if we want. But what's the point? They'll be replaced with fresh meat within the week. The guy we want is Braco. Since his kid Sergie bought it, there's been an increase in activity, lots of phone traffic. Problem is we don't have a translator. So we have no idea what they're saying. By the time we find out, it's after the fact and too far down the road to do anything."

I looked around at the computers, the four guys, the room, all the wiring, the three-foot stack of pizza boxes.

"You got all this and no translator? That doesn't make sense."

"You're right it doesn't, but those are the facts. I asked Peters if we could borrow that gal, what's her name?"

"Dziedzic?" I said.

"Yeah, that's the one. You can imagine how eager he is to share resources. You read all that shit

248

in the paper about budget constraints, well." He spread his hands palms open.

"You must be able to get someone, somewhere?"

"That's where you come in, my friend."

"Me? Sorry to disappoint, I got enough trouble communicating in English. I sure as hell can't speak Russian."

"Yeah, but Nikki Mathias can."

"Nikki Ma... it might as well be the Easter bunny. Don't you listen? I never found her."

"Yeah, I know, she found you."

"Me?"

"When old Sergie lost his head. Her name keeps coming up in the translations we received. They think she was the shooter."

"Nikki... I don't think she would..."

"What, since you couldn't find her, that makes you an expert on her? Or is it because she's a great-looking redhead who likes to stand around naked on the beach with three people who've been murdered? I've seen the photo, remember? Listen, her old man was some kind of master hunter or some damn thing. It's not a long stretch to think his kid could..."

"I was there, or well, I saw it, sort of, in my rearview mirror."

"So?"

"I just don't think she's your shooter."

"Well, Braco and everyone else seem to think she is. I do too. You find her and we're a long way toward putting this whole thing to bed."

"How am I supposed to find her? I wouldn't know where to even begin to look. I just spent the better part of a week chasing dead ends."

Hale gave me a big warm smile.

"Funny thing, we got a plan."

"Why do I think I'm not going to like this?"

"What's not to like?" Hale asked, sounding sincere. "It's simple. We just use you as bait."

"As bait? Me? Are you crazy?"

"There's been some discussion on that point."

"As bait?"

"Look, I think she has a source pretty close to Braco. Real close as a matter of fact. If we can get you to lead her somewhere, we grab her and get her to translate for us. Then we take Braco down."

"That's, that's so insane it can't possibly work. For starters what makes you think she'll show up somewhere? How will she know? I mean, are you kidding?"

"No look, the hit on Braco's kid, Sergie. She didn't follow you. She had to be waiting there. Think about it. How long did you talk to Karina, Kerri? A minute, two tops?"

I nodded.

"That's not enough time to follow, unobserved, then get to a shooting station, take up a position and fire. In a residential neighborhood? It just doesn't work."

He had a point.

"Think about it. She was in position before you arrived. She knew Sergie and his pals were going to show up. It was a setup but not for you, for old Sergie. I'm just thinking we do the same thing, again. Only this time we grab her. I'm willing to bet she wants Braco out of business a lot more than we do."

"If that's the case, why doesn't she just get in touch with the police?"

"Gee, go figure, a known prostitute, here illegally, no documentation. Some tight-ass like Peters will just lock her up the first chance he gets and charge her with Sergie's murder. Then real or imagined she'll figure Braco is going to kill her family. Too risky for her, we have to find her and convince her."

"Okay, so let me guess, meanwhile while you're trying to find her, I'm out there twisting in the wind?"

"I haven't quite worked that tiny detail out yet."

Chapter Sixty

A couple of days of doing stretching exercises, eating hot dogs, take out pizza and staring at three guys watching computer monitors put me in a slightly different frame of mind.

"So, how about this?" I said to Hale. "You set me up outside Braco's, just like I did before. I follow Kerri or Braco, whichever leaves. With any luck they'll lead me to a prearranged spot. If Nikki knows about it, she'll be waiting there, and you grab her. But, you grab me first, get me out of there. After that you can grab her. If she's hiding, you find her. If she's as good as you say she won't jump up and run away. You'll have to stumble over her. But you gotta get me out of there first. And then one other thing," I said,

"What's that?" Hale asked.

"I want LaZelle involved. Nothing personal, Hale, but he'll make sure I'm safe."

Hale nodded. "Makes sense to me. I'll try and set it up. And thanks, maybe you're not the total fuckup I was led to believe."

"Then again…" I said.

Chapter Sixty-One

Two days later I was back sitting on Robert Street. Since I was newly carless, I was parked in some sort of pimped-out ride that had been part of a forfeiture agreement arranged through a drug dealer's attorney. If I wanted to attract attention to myself I couldn't think of a better way to do it. I was sitting behind the wheel of a metallic chrome green Hummer H3 with black-tinted windows, Sprewell spinners for wheel rims and a little over a quarter ton of chrome trim that probably glowed in the dark. I was getting more than a few stares.

"You gotta be kidding me," I'd said to Hale when he had pulled this pimp-mobile into the garage.

"Look at it this way, we won't lose you in the crowd."

"Shouldn't I be wearing a full-length fur coat and a white fedora when I'm driving this bomb?"

"Yeah, well, just don't scratch this thing. It's a DEA loaner," he'd cautioned.

So I sat and waited on Robert Street sweating in the heat and humidity, trying not to doze off. I limped out of the car periodically to toss more quarters in the meter, then waited some more. In between times, I did my stretching exercises right there on the downtown sidewalk, attempting to reduce the throbbing still in my back and butt. Nothing happened. Although, at one point I thought I spotted one of Aaron's undercover guys leaning against Braco's condo building looking nonchalant. At seven that evening I drove off, made sure no one but Hale's crew was following me and returned to my bunk bed dungeon.

"A number of spurts of activity from Braco's cell," Gary said over pizza. Tonight it was sausage with onions and extra cheese.

"'Course we don't know what he was saying. Maybe he was just chatting with a girlfriend," one of the Mikes said. I could keep all of them straight by now.

Hale tilted his head back and dangled a triangle of pizza above his mouth. It reminded me of feeding time at seal island.

"Let's figure we got their attention today. If so, it would stand to reason they would set something up for tomorrow or the next day. We don't have anything by the day after tomorrow we start back at square one," he said, then gobbled the pizza slice in three quick bites.

"And do what?" I asked.

"God, I'm not at all sure," he replied through a mouthful of pizza.

Chapter Sixty-Two

Day two and the weather had changed. It was even hotter and more humid. I could feel the effect from yesterday's nine hours of sitting on my ass. I was on my donut cushion, and it wasn't helping. My butt and back were throbbing uncomfortably.

"God, I'm sore from doing absolutely nothing," I said.

"Why would that be different than any other day? Man, you oughta try hiding out on the damn floor back here," Hale said. He was stretched out on the floor of the back seat with a dark sheet pulled over him, hiding there, just in case trouble started. Aaron and a team of four were around somewhere, undercover. It was after the noon hour and I'd yet to see any of them.

"You know, it's too bad you can't take a look. The women out here are gorgeous today. I don't know how they get away with wearing so little," I lied. "I wonder how any guy could remain focused on his job working next to these beautiful things?"

Hale just sighed from the floor of the backseat.

I plugged the meter at hourly intervals. There wasn't a cloud in the sky and from about one-thirty on, the sun beat down unmercifully on the Hummer, baking it oven-like. I ran the air conditioner periodically, but the sweat still rolled off me. I drank a PowerAde, this one was blue. The previous one had been red and I couldn't really discern much of a taste difference between the two.

"You okay back there?" I asked Hale, as much in an attempt to stay awake as anything else. My head had been nodding, and my eyelids felt like they had ten-pound weights hanging from them.

"What the hell, what's happening? Anything up?" he murmured, coming awake.

"God, you're asleep back there? How come I have to sit here looking alert and wide awake?" I complained.

"We're trying to fool people into thinking you actually know what you're doing for a change. I doubt it'll work. It's pretty tough attempting to cover up someone as stupid as you are."

"You know, I've been thinking," I said.

"Well, there's a change," Hale responded.

I searched for a clever comeback just as a blue BMW Z4 drove up the exit ramp. It was Kerri's. There was no traffic coming so it could have easily turned left and driven off. Instead it waited for maybe fifteen seconds. I guessed she wanted to make sure I saw her.

"There's our BMW on the ramp, looks like just Kerri driving," I said to Hale.

"Unless someone's hiding in there, but who'd be stupid enough to try that?" he said.

From the floor of the backseat I heard him on the radio alerting our cover guys to the fact we were moving. I was suddenly very thankful that I was driving a vehicle that stood out. We turned left on Seventh, drove maybe half a mile, then took a right on Kellogg, going up the hill toward the imposing edifice of the St. Paul Cathedral. I passed on a description of our route to Hale still down on the floor of the backseat, relaying the information.

"We get to the top of this hill, I'm guessing we're either gonna turn right onto the freeway or take a left and head down Summit Ave."

"Which do you think?" Hale asked.

"I got five bucks says she'll take a right and get on the freeway. To my way of thinking it's the smart move, holds a lot more options for her."

"I'll take that bet," Hale said.

On cue the blinker on the BMW signaled a left, up Summit Ave.

"Damn it, she's taking Summit," I said, following two cars behind.

"I knew it." Hale laughed from the backseat.

"How'd you know?" I asked.

"No real surprise. I just figured the safe bet would be the opposite of whatever you thought."

I continued down Summit, five bucks lighter. We drove for almost five miles.

"You know where she's headed?" I said, a tone of surprise in my voice. "She's going right down to the River Boulevard. You don't think she's going back to that same scenic overlook where Braco's kid was shot, do you?"

"Wouldn't be the smart move, but then again…"

We took a left onto the River Boulevard. The road follows the Mississippi along the top of the river bluff. It snakes around, back and forth, turns and bends so at any given time you could be pointed south, east, or west. She traveled about fifty yards then made a right turn into a small parking lot next to a stone monument commemorating the First World War. It was just that, a parking lot, rather than a scenic overlook. A few cars had been parked by folks who walked along the miles of pedestrian paths overlooking the river. Like she had done before, Kerri climbed out of the BMW smoking a cigarette, then leaned against the trunk of the car, arms folded, staring at the Hummer.

Across the street and up a gently sloping lawn stood buildings from the St. Paul Seminary and the University of St. Thomas. An occasional student drifted aimlessly along the sidewalk.

I remained a good thirty feet away, lowered my window and looked left and right up and down the River Boulevard as far as I could see. Then I studied the route we'd just traveled, examining the cars parked along Summit for two blocks to see if there was one stuffed with muscle-bound Russian thugs with the idea of filleting me into bite-sized pieces. I couldn't see any.

"I think it looks clear, sorta."

"That doesn't sound all that reassuring," Hale said. "Maybe pull alongside her, put your piece on your lap, just in case you need it fast."

"Already there."

"Stay in the vehicle, you need to get out of here. Just go, I got your back."

I could hear him pull off the sheet cover, then shift position slightly while he muttered something into the radio.

I made a visible show of checking the cars on the road again. Kerri looked bored. She took a couple of dramatic drags from the cigarette in her left hand. Her right arm was wrapped across her chest, the hand tucked under her left elbow. If she had a pistol, and I was pretty sure she did, it could be in her right hand.

It was a cloudless, hot, humid, Midwestern summer afternoon. You couldn't buy a breeze, and I could feel the sweat running down the sides of my face. Despite the air conditioning in the Hummer I had sweated through the back of my shirt. My senses were on high alert and I was aware of the overall background hum of insects. A dragonfly flitted up and down erratically over the top of a car parked just past Kerri, wings sparkling in the sunlight.

Kerri was nodding her head ever so slightly up and down. I didn't think she was giving a signal. It seemed to be more of a hyper sort of movement, the way you might tap your foot if you were bored. She was probably screaming inside her head, "Come on you idiot, move, pull up here!"

Chapter Sixty-Three

I took a deep breath, then exhaled.

"Okay, here we go," I said. Hale didn't respond, and I may have spoken so softly he never heard me, but he could sense the Hummer moving.

"So, Dev, how have you been? Where did you get this, this car?" Kerri laughed once I stopped behind the BMW. Her right hand remained securely tucked under her left elbow. She took another drag from her cigarette.

I bit my tongue and thought, 'Gee the last time I saw you, you tried to shoot me, missed, and put a bullet through my windshield. When that didn't work you jerks placed a bomb in my car to blow me up,' instead I half joked, "Oh, you know, Kerri, I just thought this sort of fit my personality a little better, and well, the time seemed right to get a fresh set of wheels. Like it?"

She nodded, took a final drag, and then ground out her cigarette with the toe of her heeled boot. Déjà vu all over again. Just like before, she spent a long time grinding it into the ground. When she looked up, her eyes seemed a little glazed. Was it possibly a tear, or just heartless determination?

"Have you found Nikki?"

"Your sister?" I asked suggesting by my tone she was anything but "Matter of fact I think I may have."

I glanced up and down the road again, checking for vehicles. Nothing looked out of the ordinary. I turned back to Kerri. I thought she was looking at me, but her focus was a few feet beyond to the bluff.

From the bluff down to the river was parkland. The terrain was steep, wild, filled with deer, fox, raccoons, and the occasional gaggle of underage teens sneaking off to smoke dope and drink something memorable like root beer schnapps or strawberry-flavored vodka.

I saw the first shaved head struggling up the bluff, red-faced with heavy muscular arms and a thick upper body, some sort of inordinately large pistol in his hands. There were three other guys close on his heels, all armed. They were gasping and groaning, struggling to make the steep grade and pick up the pace in the final four or five feet and then they'd be virtually on top of us.

Kerri suddenly had her pistol out from under her elbow. With her right arm extended, the barrel looked to be about six inches wide and pointed right between my eyes. I hate it when I'm right.

It sounded like a slight clearing of someone's throat, sudden, brief, not at all loud.

The first shaved head was picked up and thrown back over the bluff just as he was beginning to pick up speed. It was so sudden one of his compatriots yelled something in Russian. I couldn't understand it, but the tone was more of chastisement than a warning to the others. Maybe something like 'What

the hell are you doing?' or 'Quit screwing around!'
It took them a step or two, but then suddenly they all
dropped to the ground.

Kerri quickly spun around and crouched down
behind the rear of her BMW. I seemed to have
suddenly become the least of her concerns. I
accelerated out of the parking lot, back onto the
River Boulevard and away. No one followed or shot
at us.

Hale was suddenly up, crouched in the backseat
with what looked like a MAC 10 clenched in his
hands.

"I don't think they're following," I said, giving
half a glance in the rearview mirror before
screeching around the corner, back onto Summit
Avenue and racing up a small hill. The Hummer
swayed back and forth a bit as I accelerated.

"You see where the hell that shot came from?"
Hale asked, then mumbled something unintelligible
into his radio.

"I'm thinking the college parking ramp. No
neighbors, it's secluded, and she can just get in a car
and calmly drive out like she's heading home after a
class." I whipped around the corner, forcing a
handful of college kids crossing against the light to
jump back as I leaned on the horn. Then I rocketed
down the street past the science building at the
university, heading toward the three-story parking
ramp. There were already two squad cars with lights
flashing blocking the entrance and exit ramps. In the
distance I could see the flashing lights of at least two
more police vehicles racing toward us. They'd be
here in no more than fifteen seconds.

"Pull over, pull over," Hale commanded.

I hadn't even come close to stopping before he leaped out the passenger-side door, stumbled a step or two and then hurried toward the parking ramp, half running and hopping, shouting instructions into his radio as he moved.

Chapter Sixty-Four

They got the parking ramp cordoned off quickly, more police arriving every couple of minutes. I saw Aaron a couple of times from a distance, but never got close enough to talk with him. In the end, they never found Nikki in the parking ramp. They found her car or at any rate a car, a gray 2006 Honda Accord, abandoned on the ground level of the ramp. The car was thirty feet from the exit, with the driver's door left open. She must have fled on foot the moment she saw the police squad blocking the exit. A rifle with a scope rested on the floor of the backseat, buried beneath two twenty-four packs of newborn sized Pampers. A child's car seat was belted into the rear. But no Nikki.

"Damn it, I can't believe it. We must have just missed her," Aaron said, clearly upset. We were standing on the top level of the parking ramp in the broiling sun. Waves of heat shimmered off the concrete. We'd just completed another walk through the entire ramp, while uniformed officers checked each and every one of the vehicles twice for a redhead hiding inside.

Looking out of the ramp and down toward the river I could see where the area was cordoned off with crime-scene tape. A small tent was getting set up at the edge of the bluff not quite over the body. I thought I might be able to see the body or at least where it was with a shroud draped over it, but it must have rested just that much further down the bluff to be hidden from view. There was an EMT vehicle parked in the lot at about the same place where Hale and I had been when the shot was fired. To my knowledge neither Kerri nor any of the guys who had climbed up over the top of the river bluff were in custody. A number of police vehicles were parked around at haphazard angles. The medical examiner wagon was there. I wondered if Aaron's friend Dr. Mallory Bendix was down there, but then figured her sort of arrogance probably suggested she wouldn't work out in the field with common folk.

Hale was limping, cringing with each step, most likely injured during his jumping exit out of the moving Hummer, but I guessed he may have had larger problems on his mind at the moment. The last thing either he or Aaron needed was my meddling right now.

Aaron was the senior officer on site and as such it was his crime scene. So he was dealing with a very full plate. I had just finished writing out my statement, signed it and handed it to a uniformed sergeant. Hale limped over to me, and said quietly,

"Why don't you get out of here? There's going to be enough heat without you getting dragged into the meat grinder. We got your statement. I'll square it with LaZelle soon as he gets a moment."

"You sure?"

"Yeah," he groaned. "Not like we don't know where to find you. Anything comes up I'll give you a call. Jesus," he groaned a second time.

"Look, why don't I run you down to United? You might just have a bad sprain but I'm willing to bet you broke or tore something when you jumped out of the Hummer."

"No, I'll make it. Just a little uncomfortable is all. Oh, my God!" he suddenly groaned.

"Okay, that's it, you're coming with," I said. Hale didn't argue. We did the walking wounded routine, with his right arm draped over my shoulder. Together we limped and hopped down the stairwell and across a parking lot to the Hummer.

There were news vans, three of them, parked on the far side of the crime-scene tape. Satellite dishes on top of the vans, call letters emblazoned on all four sides. Off to one side an attractive-looking woman with a microphone was wading through a crowd of casual college kids. No one paid any attention to us. The Hummer was parked on the street, just at the end of the parking ramp. There was a parking ticket beneath the wiper on the front windshield, par for the course.

I tossed the parking ticket between the front seats and pulled away from the curb. Two coeds looked the Hummer over as they passed. One raised her eyebrow and gave me an all-knowing wink, then held a suggestive grin. Her companion said something to her and they both laughed as we passed by.

Hale groaned again.

"We'll be at United Hospital in under ten minutes," I said and drove away.

Chapter Sixty-Five

I was thinking about Nikki, playing over in my head what I would do. She was probably dressed in unassuming clothes, just in case. She took a shot, then as everyone scattered she tossed the weapon in the backseat of her car, then pulled the Pampers down on top of it. Proceeded to drive out of the ramp, only the exit was blocked. The timing had to have been close. I guessed the police squad wasn't quite there as she got to the ground level in the ramp. She was probably heading for the exit just as squad car pulled up and blocked it. She got out of her car and calmly walked away.

If she remained calm she could blend in with the college kids. God, could she have been in the group I almost mowed down when we came around the corner? She stuck with the group or a group, moved across campus, then exited on the far side. She was on foot. Would she carry any I.D.? Did she bring a purse in the car? Maybe, maybe not. She was walking away from the campus, but didn't want to attract any attention so she might have stayed on busier streets where there's pedestrian traffic. Without a purse she may not have money for a bus or taxi. So she was going to walk away, steadily, just a woman out for exercise.

There were a lot of 'maybes,' but I had an idea. I skirted around the roughly six-block campus area, down to Marshall Avenue. It was busy, lots of cars, people walking, there were shops, a couple of restaurants, and a lot of people on the street. I drove almost two miles, looking.

"You're taking your sweet time getting me to the damn hospital," Hale groaned.

I could see he was talking through clenched teeth.

"Yeah, okay, let's get you there," I said, picking up speed.

"I can hop on the interstate at Snelling and make up for lost time. I can see the stoplights for Snelling about three blocks ahead. I'll take a left there and, and, and…"

I focused on a figure up ahead walking on the sidewalk, not running, but making pretty good time.

"Hale, look, up ahead, you see her? The redhead? That our girl? The baseball cap, with the ponytail."

Hale took a deep breath, then exhaled, attempting to override the pain.

"Jesus, I don't know."

"How may women do you know go out to walk a couple of miles in boots with a pointed toe and six-inch heels?"

"Christ, go over the curb and pull up alongside her. I'll jump out," he said.

"Are you kidding? And what? Hope you land on top of her and pin her to the ground? You can't chase her with that leg. Christ, you can barely stand."

I pulled over to the curb.

"Give me your cuffs," I said, holding out my hand. "She's focused on just moving away from here. I can come up behind and get close to her. You just be ready to pull up as soon as I'm there."

He slapped the cuffs in my hand and I was off walking quickly to catch up to her. Any sound I made moving along the sidewalk was drowned out by the constant flow of traffic. In short order I was no more than thirty yards behind her, and Hale was creeping along behind me in the Hummer, a city bus coming up behind him. As the noise from the bus increased I began to run. It was an interesting experience. I don't like to run, and I certainly hadn't done it since the bomb blast last week. As the bus roared past, I closed to within fifteen feet. More than one person on the bus was watching with a look on their face wondering exactly what in the hell I was going to do. I came up behind her, and called out her name,

"Nikki, Nikki."

She turned around reflexively, just as I leapt. I landed on top of her and knocked her to the ground. She got a solid elbow into the bridge of my nose just as we hit the ground together. I heard something crack. Somehow I got one of the cuffs around her wrist, then felt the nails from her free hand scrape down the side of my face. The Hummer was over the curb, screeching to a stop on the sidewalk. A second car screeched from somewhere.

She tried to knee me and I turned my thigh to block her. It still hurt. I was wrestling for her free hand. She gave me another elbow, this time to my mouth. God, that hurt!

I caught another elbow with my lip, twisted her hand behind her back, clamped the handcuffs around her wrist. I sat up on top of her, took a deep breath, and felt an explosion on the side of my head.

"The fuck you doing, buddy?" someone yelled. It wasn't Hale. Another boot, this time to the back of my head, partially knocking me off Nikki. I saw stars and things went black for a second or two.

"Get the hell off her, man. Get off. Leave her alone ya pervert!"

I was aware of two massive tree trunk legs stepping over Nikki and coming after me. I rolled a couple of times, hoping to avoid the boots. It didn't work. I caught a glimpse of Nikki up and running, then she was down on the ground again.

"Police, police," I screamed. Two or three well-aimed kicks arrived before he stopped.

"Y'all cops?" followed by a pause that allowed the pain to begin to register. "Shit, sorry there, officer. I didn't know. Honest."

He was overly large. Shaggy brown hair, full beard, dirty Budweiser T-shirt, jeans, what felt like steel-toed boots and a very worried look on his face.

Hale had the MAC 10 pointed at the guy. His left foot had Nikki pinned to the ground by her ponytail.

The big man bent down to help me up.

"Shit, you all working undercover? I didn't know, honest. I thought you were rapists or something, you know? Thought I was protecting that little gal is all. Man, you guys oughta wear a badge or something. Ain't that the damn law?"

Hale grimaced, lifted his shirt, and exposed the badge pinned to his belt.

"Okay, there's the damn badge, now beat it, before I charge you with interfering with an officer."

"Look, didn't mean no harm by it, like I said..."

"You wanna get charged or you wanna drive away and enjoy the rest of your day?"

"Drive away, I reckon."

"Okay, good, right answer. So go, take off, get outta here."

Chapter Sixty-Six

Hale phoned the Mikes and Gary. The Mikes transported Nikki back to the bunk bed dungeon. Gary drove us to the hospital, five stitches for me, and a walking cast for Hale's broken ankle. It was after five before we got back and were able to begin talking with Nikki.

She was a little scuffed up from our grab. She wore no makeup and was even more beautiful in person than the photo of her standing naked on the beach. She was also more than a little suspicious, but then who could really blame her?

We were sitting on the couches. Hale was asking the questions, his injured ankle encased in a gray walking cast with his leg extended and resting on a stack of pizza delivery boxes.

I sat at the far end of the other couch, directly across from Nikki. I held a cold can of Coke wrapped in a T-shirt. I alternated pressing the can gingerly against the stitches on the broken bridge of my nose and then the stitches in my swollen bottom lip. It didn't seem to be helping much.

Nikki was sitting in the corner of the couch, knees together, feet flat on the floor, arms folded tightly across her chest. She was looking at Hale, almost glaring at him, mouth set firmly, lips clamped. I could see her chest rising and falling with each breath, and I could hear her exhale.

"You knew Sergie Alekseeva?" Hale asked.

She nodded ever so slightly.

"Can you tell me anything about him?"

"I can tell you he is dead," she said, almost spitting the words out. Her accent was much more pronounced than Kerri's and when she made the statement she raised her chin ever so slightly, but defiantly.

"Yeah, well, that was in all the papers, but can you tell me anything about him?"

"What is there to tell? A pig, better off he is dead." It was almost as though she was talking to herself. She didn't look at either of us, just stared blankly at the wall behind me.

"No argument from me," Hale said. "But what we're after, Nikki, is arresting Sergei's father, Braco Alekseeva, and putting him in prison for good. We want to close down his organization. Understand?"

She gave no indication she had even heard him.

"We believe he's involved in human trafficking. Transporting girls over here, forcing them to be prostitutes. Raping them, getting them hooked on drugs, ruining their lives, maybe even killing them. But we need more proof before we can arrest him."

"You can't stop him," she said quietly, almost offhandedly, like it was a given, akin to darkness falling every night.

"We can't stop him without help, and that's where you come in. Look around you, you're not in jail. I haven't asked you what you were doing before we found you walking along the street. Right now, I don't really care. I just need your help in bringing down Braco Alekseeva. That's all I care about. I don't care what you've done. I don't care if you don't have a visa or you don't have a passport. Stopping Braco is the only thing I care about. And, when I'm finished with Braco, we're going to shut down Kumarin and his gang down in Chicago. Now, I think we can help each another here, but it's up to you."

Nikki gave a slight scoff, then shook her head ever so slightly, unconvinced.

I moved the can of Coke to the side of my throbbing head where I'd been kicked. The welts and scrapes from Nikki's scratch still felt raw and burned down the side of my face. Both my eyes were already purple and getting worse from the broken nose she gave me.

Hale looked at her for a long moment, then called across the room, "Gary, bring some of those transcripts over here, will you? Maybe that stuff concerning Miss Mathias and how Braco planned to deal with her."

It took a few minutes before Gary placed a pile of transcripts on the couch. Hale pushed the pile toward Nikki until it spilled toward her.

"Go ahead, look at these. It makes for some interesting reading. You might even be aware of some of these conversations. One of our problems is, by the time we get these damn things translated, it's after the fact, so whatever was discussed has already happened. So they're worthless as far as stopping Braco. But they do present a fairly complete picture of what's going on. Maybe they'll make some interesting reading for you. So go ahead, take your time, and read through them. And, while you're reading, remember that as long as you stay silent the only person you're helping is Braco, no one else. And, if you're worried about family back home they would be a lot safer if Braco and Kumarin were locked up for the rest of their lives."

With that Hale grunted and groaned to his feet, hobbled over to the computers, and looked over Gary's shoulder.

I studied Nikki for a moment. She was biting her bottom lip, thinking, maybe. Then she focused on me and glared, her face an unreadable mask. I decided it might be safer standing over with Hale.

Chapter Sixty-Seven

At least it wasn't pizza again for dinner. It was Chinese takeout, some sort of stir-fry with an awful lot of fried rice, which I love. One of the Mikes delivered a bowl to Nikki, along with a cup of tea and three or four small Butterfinger candy bars. The perfect balanced dinner.

Nikki was still in the same corner of the couch, but she had curled her feet up beneath her and was reading as she ate. She was maybe three-quarters of the way through the stack of transcripts when Hale pulled another pile of equal size and had one of the Mikes deliver it to her. She didn't protest, just laid her unread portion on top of the new pile, pulled the whole thing a little closer to her and continued to read.

At some point Hale talked to Aaron on the phone. It was a short conversation and I guessed he never quite got around to mentioning that we had Nikki. From what I could tell, the conversation wasn't heated. Hale had just checked in to eliminate one more thing from the laundry list Aaron was probably working on.

A little after nine Nikki raised her arms over her head, stretched, and headed for the bathroom.

"Is okay if I go to bathroom?"

"Be my guest," Hale said. "Would you like a mug of tea? I'm putting some on."

"Please." She nodded then headed for the bathroom just behind the kitchen area.

In lighter moods I might have offered to accompany her, but I was still smarting from the beating she gave me earlier in the day and wasn't about to attempt surviving another.

She was in the bathroom for about ten minutes. One of the Mikes had just asked if he should check when the door latch clicked open and Nikki came out.

"Tea will be ready in a minute. Let's sit on the couch and have a little chat," Hale said. "I don't get off this damn ankle soon I'm going to scream."

Nikki nodded and maybe smiled ever so slightly. I couldn't be sure.

Chapter Sixty-Eight

We were all seated around the couches, Nikki in the same corner with her feet tucked comfortably beneath her. Hale at the other end, leg resting on the stack of pizza boxes. Gary and I sat on the opposite couch. The two Mikes wheeled their desk chairs over and nibbled on remnants of cold dim sum. Nikki and Hale were drinking tea. I held a mug but hated the stuff. Gary sipped a Coke.

"So," Hale slurped tea. "You see some of what we're dealing with. What do you think?"

Nikki looked very smug, smiled at Hale, and said,

"I am a very big pain in the ass of Braco."

"Yes, you have been. And if you learned that much you must have also read that they want to put a stop to that."

Nikki smiled almost to herself. She sipped some tea, looked off somewhere, then said, "They plan to kill me. They will rape me for a few days, maybe a week if I last. And when there is nothing left to rape, 'The Butcher' will be there and cut me into so many little pieces. No one will ever find me. And then the last lesson, I will be the example to the others that you cannot win against Braco."

"You're right. That is their plan," said Hale. "Now what's your plan?"

"My plan?"

"Yeah, do you want to end up in little pieces? Or would it be better to see Braco and Kumarin go to jail for the rest of their lives?"

"But I don't know what…"

"Look at it this way," Hale interrupted. "On your own you have been a very big pain in the ass of Braco, as you said. If we work together, all of us, and some others, we'll beat Braco. Beat Kerri Vucavitch. And, beat 'The Butcher.'"

"Humpf, Crvek, 'The Butcher'," she said absently staring at the floor, holding her mug tightly.

Hale shot me a quick glance, then refocused on Nikki.

"We can lock them all away, forever if you help us. Will you help us?"

Nikki seemed to stare at the floor for quite some time, then looked at Hale and nodded.

"I will help you to put them all away or kill them. It makes no difference to me. Just so long that my family will be safe, finally."

"And you, you will be safe too, Nikki."

"We will see," she answered.

Chapter Sixty-Nine

Nikki began in earnest the following morning over breakfast. She turned to Hale and said, "If you want to get to Braco it is important to cut him off from his money. Not only the girls who have to whore for him, but the drugs as well. Without those two, he will quickly go desperate."

She then proceeded to give a list of the girls she knew, who were working for Braco, where they lived. The outcall services they worked through. She listed his lieutenants, the ones she knew, and where they could be found. Then she told what she knew of his drug operations, which didn't seem to be all that much, except for one important aspect.

Braco had aligned himself with a small bank out in Valdem, Minnesota, almost on the South Dakota border. Nikki thought he might own part of the bank or maybe even all it, she wasn't sure. The important fact was the bank operated a number of Casas de Combio's in the banking industry known as CDC's. These were currency-exchange houses where people could send funds to Mexico. With two large regional packing plants within twenty-five miles of Valdem there were plenty of individuals sending money back to their families in Mexico. It became the perfect money-laundering scheme.

Using fake accounts, Braco transferred funds to purchase drugs in Mexico and then transported the drugs back up to Minnesota. It turned out the beach photo, with the Lee-Dee guys and little Mai, had been an excursion to set up the Mexico end of things. Once they were set up, Braco planned to kill everyone who knew the particulars. Nikki was the final loose end. That was why Kerri had hired me in the first place, to find Nikki so they could kill her. Charming.

Nikki didn't have account numbers, but she had some of the false names under which funds had been transferred. She gave the names to Hale, who passed them on to the Federal Crimes Enforcement Network and Peters at the FBI.

Then Hale called Aaron and the two of us went down to his office to let him know we had Nikki and that she was working with us.

Chapter Seventy

Aaron had dark bags under his eyes and looked like he was operating on about three hours of sleep. He looked at the two of us as Hale hobbled in behind me.

"What the hell happened to you two? You look like shit."

"Well, that's a marked improvement over yesterday," I said.

Hale groaned into the chair. I stood against the door frame. After thirty seconds of pleasantries Hale gave me a nod and I decided to drop our bomb on Aaron.

"Look, Aaron, we got Nikki Mathias," I said, just throwing it out there. I felt relieved just getting it off my chest. I didn't like keeping information from him.

"Yeah, that's what I figured," he said off handedly.

"Huh?"

"I got a call from Peters earlier this morning, bragging about how they'd tracked down some bank in the middle of nowhere, had account names, and were going to descend on the place armed with federal warrants. I didn't think the Feds could put that together. They're too busy covering their asses to get their hands dirty. That info had to come from somewhere and when you clowns were conspicuously absent it wasn't a long leap to put two and two together."

"Look, it's not like we were trying to keep you out of anything, you just seemed to have your plate pretty full at the time and well, we…"

Aaron raised his hand to quiet me.

"What's done is done. It took awhile, but something good had to come from yesterday. You've seen the news?"

We shook our heads.

"Seems we got a serial killer out there shooting innocent citizens as they walk along the river. Jesus, Sergie Alekseeva, and this moron yesterday, Villas somebody. Innocent citizens, God help me. So, how'd you find her?"

"Oh, just sort of ran into her," I said, hoping to move on.

"Looks like you may have run into her pretty hard."

"She's given us a lot of names and places. I think you guys might be able to shut down a good portion of Braco's revenue stream," I said.

"Revenue stream? Who have you been talking to?" he glanced at Hale.

"We got addresses, names, what the security situation is like. If you moved on this, I bet in twenty-four hours you could do Braco some real harm," I added.

"It would sure take some heat off."

"She's giving us information you guys can act on. You can judge whether it's good or not."

With that Hale handed Aaron two sheets of paper with names and addresses Nikki had provided. Aaron read through them, picked up the phone, and spoke to someone named Norm, who entered the office a moment later. Aaron introduced us all around. Norm nodded, took the list, and left.

"Any chance I can meet the ever-popular Nikki?" he asked.

"That's not a problem. I don't think. Let me tell you what I have in mind," Hale said. He went on to explain how Nikki was key to bringing down Braco and important, though in a lesser role, in doing the same thing to Kumarin down in Chicago. He finished up with,

"So you can see how her arrest would not be in our best interest."

"Okay." Aaron nodded, and that was all he said.

Chapter Seventy-One

Two days later we began to shut down Braco's empire in earnest. The call centers were the first priority. Hundreds of Internet ads were out there listing cell-phone numbers with bogus photos. The ads funneled back into maybe a half dozen different call centers, which then contacted and sent transport to pick up and deliver the girls, not to mention extract payment.

I envisioned some sort of secure facility. High-tech cameras, armed guards, bars on the windows, and something akin to a vault door that was impossible to breach. I could not have been more wrong.

They were operating out of a series of nondescript offices. Where two or three woman manned computers to constantly update ads on dating networks and a variety of search engines. They answered the calls and set up the appointments. They were just like Da'nita Bell, only not in a wheelchair and still alive.

At the first place we knocked on we found an office door that was locked. Nikki called someone's name and answered whatever was asked in Russian.

We heard light footsteps and then the door opened almost immediately.

Aaron, Norm, and two other guys barged in wearing bulletproof vests with their weapons drawn. It got the girl's attention. Hale and I followed. Once it was secure, I brought Nikki in. One of the women, a mean-looking blonde, spat some invective in Russian at her, kicked out, and caught me in the shin. It really hurt.

Nikki half screamed something back at her. The three women, in the process of getting handcuffed behind their backs looked at one another like deer in the headlights.

We placed them in different corners of the office. Two of Aaron's guys led the mean blonde out to a squad car. Once she was out of the room Nikki walked over to Hale and me, then whispered,

"The dark-haired one might have something to say. She has been knocked."

"You mean knocked up?" I asked, still rubbing my shin.

"Has baby in her."

Aaron gave the nod to the other two guys and they led a thin brown-haired girl out, holding her by the elbows. She looked like she needed a bath and a meal, and appeared to be somewhat drugged and not completely aware of what was going on.

Nikki approached the dark-haired girl. I gathered around with Hale and Aaron. She resembled a frightened puppy, large dark eyes, visibly shaking, blinking back tears. In a soft voice Nikki translated their questions and the young girl's answers. At one point she gave the girl a hug, wiped the tears from her face, then finally kissed her on the forehead just before they led her away, crying.

We hit four of the places, made sixteen arrests, and confiscated twenty-one computers, which were delivered to the bunk bed dungeon for Gary and the Mikes to begin sorting through.

At our final stop we could hear what sounded like women arguing. Nikki knocked and a male voice answered, gruff sounding. Nikki looked at Aaron, shook her head to indicate she didn't know who it was, then knocked again and said something. The male voice shouted something back, loud, angry. Nikki replied, sounding like she was pleading. The door flew open and a fat, bald man stood in the doorway. He was shouting, wearing white jockey shorts and a mean look.

Aaron's fist brought whatever he was shouting to a close. The entry team trampled over him in the process of surging into the office. Two paunchy, middle-aged women stood together in jeans and bras. Their upper bodies looked like bread dough covered with knuckle imprints and hung heavily over their waistbands. It made you wish they'd quickly find their tops. Cigarettes smoldered in their left hands. They were sipping what looked like vodka. One of them held the bottle and apparently had just finished refilling their shot glasses. They stood completely still, eyes wide with shock.

On a couch against the wall was a very young girl, no more than sixteen maybe seventeen. She wore jeans, unzipped and half pulled down, no top and was either very drunk or drugged. She was aware we were in the room, but as she attempted to stand she fell to the floor, got up on all fours and then vomited.

The bald guy in the jockey shorts was kneeling, hands cuffed behind his back, beer belly resting on his thighs, blood was dripping from his nose onto his chest. He half shouted something, then spit at Nikki.

She was wearing the same stylish boots she'd worn the day we spotted her, sharp pointed toe, narrow six-inch heel. She calmly, quickly took a very graceful three-paced hop, kicked him in the crotch, full force, like she was attempting a fifty yard field goal.

He collapsed with a groan and fell forward on his side, moaning.

"Oh, no, don't, please stop. You'll hurt him, stop, stop," I said softly, dead pan, not meaning a word of it.

Nikki turned, gave me a smile, then brushed something imaginary off her jeans. She muttered something in Russian just loud enough for the two women to hear. They both nodded respectfully, then stared down at their feet.

"Please put their tops back on," Aaron pleaded. "Probably call the paramedics for the kid. I'm guessing she'll need forty-eight hours to clean out her system."

Nikki bent down next to the girl, asked her something. It sounded like she asked the same question three or four times.

"She said she just wants to go home. She wants her mother," she said, standing and making her way back to fatty in the jockey shorts.

He began talking loudly, scrambling backwards on his knees, maybe pleading.

I would have loved to let her go at him again, but I grabbed her arm and held her back. She fought, but not that hard.

Fatty had half crawled behind Norm, peeked out from behind him, smiling through his bloody nose and began to shout something at Nikki. Norm kneed him in the side of the head, bouncing his head off the door frame,

"Oh sorry, I didn't see you there," he said, then grabbed the guy by his ear and yanked him upright.

Nikki took a step in his direction and the guy visibly flinched. I don't know what she said to him, but I'd had women direct that sort of tone at me enough times to know it was rather unpleasant.

Chapter Seventy-Two

That night we had a celebratory feast of
takeout pizza, garlic bread and Cokes. Aaron and his
team joined us, and we planned the next day's
activities. If we'd taken out a good portion of the
call centers today, tomorrow would be spent
rounding up the worker bees. Armed with warrants
we started at six o'clock the following morning,
hitting apartments.

In the first apartment we placed six girls under
arrest. I pegged them at an average age of about
twenty. All asleep, some still groggy from whatever
chemistry they'd been on the night before. We
found a couple of box cutters they must have carried
for protection, otherwise their purses held cheap
makeup and no identification. There was a small pot
of something with mold growing on it in the
refrigerator, a note in Russian taped to the lid.

For a place housing six young women it was
remarkably empty. In the closet there were a couple
of T-shirts on hooks, one blouse half-way hung up
and three skirts that were so small I thought they
might be belts. Seven high-heel shoes of varying
sizes were scattered across the floor along with a

variety of undergarments. No food to speak of. Two empty plastic vodka bottles rested beneath a torn and threadbare couch, along with someone's thong. There was a metal mount on the kitchen wall for a phone, but no phone. Three of the girls had pay-as-you-go phones, none of them with more than an eight-dollar credit.

As they were being led out, one of the women turned to me.

"I do you cheap, you enjoy, then let me go, no?"

"No," I said. "God, all I rated was a discount, not even a freebee," I complained to Aaron.

"She probably knew you," he said.

We raided a number of places throughout the day, all pretty much the same, depressing. The women were taken to a facility for Immigration and Customs Enforcement processing and I guessed eventually returned to wherever they came from.

Back at the bunk bed dungeon, Nikki was busy translating reams of transcripts from Braco's email and phones when she wasn't turning up her nose at the Canadian bacon and pineapple pizzas we'd ordered for dinner.

"You will all be fat as pigs. The eating here is not healthy," she said, shaking her head. "I cook tomorrow, something good for you, and me."

There was no further discussion.

The following morning Hale and Aaron had us sit tight after we received a call from one of Peters' lieutenants. I guessed it was one of the shiny-shoed, pressed-suit clones that hovered around Peters in the conference room during the meeting where I met the lovely agent Dziedzic, not that it made any difference.

Armed with federal warrants, the FBI was going to shut down the State Bank of Valdem, Minnesota, and deny Braco access to funds in a number of accounts. The guy went on for a couple of minutes about the extensive federal investigation that had resulted in the information to obtain the warrants and ultimately shut down the bank. Then he added, none too subtly, that it would be nice if we put our little sideshow on hold for a bit, lest we screw up the Bureau operation. Hale reminded him our 'little sideshow' had given them the information their extensive investigation seemed to have missed. The phone conversation ended shortly after that.

The day was spent monitoring Braco's communications. In between times, Nikki made a stew, a salad and roast potatoes. Washed down with a couple of cold root beers we all admitted it was a pleasant change of pace from pizza and garlic sticks.

The five o'clock local news led with the FBI moving on the bank in Valdem. Amazingly, the cameras just happened to be present as Peters stormed into the bank armed with his federal warrants and a platoon of pressed suits.

"Great, but I'm willing to bet these guys are going to grind our end of things to a screeching halt," Hale said to Aaron between bites of stew.

"They'll be going after the bank. National media has no doubt already been alerted. It's probably the smart play for the Bureau. They sort of care about Braco the Whacko, but nailing a bank, and the impact that has on everyone else involved in this kind of money laundering, that's the bigger score for them. I don't like it and there's not a hell of a lot anyone can do about it," I said.

"Be nice to know what they have in mind," Hale said, slurping the last of his stew, then getting up to refill his bowl.

"You could ask Peters," Aaron scoffed.

"I might know someone who could help. We'd have to let her in on the fact we have Nikki. But she might help, if we could help her," I said.

"And just who would that be?" they asked in unison.

So I told them. As I finished I mentioned I hadn't seen the lovely agent Dziedzic on the news with the other Bureau types and wondered if it wouldn't make sense to give her a call.

Chapter Seventy-Three

"Yes."

"Valentina Dziedzic, please."

There was a bit of a pause before she answered.

"Finally make bail, Mr. Haskell?"

"Not to worry, I'm sure I can beat those charges and please call me Dev, will you? Otherwise it sounds like you're going to arrest me. How've you been?"

There was just the hint of a chuckle. I knew my charm was working its magic.

"Fine, just fine. From what I hear you've been busy," she replied.

"Oh, you know, never busy enough. Hey, I saw your guy Peters on the news with a bunch of guys who looked like they didn't want to get their suits dirty. Were you in on that? I didn't see you charging into the bank with all the other earnest agents."

"No, I guess there wasn't a need for a translator out there on that operation."

I thought I could just pick up the slightest hint of something in her tone.

"How fortunate the camera crews from the local stations and amazingly FOX, just happened to be passing through Valdem, Minnesota, at the time."

"Timing's everything," she said frostily.

"So do you go by Val or Tina?" I asked, hoping to get some more positive vibes going in our conversation.

"You can call me Agent Dziedzic," she said.

Something must have been wrong with the connection. My charm didn't seem to be getting through.

"Okay, Agent Dziedzic, I…"

"Just kidding, I go by Val. But if we're talking business it should probably just remain Agent Dziedzic."

"Okay, Val, listen, the reason I'm calling is I'm wondering if we might get together. There might be some business involved, but that doesn't mean we couldn't enjoy ourselves in the process."

"Does that actually work?"

"Enjoying our…"

"No, your lame line, enjoy ourselves in the process? You gotta be kidding me."

"Well, actually, I was thinking that we could get together. There's someone I'd like you to meet. I think you might find her interesting. Almost as interesting as me, but not quite."

"This have anything to do with the Alekseeva investigations?"

"It might."

There was a long pause.

"You know, they basically have me doing gofer work on that, running for coffee if they need some, taking messages. So if you're hoping to work some sort of deal or trade or inside scoop, I'm not in the communication chain. You'd have to run anything like that through Agent-In-Charge Peters." Her disdain was almost palpable when she said his name.

"I'm guessing you might have a little more to offer than running for coffee and if nothing else, you might be able to pick up a good bit of background information. Would it be a good career move? I don't know, you know what they say, nothing ventured, nothing gained."

"Peters know about this?"

"If he knew, do you think I'd be making the call?"

"Where can I meet you?"

Chapter Seventy-Four

We met in a Holiday station. I had to gas up my new loaner, a nondescript Toyota Camry. Just about anything would have been a step up from the pimped-out Hummer.

"You sure know how to romance a girl," she said, after pulling alongside and climbing out of her car.

It was a warm day, but not insufferably hot, and the humidity had blown out of the region at least for the moment.

Dziedzic wore sandal things with little heels, a form-fitting pair of jeans, and a white blouse, two buttons casually undone. The curls in her hair bounced as she walked around her car. The highlights in her hair shone in the sun. She did not look like my perception of an FBI agent.

"Oh, charming. Health food?" she said, leaning into my open window.

I was sitting behind the wheel, wolfing down a very large Butterfinger candy bar. The humidity may have dropped, but it was still warm enough to melt the chocolate. In an effort to avoid any mess, I had created just that, crumbs melting on my shirt and a smear of chocolate on the edge of my mouth, which I now proceeded to wipe off and then licked the chocolate off my fingertips.

"Oh, so sexy," she said in a tone that suggested the exact opposite.

"I'm practicing working undercover and blending in. Thanks for coming, Val."

"I think you'll need a lot more practice. And what happened to your nose?" she asked, looking at my stitches.

"Oh, just ran into someone I'd been looking for."

The claw marks down the side of my face had more or less healed. The swelling on my lip had gone down, although it was still split. There was still a major gash across the bridge of my nose, bits of thread exposed from each of the stitches. My black eyes had mostly faded, but in their fading left yellow and green bruises.

"Hey, hop in. I'll take you over," I said.

We exchanged pleasantries on the five-minute drive. As we approached the park where we were going to meet Hale and Nikki, I pulled over to the curb and turned the car off.

"Okay, here's the deal. We're going to arrest Braco Alekseeva. We have an informant who has given us information. Some of which was passed on to you guys."

"Is that what got Peters all hot and bothered about that little bank?" she asked.

"Yeah."

"I knew he wouldn't move that fast unless there was someone pushing him."

"We didn't actually push, but I think he figured he had an opportunity to move way past one local bad guy up here in flyover land. Make it look like he was taking a real hard line on money laundering operations all over the country."

"And he told you guys to what, back off?"

"Actually, no. He had one of his toads tell us to back off, not to do anything that would screw up their investigation."

"Agent Fahey?"

"Fahey?"

"Bayard Fahey, sort of soft-featured, blondish hair, rosy cheeks, blinks incessantly."

"I don't know, could have been. Actually the guy just made a phone call. We never talked to him in person."

"Charming, can't beat the personal touch."

"So here's the deal, Val. We'd like you to talk with our source. I can tell you she has been instrumental in just about completely shutting down Braco's trafficking operation, cutting his Internet brothel off at the knees. And, she is the source for all the information regarding the bank in Valdem. She's provided account names and sort of assisted in the recovery of a number of women and girls forced into prostitution. We're not asking you to derail any investigations or federal indictments or anything like that. We'd just like you to talk with this source, see if you can help us, and maybe help yourself and her at the same time. Fair?"

She seemed to consider this for a long moment.

"I'll talk with her, see what comes out of it. If there are any illegalities I can't ignore them or if you're looking for some sort of federal exoneration it is not in my purview to offer such."

"Yeah, we understand that. We just don't want Braco to get away, maybe relocate in Chicago or somewhere else and continue to make life miserable for everyone he comes in contact with."

"Okay, I'll certainly listen."

Chapter Seventy-Five

We followed a winding road past a couple of ball-fields, past a playground with swing sets and monkey bars, then drove on a little farther to the picnic area. Aaron, Hale, and Nikki were sitting at a picnic table in the shade, drinking coffee. We parked and walked the short distance from the street up a slight hill.

"Val, I think you know Billy Hale with I.C.E, and Aaron LaZelle with St. Paul," I said once we were in the shade.

"Agent Dziedzic, sorry I don't have any coffee to offer you. I foolishly thought Haskell here might have had a little more on the ball," Hale said. His ankle was still in the walking cast and extended along the length of the picnic-table bench. Nikki sat across from Hale with her back facing us as we approached. Aaron sat next to her.

"Val, this is Nikki Mathias, the woman who's provided so much assistance to us. Nikki, Agent Val Dziedzic with the FBI."

Nikki appraised Val coldly.

Val said something in Russian, smiled and extended her hand. Nikki replied, took her hand tentatively, then quickly let go and stared at the tabletop.

"Please, please sit down." Hale directed Val next to Nikki, then started to bring her up to speed as I grabbed a spot next to his foot.

"I'm not sure what Dev has already told you, so let me start at the beginning. Jump in with any questions. Aaron, Nikki, I get anything wrong, you correct me, okay?"

Nikki nodded, Aaron smiled ever so slightly.

Hale began with a general overview of the Task Force dating back twenty-four months. Then walked his version forward, looking a couple of times at Nikki for agreement. She nodded her head occasionally, but continued to stare at the tabletop. Having come to know her a little better, I was pretty sure there wasn't much, if anything, she missed. He casually skirted around the shooting of Sergie Alekseeva and Villas whatever his name was, storming over the top of the river bluff a few days back. He did mention the call centers, the illegals, the underage girl forced to drink vodka and about to be raped by a fat guy in jockey shorts. Maybe embellished, with a little positive spin, Nikki's role in stopping that particular activity, gave a not-so-flattering take on the FBI's role and Agent Peters by extension. Val didn't blink. Then Hale concluded with,

"So, while I understand the importance of the bank, the money laundering, and how that particular prosecution will relate to a broader picture, my concern, our concern, is the trafficking aspect of things. Braco in particular."

"I hope you can understand our situation down here on the local level," Aaron added. "We still need this guy put out of business, now. Not another twenty-four months from now. Since the money laundering out in Valdem surfaced, we can't seem to reach Peters. He has our calls routed through some sort of communications office like we're a local newspaper instead of members on the same Task Force."

Val nodded, then looked at Nikki and said something in Russian.

Nikki didn't look up, but replied.

Val seemed to be considering whatever Nikki had said, looked over at Hale, then to me, Aaron, then back again to Hale. She took a breath, then said, "Well. I can tell you Peters will be focused on the bank. He's going to ask you, ask is my word by the way, basically he'll insist. But he's going to ask you to wait on Braco Alekseeva so he can establish a trail. Which, from what you tell me, he has a pretty good chance of doing. But you are looking at another twelve to eighteen months, minimum. Meanwhile, like you said, Braco Alekseeva will continue to operate." She said something to Nikki in Russian again.

Nikki responded, Val nodded.

"Nikki thinks he has other sources to rebuild his laundering scheme. A guy like that is too smart not to. Problem isn't if, but rather when he reestablishes, he'll have the funds and the attorneys to fight this thing indefinitely. I think you're sort of in the eye of the hurricane. It's safe, relative to legal maneuvering, to go after him but there is a limited window. I'm talking days, not weeks."

"Do you think Peters could be talked into doing both, nailing the bank and Braco at the same time?" I asked.

"That would be the bold move, but in the end Peters is a career corporate man. He didn't get to the level he's at by being bold and taking chances. No, he'll follow the sure thing, the bank. It's more his style, less chance of getting his hands dirty, less chance of anything going wrong."

"I'm not his biggest fan, but are you telling me he's okay with Braco getting away?" I asked.

"No. He's okay with going after a bank that has been laundering drug money. That's his main focus now. If, in the process, some pimp running a few girls postpones his day of reckoning, well, that wasn't the intent, but it's how things played out. That's how he'll view it."

"You're kidding me?" I said, looking over at Aaron.

"No, she's probably right. They'll go after the bank and the CDC's, the Combio's, you can see them closing those things down for the next couple of years. Think of the headlines, with all the bailouts and the foreclosure problems. I mean, who wouldn't love to see a banker or two marched off to jail? And they'll learn something here, they're not stupid. I'll lay you odds any bank working with Combio's is going to be looked at very closely, effective yesterday."

Nikki said something to Val, and they spoke back and forth in Russian.

Hale said to me, "I think from my standpoint we've got more than enough to go after Braco." He drummed his fingers on the picnic table for a

304

moment then said, "Yeah, I'd like to do it. I don't want to see that animal on the streets any longer than necessary. You?" He looked over at Aaron.

"That's what I've wanted to do all along," Aaron replied.

Chapter Seventy-Six

The volume of Braco's communication skyrocketed with Peters' high-profile news coverage. Peters continued to route calls from Aaron and Hale through a communications officer. So much for the Task Force.

Val kept us fairly informed, nothing top secret, but her information proved our initial assessments had been correct. The idea of arresting bankers and shutting down an institution involved in money laundering, along with all the headlines, had proven just too tempting.

Aaron and Hale planned to move on their own and arrest Braco Alekseeva, Kerri Vucavitch, and Tibor Crvek, 'The Butcher'. They planned to go after them on a laundry list of charges including murder, extortion, racketeering, money laundering, human trafficking, and prostitution. They were in the process of having a stack of warrants prepared when events took a dramatic course of their own.

Val received a call directly from Peters, still out in western Minnesota. He instructed her to get involved in the missing-person investigation of a sixty-five-year-old St. Paul accountant by the name of Marvin "The Manipulator" Lepke. Mr. Lepke, a CPA whose state licenses had been revoked some ten plus years ago, had just one client, Braco Alekseeva. Lepke was reported missing by his wife within twenty-four hours of the Valdem bank story breaking.

Aaron, Hale and I arrived at the Lepke home. Marvin "The Manipulator" wasn't a complete stranger to anyone who read local newspapers. His legal problems some years back had been in all the papers. He was fat, bald, ill-tempered, and touted as an accounting genius up to the time of his arrest and subsequent incarceration on embezzlement charges.

"If you even open your mouth, I'm going to drop kick you out of here," Aaron said to me as we walked up to Marvin Lepke's front door.

The home was situated in the posh, staid, Crocus Hill area of St. Paul. A massive two and a half-story red-brick colonial with white trim, a white picket fence, and pink roses climbing over lattice work. An overweight golden retriever was sleeping on the front step. He lifted his head at the sound of the gate closing, wagged his tail once or twice in hopes of a scratch behind the ear, but other than that, never moved.

"Great watchdog," Hale laughed.

Aaron rang the doorbell.

An attractive blonde woman answered the door and invited us in. She might have been forty, but looked no more than thirty-five. She did a fantastic bit of justice to the pair of black stretch pants clinging to her perfectly toned form.

"Hello, I'm Lori Lepke," she said.

Lepke's daughter I guessed.

Aaron introduced us, and I responded with a slight nod.

"An agent from the FBI is already here, back in the kitchen. Thank you for coming. This way, please," gorgeous Lori said, then turned and we followed.

The elegant interior of the home really didn't register. I was focused on Lori's sexy walk. Entering the kitchen I spied a set of luscious dark curls and returned to reality.

"Agent Dziedzic," I said.

Aaron cleared his throat as a warning.

"Gentleman," Val said.

"Oh, you already know one another?" Lori asked.

"We've worked together on other projects," Aaron replied.

"Coffee?" Lori asked, pulling three matching mugs from one of the spotless white cabinets on the wall. She must have worked on her figure twenty-four hours a day, seven days a week. Very firm and very beautiful.

"I told all of this to the other officers earlier in the day. But, well, as I was just telling agent Dziedzic, my husband, Mr. Lepke, is a creature of habit and when he didn't come home, didn't call, I became very worried. After all…"

Husband? That toad? It couldn't possibly have been the first time Lori Lepke had seen a shocked look on someone's face when she identified herself as Marvin Lepke's wife, Mrs. "Manipulator". Despite my sense of having just been banged over the head with a heavy shovel, I regained control as she continued on with her story.

308

"… hours, but that's just not Mr. Lepke. He's never missed a night with me since the day we married."

Small wonder, I thought.

"How long have you been married?" Aaron asked, taking a mug of coffee from her and nodding thanks.

"Two years and three months," she said, dispensing mugs to Hale and myself. She made it sound like she had been serving a sentence.

In response to Aaron's puzzled look she said,

"Yes, I know what you're going to say, and yes, we met while Mr. Lepke was still in prison. We were married a week after his release. A week after he paid his debt to society," she added, sounding a little more forceful behind her disarming smile.

"Has he been practicing again?" Hale asked.

She smiled sweetly, innocently, perfect white teeth.

"Not in so many ways. I mean, he is a genius as you know. But he was acting more as a consultant. As far as I know he never signed off on things, just advised if that's what you were getting at. He's always been one to obey the law."

"Since his release," Aaron added.

"Exactly."

"Who did he advise?" Aaron asked.

"Come now, Lieutenant, you probably know better than I do. Why Mr. Alekseeva, of course. That was his only client. But with all the various holdings and businesses he was very busy with just that one client, advising."

"No doubt," said Aaron.

"So as far as you know, Mrs. Lepke, where was the last place your husband would have been?" Hale asked.

"Like I was telling Ms, I mean, Agent Dziedzic when you arrived, he was at his office." She set down her coffee mug and pulled business cards from a small, brown leather holder. The kind someone might carry in their pocket.

"This is Mr. Lepke's office address. As far as I know that's where he was. I just don't know where he may have gone."

"Accounts Services. He could be a window washer for all we know," I said.

If my remark made any impression you sure as hell couldn't tell.

"Did you go to his office?" Aaron asked.

"No, I phoned about seven-thirty, but there was no answer. I would have gone over there but I don't have a key. Mr. Lepke was a very private person in regard to his business activities. As I said earlier, when I didn't hear anything back I phoned the police," she smiled sparkling white teeth again.

I took out my cell phone, made like I was reading a text message, then shot a couple images of Lori without the flash. She glanced at me, but I didn't think she knew I had photographed her.

"Excuse me, sometimes these things are like a leash," I said.

Lori smiled another assault of sparkling white teeth.

We asked a number of other questions, most of which the lovely Lori answered perfectly. She smiled, we smiled, then thanked her and departed.

Chapter Seventy-Seven

Back at the bunk bed dungeon, I asked the question I presumed was on everyone's mind.

"Okay, riddle me this, Batman. How does some low-life like Marvin Lepke score the likes of the lovely Lori? While he's still behind bars?"

"I think that's why they call him "The Manipulator"," Aaron said.

"You mean Mr. Lepke?" Hale joked.

"Him too," Aaron answered.

"I would say the timing of his disappearance is interesting on two fronts. Obviously with the Valdem Bank all over the news it gives one reason to pause. The other thing is, don't you sort of wonder if old "Marvin the Manipulator", when he wasn't preoccupied with lovely Lori, hadn't returned to his old embezzling ways? This time possibly underestimating the guy he was embezzling from?" I asked.

Hale smiled, "Do you mean to tell me that despite what his wife said, Mr. Lepke hadn't completely learned his lesson?"

"Or, once he learned it, he then promptly forgot it," Aaron added.

"She's not exactly what I would call wracked with concern or fear," Val said.

"The wife, Lori?" Hale asked.

"Very strange," Aaron added.

"Yeah, how nice of you to come. I'm perfectly made up, I have a great figure. By the way, check out how I can move this fantastic ass when I walk. Care for some coffee? Oh, and did I mention, Mr. Lepke seems to have gone missing. Like he was an attachment to the vacuum, or something," I said.

Nikki was sitting on the couch, in what had become her corner, making notes on what looked to be a six-inch stack of transcripts.

"Nikki, do you recognize this woman?" I asked, showing her the image of Lori Lepke on my phone.

Nikki studied the shot.

"There's two more after that one," I said.

She was already shaking her head, then advanced through the other two images.

"Very pretty, but I have not seen her before, I think," she said and handed my phone back.

"I'm guessing she might end up with a pretty tidy sum should Marvin go missing. Given Braco is the other player, was she involved? Or, just fortunate? I don't know," Hale said.

"Well, I think I know," Val said. "There is either an element of the Stepford Wives in this whole thing, or she really is a dumb blonde. I'm not sure which."

"Any unusual activity in Marvin Lepke's bank accounts might tell us something. Or at least point in a direction. I can get a warrant for his offices. I wonder if it wouldn't make sense for you to report to Peters, maybe let him know we're going to

312

Lepke's office and it might be a good idea if you were there," Aaron said. He had his phone out and was dialing.

"I'm due to report in anyway. Maybe they've come across something out there," Val said and reached for her phone.

Chapter Seventy-Eight

Val reported in to Peters, who was as consistent as ever, having absolutely nothing to add.

Aaron picked up the warrant on the way to Lepke's office and a license number from the DMV on Lepke's car.

"Not bad, old Marvin's tooling around town in a Mercedes CL600 coup. They start somewhere over a hundred grand. Nice set of wheels for an ex-con little more than twenty-four months out of the slammer, obeying the law, and just working to try and get his life back together."

"Who says crime doesn't pay?" I said.

The four of us met in the parking lot behind the building. Located in a forgettable two-story structure, Lepke's office felt remarkably similar to the call centers we had raided earlier in the week. The Tenants Directory identified Accounts Services as unit 6B.

Since we didn't have a key, Aaron located a building maintenance man who let us in with his passkey, then hung around until Hale told him we'd call if there was anything else we needed.

Marvin the Manipulator's office was tastefully furnished if 1969 was your thing. A waiting room was inhabited by a matching upholstered couch and chair, big gold flowers haphazardly splotched all over them. Both the chair and couch were covered by heavy protective plastic. There was an Early American style coffee table positioned in front of the furniture with not so much as an outdated <u>National Geographic</u> on it. In the corner, between the couch and chair, was a brass lamp pole stretching from floor to ceiling with three brass lampshades, angled in different directions. None of the lampshades held a light bulb.

"The place just makes you want to shout 'sock it to me'," I said.

"Wouldn't want anything to harm that gorgeous upholstery," Val laughed.

There was a doorway beyond the couch, which Hale entered. It was the office. We knew that because there was a desk with a black leather chair on wheels behind it. And not much else.

"When was the last time you saw an office without chairs for clients to sit in?" Hale asked.

"Maybe when Mr. Lepke was advising they just stood at attention," Val said.

"You know, based on his taste in decoration it's probably safe to say he wasn't on the cutting edge of current. But, wouldn't you think that even someone who was just advising would have a computer? A typewriter? Something?" I asked.

"He did, or does," Aaron said walking behind the desk. "You can see dust on the desktop where the keyboard and screen were positioned and there's an indentation back here under the desk. I'm guessing that's where a terminal was located."

He slipped a pen under a drawer handle and pulled it open.

"Surprise, surprise, empty." Then proceeded to open all the drawers, all empty.

"A clean office, as in cleaned out," I said.

More indentations on the carpet suggested the recent removal of two file cabinets.

"Just a wild guess, but unless Marvin went on an unplanned vacation somewhere without his bride, I'd guess the odds might be pretty good he's not doing so well right now," Hale said.

"All roads still seem to lead to Braco Alekseeva," Aaron offered, and so we took one.

Chapter Seventy-Nine

Armed with the laundry list of offenses and
now the missing Marvin Lepke under seemingly
suspicious circumstances, Aaron secured warrants
and a swat team for the arrest.

Braco's red Lexus, the apparent recent recipient
of bodywork, was parked and gleaming in its
reserved spot in the parking garage beneath his
condo building. Gleaming two parking spots away
was the dark blue BMW registered to the Lee-Dee
guys that Kerri drove around town.

"Just to be on the safe side, I'll have these
vehicles towed to the crime bureau and checked for
signs of Marvin Lepke," Aaron said.

"Maybe check for Da'nita Bell and her
wheelchair on the Lexus," I added.

"That too."

We rode the elevators up to the thirty-fourth
floor, then had to get out and take a private elevator
the final two floors up to Braco's penthouse on
thirty-six. Aaron had a small army assembled in the
lower lobby before we moved on Braco's penthouse
unit.

His private elevator was paneled in some elegant kind of wood, definitely not knotty pine, a plush red carpet on the floor, and framed mirrors with beveled glass on three walls. There were enough of us that it was going to require at least three waves, plus additional guys creeping up a fire stairwell.

Just as we were beginning to load into the private elevator, Aaron's phone rang. I heard one side of a conversation and heated, garbled responses emanating from his phone.

"Agent Peters, nice to finally hear from you. Thank you for returning my calls from the past week," Aaron calmly said.

"Yes, Agent Dziedzic is here, in a courtesy role only. She is viewing the operation, from a distance," Aaron said, nodding at Val.

"Little late for that, I'm afraid, we're set to go in."

"No, we will not stand down. I have warrants. I'm in the process of dealing with what we suspect is at best a kidnapping and what we fear could well be a murder. Time is of the essence."

"Oh, I see. Well, let me rephrase, Agent Peters. At this point you're wasting my time, which means you're endangering the lives of my people. Good day," he said and clicked off his phone.

"Let's go," Aaron nodded to his swat guys and entered the private elevator.

When the doors opened, I guess it was more a combination of Scar Face meets the Big Lebowski. I wasn't allowed up until the third wave and only then because they assumed I had to be someone of authority, since I was up there to begin with.

No shots had been fired. By the time I got up there, a Swat team guy wrapped in Kevlar was reading Miranda rights to two thugs with shaved heads who were handcuffed and facedown on the floor of a hallway. Val was there, translating. Across the hallway, large paneled doors opened into a massive living room with skyline views on two walls. Even with all the windows, the room seemed dark. Despite the summer sunshine, the fireplace was roaring and stacks of files about three-feet high were lined up next to the fireplace. Remnants of burning files flew up the chimney. Hale, hobbling in his walking cast was busy pulling singed files out of the fireplace.

Three long black leather couches were arranged in a large U in front of the fireplace. A massive coffee table about the size of a double bed sat in the middle. The table was trashed with empty vodka bottles, dirty glasses, some serious stacks of cash and what I assumed was a mound of cocaine next to a mirror. A couple of rolled-up bills were stuck in the mound like haphazard birthday candles. A pistol lay on the floor between the couch and coffee table.

Kerri was there, wearing a black negligee that perfectly complemented a swollen, nearly closed black eye. She seemed catatonic, with heavy powder residue on her upper lip, chin, and dusted across her chest. Her head lolled to the side and she drooled slightly, I guess in acknowledgment.

Further back in the room, close to what was a wet bar area, a group of officers stood around a fat little bald man with a wispy ponytail lying on the floor. He had a Van Dyke-style goatee and was clad in a blue and gold paisley robe that looked to be silk.

The robe was disheveled and exposed a very fat, very pink rear end. Although I hadn't heard a shot, he appeared to be wounded. One of the officers was applying a compress to his head as I approached.

"Stupid bastard ran straight into the doorframe at full speed and cracked his head open," the officer was explaining to Aaron.

I noticed there was an empty gun holster belted over the silk robe beneath a massive beer belly.

"The infamous Braco the Waco," Aaron said as two swat guys raised the paisley-clad troll to his feet.

I'm not sure what I expected, but it wasn't this. I'd been thinking maybe someone around six foot-five. Braco couldn't have stood much more than five and a half feet. Instead of lean and muscled with piercing eyes that shouted a warning, he had triple chins, bags under his eyes, florid cheeks, and looked more like an Elizabethan English professor than some Russian gangster in a human trafficking scheme.

Aaron smiled, took out his Miranda card.

"Agent Dziedzic, if you'd help with translation when you have a chance," he called over to Val.

__Chapter Eighty__

Suddenly there was shouting from one of the
back rooms, followed quickly by three or four shots.
Everyone flinched and ducked, except for Braco,
who wobbled for a moment, then just dropped to the
floor. He hadn't been shot, he just flopped over or
passed out.

Aaron moved forward with four officers,
crouching as they went.

"Just stay put and don't get in the way," he
directed me.

I followed at what I assumed was a safe
distance.

The shots seemed to have come from a dining
room area, and the shooter had retreated into the
kitchen. Swat team guys were crawling along the
side of the dining room table. Once they were in
position, the team leader waved two more into the
room along the opposite wall. I took Aaron's advice
to heart and hung back, way back, halfway down the
thick-carpeted hallway.

"Tell whoever it is to throw their weapon out,"
Aaron said to Val.

She called out in Russian, then repeated the sentence.

We waited.

"Again," Aaron said after what seemed a very long time.

We waited awhile longer and then someone suddenly grabbed my collar from behind and yanked me to my feet shouting something in Russian as a pistol barrel cracked into the back of my head.

"Don't fucking shoot!" I pleaded just in case someone didn't get the message.

Aaron's eyes were wide, Hale looked deadly serious, and Val said something in Russian.

A response hurled back from behind me. I had other things to worry about just now, but I was keenly aware of garlic breath. The hand on my collar forced me forward, repeated a growled phrase in Russian again and again, all the while using me as a human shield. We slowly made our way toward the elevator, our backs against the wall.

"Everyone stand down. Just let them go, let them go," Aaron said, while Val translated.

The hand grabbing my collar seemed to take a larger hold and tightened around my neck.

I couldn't spot Braco, not that I needed to talk with him at the moment. Kerri was cuffed and looked to be unconscious, kneeling on the floor with her ass against the coffee table and her head on a couch.

The voice behind me growled something.

"He wants you to pick up a bundle of cash," Val translated as I was pushed toward the coffee table.

I picked up two just to stay on his good side, then stuffed them in my pocket.

We made our way into the hallway, across to the elevator, and then inside.

On the short ride down I stared wide-eyed at the reflection of my pale faced image while a sneering Tibor "The Butcher" Crvek held my collar, banged a very large pistol against my head, and giggled insanely.

"Don't shoot, please don't shoot. Very sensitive situation here," I pleaded to a group of cops milling around the lobby area two floors down. The Butcher moved us against the lobby wall and snarled something in Russian. Then snarled again.

Footsteps came pounding down the fire staircase. Aaron, Val, and half the St. Paul police force.

The Butcher snarled again.

"Jesus," I sobbed.

"He wants everyone to back up. Let him get to the other elevator," Val said.

"We'll lose him," someone shouted.

"Stand down, stand down everyone, back up, come on, move," Aaron commanded.

"Oh, fuck," I whined.

The Butcher shoved me against the wall, growling.

"Push the button for the elevator, Dev. Push the down button," Val translated.

As instructed I pushed the down button and then thought once we got onto the elevator I didn't stand a chance. I would be dead about one second after the door closed.

I looked Aaron in the eye, blinked slowly a few times to signal something, what? Just to signal I guess. The elevator arrived a lot sooner than I had hoped, gave a soft ding a moment before I heard the door slide open behind us. The Butcher grabbed my collar even tighter and began to pull me, half chuckling, taunting the crowded lobby as we backed into the elevator.

Throughout my life I have found abject fear to be a particularly good motivator.

I took two small steps backward as The Butcher dragged me. With the third step I pushed back as hard as I could, bringing my right arm up, hoping to turn out of the way and grab his gun. It didn't quite work that way. The gun fired before I could completely turn. The roar deafened me, but apparently missed as we fell. I rolled off him just as we hit the floor. A number of weapons fired and his body jerked repeatedly.

"Hold your fire, hold your fire," Aaron screamed.

The Butcher was on the floor, very still, half sitting, leaning to the left and staring vacantly. There was a small hole, surrounded by powder burns along the right side of his nose, and a larger exit wound on the left side of his face, just in front of his ear. Blood was pooling on the plush carpet.

My ears were ringing and I could feel a burning sensation on the back of my head and neck just before I passed out.

Chapter Eighty-One

I awoke sometime in the middle of the night. I could see it was raining out, although I was having trouble hearing anything against the window. The hospital room was empty except for some equipment quietly blinking next to me. There was a soft light on over the bed and I drifted back to sleep.

When I woke next it was to a nurse looking at a chart as she wheeled a breakfast tray in front of me.

"How'd we sleep?" she asked. What I could hear of her voice sounded muffled, like I was wearing earplugs.

"Okay, I think," I said groggily, not recognizing my own voice.

"My hearing is screwed up, I think."

She nodded, said something I didn't catch, then smiled and left the room.

I devoured a stack of pancakes with bacon, a glass of orange juice and some coffee. I kept trying to open my ears by yawning and swallowing, but nothing seemed to work. There was a greasy substance on the back of my head, a salve I guessed, maybe for powder burns.

I thought of The Butcher on the floor of that elevator, glazed eyes staring, toward what? Maybe the gates of hell. I felt absolutely no remorse.

I attempted to listen to the television mounted on the wall, but I was having trouble hearing it when a nurse came in and turned the sound down, then waggled a finger at me, and mumbled something I didn't quite understand.

Sometime in the early afternoon a doctor came in and talked to me. I couldn't hear most of what he was saying, but I caught the part about release forms and going home. I thought about calling Heidi for a ride, but why bother? I wouldn't be able to hear the phone ring, let alone her response, and my natural aversion to text messaging made it all just a lot easier to climb into a taxi.

Chapter Eighty-Two

Three nights later I was sitting in The Spot bar, minding my own damn business, content in a mild and steadily growing alcoholic haze. A bit of a private celebration after discovering two thick packets of hundred-dollar bills still stuffed into my pockets when I pulled on my trousers before leaving the hospital. Compensation from Braco I figured, and justly earned.

I failed to mention the cash in my after-action interview with the police department. They didn't ask, and I didn't offer. Aaron had fired at least two of the rounds into The Butcher and, according to department policy, had been placed on a mandatory week of clerical work.

"Get you another Jameson, Dev?" Jimmy asked.

A little voice inside my head said '*Just finish this one and go home*'.

"Yeah sure, why not?" I replied. My hearing was mostly back. I missed the occasional word here and there, but in general it had returned. I could use a phone anyway and the new Jameson made me think I might turn the night into a complete celebration. After a couple more healthy sips to build up courage and with very little reflection, I phoned Heidi.

"What?" she answered.

"Whoa, hell of a way to greet a hero," I said.

"Hero? You haven't answered any of my calls and I ..."

"Did you hear any of the news reports? I couldn't even hear the phone ring, let alone anything you'd say."

"Well, I'm kind of busy right now."

"Not your gnarly hairdresser pal, again? I thought you..."

"What I said was never mention that piglet to me again. Ever. No, I'm with Keith tonight. He's an artist, if you must know."

"An artist?"

"Tattoos actually."

"Tattoos? You're getting tattooed?"

"In a manner of speaking, with any luck. Look, I'd love to chat, but I have to get going here. I'll phone you in the next couple of days."

Yeah, sure you will.

"Hello."

"Hi, Val, Dev Haskell. How you doing?"

"Dev, oh good to finally hear from you. Yeah, well, you sort of caught me at a bad moment. I wonder if I might call you back in a bit?"

"Yeah sure. Look, I was just thinking I sort of wanted to get your take on everything that happened in that elevator. I'm missing some critical moments, you know? Would you have time to stop by, maybe later tonight say for a nightcap?"

"Oh, I'd love to, but actually I'm out in DC right now. Maybe we could link up later on. If you look on my business card, my email address is on there. Send me an email and I can forward after-action reports to you, and let you read through those."

"To tell you the truth I wasn't thinking of reports, exactly."

"Oh, you know in a warped sort of way that's sweet, Dev. But, things are going pretty well all of a sudden and like I told you once before, you probably wouldn't be the best career move for me. You know?"

"Yeah. Look, I'll send an email to you for those reports. I'm looking at your card right now. Good luck, all the same."

"You too, Dev. Stay in touch, okay?"

"Yeah sure. Talk to you later, Val."

I sat drumming my fingers on the bar trying to come up with someone who hadn't sworn "they never wanted to see me again, ever!"

"Here you go, Dev," Jimmy said, setting a fresh Jameson down.

"Jimmy, am I losing what's left of my mind, did I…"

"From the lady."

"Lady?"

"That redhead, she's," Jimmy looked back over his shoulder. "Well now, where in the hell did she go? She was standing right there a minute ago. Maybe she ducked into the ladies room."

"Redhead? Accent?"

"Yeah, she's got an accent."

"Good-looking?"

"Very, that's her, wherever in the hell she went," Jimmy said, looking around again.

"She's gone."

"What do you mean gone? She was really a knockout."

"You should see her naked on the beach."

"What?"

Chapter Eighty-Three

The following morning I wandered up to Bon Vie, wearing sunglasses and staying in the shade as much as possible. Okay, it was a little past one in the afternoon but after a night of being over-served it was still breakfast time for me. I was trying to be positive, thinking there may have been a spark between that cute waitress Madeline and myself.

"Oh, you. Do I need to warn our customers or is this going to be a social visit?" Amy asked as I entered, but then she smiled, sort of.

"I was thinking breakfast."

"I suppose Madeline's section," she said, making her way toward the back of the small room. "Here, take this table and try not to disturb any of the other customers around you."

Madeline arrived with a mug of coffee, a menu, and sporting a shiny new diamond that she waved under my nose as only recently-engaged women can.

"Thanks, Maddie. Gee, did you get engaged?"

"Oh, you noticed. Yeah, we just decided ...."

I settled for Eggs Benedict as I heard exactly how some wretch popped the question and ruined my plans for a fun night or two. My phone saved me from hearing their honeymoon plans.

"How's the head?" Aaron asked.

"Good. Hearing just about back to normal," I said.

"Anyone trying to kill you?"

"Not so far. 'Course its still early in the day. You back on the job?" I asked.

"Couple more days of clerical, but thought you might be interested. They found Marvin Lepke yesterday."

"Really? Where? Vegas, L.A.?"

"Not quite that far. Actually in the BMW we had towed in. Searching it was put on hold after Braco's arrest and the shooting. Marvin was wrapped up in about fifty different packages, frozen. It looked like they planned to leave him scattered across a five-state area. He eventually thawed and attracted someone's attention once he started leaking into the parking lot."

"His wife Lori involved?"

"Probably, not that we'll be able to prove or even want to pursue. Bail has been revoked for your pal Braco and his girlfriend, Kerri Vucavitch. Flight risks. They'll be looking at a couple of consecutive life sentences, no chance of parole. I don't know if you caught Peters on the news?"

"Peters? No, not really. What's his angle?"

"He's putting the success of the operation all down to the Task Force, naturally, since he heads up the thing."

"You gonna blow the whistle on him?"

"Not in so many words. We got a lot of bad guys off the street, shut down a major trafficking operation. We're happy enough with that for the time being. You okay?"

"Okay?"

"Yeah, I mean the mental part of it. Hearing will most likely return. You having nightmares or anything?"

"Nightmares? No, no trouble there, just having a tough time finding a date is all."

"Yeah, well the word is probably out on you."

"Thanks."

"Yeah, not a problem. Dev, glad you're okay. Stay safe."

I left a tip, wished Madeleine well. Amy thanked me for not causing a scene and I congratulated her for scrubbing most of my blood from the front sidewalk.

I'd walked fifteen feet from the restaurant when a horn honked. I looked at the attractive redheaded woman behind the wheel. She waved me over, smiling,

"You maybe buy me a drink now, no?" she said.

"Yes."

The End

Hey, thanks for taking the time to read Russian Roulette. Please don't miss the following sample of Mr. Swirlee.

Mr. Swirlee

<u>Chapter One</u>

"What did they do?" Mr. Swirlee screamed, his bald head immediately going from beet red to dark purple. "You idiot. Did you hear anything I said? They tried to kill me for God's sake."

His real name was Weldon Swirlmann. Although he insisted I call him Mr. Swirlee. Screaming made him even more red-faced than normal. His crimson face propped up on the pile of starched white hospital pillows looked even more outlandish. Blips on the monitor screens arraigned alongside his bed jumped accordingly with every outburst.

"I'm telling ya, they wanted to murder me. Only those brats showing up on their bikes stopped things from getting any worse."

"What did the police say?" I asked.

"The cops! You think I trust them? They were probably in on the deal, the bastards," he screamed.

Beep, beep, beep, beep, beep. One of the monitors had now switched to alarm mode.

"Oh, these goddamned things." He reached up to yank the cord out of the monitor.

The young woman introduced to me as Lola sat up just a little straighter in the vinyl visitor's chair near the end of his bed. Using my acquired skills as a private investigator I deduced she was Mr. Swirlee's daughter. She adjusted her blouse with both hands, pinched the cream-colored silk between thumb and forefinger, just above her belt line then tugged.

Each one of her elegant, long red nails sported a delicate little gold design, and she seemed to function effortlessly despite the long-nail handicap. The tug exposed another inch or two of deep cleavage. She was beautiful, in a sort of peroxide way.

For the first time in twenty minutes she spoke, cautioning Mr. Swirlee in an exceptionally high, squeaky, little-girl voice.

"Careful, precious, remember what Doctor…"

"That quack? He should just stick to his job, which is getting me the hell out of here. Damn it, Haskins, they tried to kill me."

"Actually, it's Haskell, Devlin Haskell."

Mr. Swirlee glared at me for a couple of long seconds.

"Whatever. The bastards tried to kill me. They couldn't buy me out, couldn't run me out, so now they finally tried to kill me."

"Who's they?" I asked.

"What in the hell am I paying you for? That's what I want you to find out. You're supposed to tell me just who in the hell did this." With a wave of his hands Mr. Swirlee indicated the bandages wrapped around his left leg propped up on a series of pillows.

"Actually, Sir, no offense, but you aren't paying me. At least you haven't yet. The first I heard of this was the message from your daugh… from Lola last night." I nodded at the smiling Barbie doll sitting up straight in the vinyl chair.

She winked back slowly and licked her lower lip.

"So anyway, you haven't paid me. Not that that's the point. What makes you think this was intentional? I mean your car was…."

"Car? That wasn't just a car. That was a Mercedes CL 600. Know what they go for, Haskins?"

"Haskell."

"They start at about one twenty. Damn it, grounds right there to shoot the bastards."

"But what makes you so sure it wasn't some idiot involved in a simple hit and run?" I asked.

"Simple! Does this look simple to you? I got a damn business to run. Think I can do that while I'm stuck in this nut house? Simple, he says, Jesus, I ought to…"

"Thank you, Mr. Haskell, we'll be in touch," Lola squeaked in her cartoon voice then slinked to her feet. With the six-inch stiletto heels she stood about five foot eight. Her skirt was just a little longer than the black belt with the rhinestone buckle wrapped around her slim waist. She extended her right hand. When I took it she rubbed the back of my hand with her left, then raised an eyebrow and flashed a lustful smirk.

Or was I just imagining that?

Mr. Swirlee looked out the window, unaware. His monitors had returned to a normal pattern.

"Let me see about clearing my calendar, and I'll get back to you tomorrow."

"We look forward to it." Lola smiled, still rubbing the back of my hand, in no apparent hurry to let go. She suddenly tickled the palm of my hand with her finger.

"Just find out who in the hell did this." Mr. Swirlee grumbled from his bed, then turned back to the window, clenching and unclenching his jaw.

Chapter Two

I didn't really have a calendar, let alone one to clear. I dropped by The Spot bar, just to see if anyone was looking for me. No one was.

Mr. Swirlee ruled an empire of ice cream trucks. A fleet of pink-and-blue trucks every parent in the seven-county metro area had come to despise. The trucks crawled through neighborhood streets, playing a chimed version of "Oh where, oh where has my little dog gone?" until you wanted to scream.

Children ran back into their homes, begging for two or three dollars for one of Mr. Swirlee's overpriced ice cream treats. Frankly, there was a part of me that was more than a little amazed some crazed father hadn't tried to kill Mr. Swirlee long before now. I decided to do some checking.

"Economic development," the voice cooed into the phone.

"Connie Ortiz, please," I rasped back, hoping I'd disguised my voice.

"Who may I say is calling, please?" You could almost hear the frost forming on the words. I knew it wasn't going to work, but I foolishly tried anyway.

"I'm calling on behalf of Haskell Investigations," I said.

"And your name?" she asked, a chilling accusation in her voice.

"Devlin Haskell," I said grimacing, waiting for the expected blast. I wasn't disappointed.

"Oh, I didn't recognize your voice at first. Just a cold? Hopefully."

"Is this Sandy?" I asked, hoping to charm my way past the minefield.

"Who exactly did you expect to be answering the phone?"

"I…I wasn't sure. I thought it might be you, Sandy, but I really didn't recognize your voice. It's been awhile, you know?"

"Mmm-mmm. Let me see if she can take your call. Hold please."

I knew the drill, I'd be on hold for three to five minutes, and Connie Ortiz would be unable to take my call. The truth was Sandy wouldn't even try. Still upset about a minor fender bender I had driving her car a couple of years ago.

We had been heading to my place. Sandy was way too over-served to drive, so I thought I'd help. Under the circumstances, it had seemed like a good idea at the time to just walk away from the accident scene. At three in the morning we quietly staggered away from what was left of the parked car and Sandy's damaged Toyota. No good deed goes unpunished.

"I'm sorry, she must have stepped out. May I take a message and have her return your call?"

Why bother? It's the same every time I call. I knew Sandy never tried to reach Connie Ortiz. If I leave a message, Sandy won't deliver it. It served me right for calling Sandy's PMS hotline I thought, then said,

"Okay, thanks for trying Sandy. If you could have her call me? She's got my number. Great to talk…"

Sandy abruptly hung up. I'd have to reach Connie at home later tonight.

"You want another one, Dev?" Jimmy, bartender extraordinaire, nodded toward my empty Leinenkugel's glass.

"Thanks Jimmy, but I better not. I've got a pretty busy day," I lied.

"Really? You got some business?" Jimmy sounded genuinely surprised.

"Yeah, checking a few things out for Mr. Swirlee. It shouldn't take…"

"That ice cream guy?"

"Yeah, that's him."

"I could have killed that prick a half dozen different times when the kids were little. It never failed, one of his damn trucks always showed up just before dinner. Damn kids screaming for ten bucks worth of ice cream. Ten bucks…hell, we didn't have a dollar to our name back then. And that song still makes my blood boil, that dog song, you know? They got that chime thing going with the damn bells. Son of a bitch always seemed to park right in front of our house. God, I don't miss those days," he said, shaking his head.

"Yeah, I know what you mean."

I made a mental note not to mention Mr. Swirlee again.

"You know who works for him, or did awhile back? Bernie!" Jimmy said.

"Bernie? You mean the burnout?"

"Yeah, you got him, Bernie Sneen. You know him, right?"

"Not really, except that he's sort of missing a few cards from his deck."

Well, yeah…anyway, he was driving one of those trucks last I heard. Might explain the drug use. Listening to that damn dog song chiming away, it'd drive anyone nuts."

"Bernie? They let that guy near kids?"

"Yeah, I guess so."

"God."

__Chapter Three__

__I found Bernie Sneen__ in a different bar. There were at least four places he was a daily regular. He was in the third place I checked, Dizzies.

You could say Dizzies was a bit low on ambience, but then that would suggest there might be some. Dizzies was all business, and the business was drinking. The bar itself was no more than twelve feet wide from the back of the bar to the opposite wall. If you were looking for food, casual conversation, a fun night out, or pleasant company, this was not the place.

It was dim, unfriendly, and smelled like the men's room at a bus station. Bernie Sneen sat three stools in from the front door, bathed in the light of the overhead television displaying a soundless episode of "Skating with the Stars." He seemed to be muttering to himself as I climbed on the worn vinyl stool next to him.

"Hey, Bernie, long time no see. How's it going?"

He looked over at me and nodded, his lips moving, but involved in some other inner conversation. He put a hand up, signaling me to wait a moment.

"What can I get you?" the bartender asked a moment later.

"I'll have a Leinenkugel's. Give Bernie whatever he's drinking."

"Ouzo and Heineken's," the bartender replied by way of explanation.

Bernie's lips continued to move for another minute, until the drinks were delivered. He raised his glass of ouzo, nodded, then took a sip.

"You're that goofy P.I., right?" he asked after setting his shot glass down.

"Dev Haskell, we've talked a couple of times, I think in The Spot," I said, trying to steer things in a little more positive direction.

Bernie nodded, then just stared at his beer.

Eventually I asked,

"Hey, weren't you driving an ice cream truck for Mr. Swirlee?"

"That bastard," he said, shaking his head.

"Yeah, Mr. Swirlee. You still driving for him?"

"Nah, bastard laid me off. Didn't like me drinking while I was driving, I guess. Jesus, what was I supposed to do, crawling along them streets about two miles an hour."

He was quiet for a minute or two, then looked over at me and grinned idiotically. For the first time I noticed his glazed eyes blinked furtively in time to a slight facial twitch.

I nodded, suggesting he actually made some sense.

Bernie was one of those guys that no matter how you tried to clean him up he always looked like

344

he needed a bath. At about six foot one he was two inches taller than me. I put his weight at forty pounds less, no more than one-fifty. He had dark, thinning hair, too long and slicked back against his skull. Not so much a particular style as it was just unkempt. Sallow skinned, he was in need of a shave and sported an Adam's apple the size of a golf ball on his scrawny neck. Not what you'd call attractive.

"They catch you eating all the ice cream?" I joked.

"Yeah, right," he said again with the idiotic grin. I noticed a dark hole on the left side of his mouth, about four teeth back.

"You ever deal with Mr. Swirlee, himself?"

He glanced at me. I was quickly becoming an irritant now that he had finished the Ouzo and was more than halfway through the beer I'd purchased.

"That bastard? I had to talk with him when I got my route, then the night post."

"Night post?"

Bernie looked over at me, twitched a few times then stared straight ahead and sipped his Heinekens. I was definitely an annoyance.

"What do you mean, night post?"

"Look, I don't want to talk about it, if you don't mind."

"Just asking."

"You work for the cops?" he asked, then proceeded to drain his glass.

"The cops? Me? No. Just curious about the night post thing."

"And I said I didn't want to talk about it. Jesus, what is it with you?"

"Look, Bernie, I…"

"Nice chatting," he said, and jumped off his stool, twitched at me briefly, then quickly walked out into the sunshine, hands thrust deep in his pockets. I noticed his shoes. Unlaced black high tops faded almost grey, with bright red laces. Bernie was ever the trendsetter.

"Get you anything else?" the bartender asked, clearing away the empty shot glasses, then looked at my untouched beer.

"No thanks," I said, shaking my head. I took a cue from Bernie, climbed off the stool, and went out the door. I figured my beer wouldn't go to waste. The bartender would probably serve it to the next person who came in.

Chapter Four

I called Connie Ortiz at home a little after 7:00 that night. We'd dated a few years back until Connie came to her senses and dumped me, although it was really one of those mutually agreed decisions. We got along well, and joked when we ran into each other, which wasn't too often.

"Hi, Connie, Dev Haskell."

"Hi."

"Hey, you got a minute to chat?"

"Yeah, but really not much more than that. Kind of crazy, you know? But go ahead, what can I do for you?"

"I wanted to ask you about a business. In fact, I tried to reach you at your office earlier."

"Today? I didn't get a message."

"Well, I spoke to Sandy. She..."

"Sandy? Oh, yeah, well...I think she's still upset about that reckless driving charge a few years back."

"Yeah, I know. I got the thing pled down for her. Jesus, they were going to charge her with a DWI and leaving the scene. Under the circumstances she could have been looking at some jail time not to mention losing her license. She just can't seem to get it through her head that…"

"Well, I don't want to get into it, but you know she maintains she wasn't even behind the wheel."

"Yeah, I know. You're right, we probably shouldn't get into it."

I'd always wondered since Sandy had passed out, how could she possibly remember I'd been behind the wheel?

"So, how can I help you? I'm guessing you didn't call about Sandy's driving record."

"Oh, yeah. Look I'm working on a project for a client. Can you tell me anything about Mr. Swirlee?"

"Mr. Swirlee, the ice cream trucks?"

"Yeah."

"Who's your client?"

"I'm going to have to interject client privilege here and not say."

"Okay, I guess. Mr. Swirlee, well, they're pretty big. I'd guess they employ over a hundred people in this town."

"What about competition?"

"Competition?"

"Yeah, is Mr. Swirlee the only show in town? I've sort of been out of the ice cream demographic for about thirty years."

"I can think of a couple of competitors, but they're really small. Competitors in name only, and I can only think of one now that I mention it. I don't know, but I would guess Mr. Swirlee has about 99-plus percent of the market."

"You ever dealt with him?"

"I've met him a couple of times over the years. Wendell something."

"Weldon," I corrected.

"Yeah, that sounds right. Like I said, I've met him, but not what you might call dealt with him. I would say he is a very focused individual."

"That's a nice way to put it."

"That's why I'm in the position I'm in."

"You know of any group or individual who might wish him harm?"

"Off the record?"

"As always."

"No, to answer your question directly. Any competition he has, on the ice cream level, would be small players. I can't see anyone doing something illegal if that's what you mean. On the other hand, as I said, he is a very focused individual. I hear he can be rather difficult…ruthless may be a better term. Of course, there have always been the rumors of the gambling thing."

"Yeah, I've heard some of those rumors, too. What do you hear on that front?" I asked, wondering *Gambling?*

"Well, it's always been alleged he's involved in gambling, but the flip side is the term 'alleged'. To my knowledge nothing has ever been even remotely proven. I think there may have been a handful of incidents with some of his drivers, but then again, what sort of person wants to drive an ice cream truck for a career?"

I conjured up a brief image of twitching Bernie Sneen.

"I would expect he has to be fairly careful during the hiring process. Background checks, credit checks, that sort of thing," Connie continued.

Another image of Bernie popped into my mind.

"Okay, but Connie, to your knowledge no one offers a competitive threat to him."

"A competitive threat to Mr. Swirlee, for ice cream? No, I can't imagine anyone providing much of a threat. It would be so expensive just to get started, let alone the overhead required with today's fuel prices. I mean he loses six months a year just with bad weather. I just can't see it. In fact, it's nothing short of amazing that he's done as well as he has. You know, who you should talk to is the Scoop people."

"Scoop people?"

"Over on the West Side, Double or Giant Scoop, something like that. I think they have a couple of trucks. They might be able to answer some of your questions. But now that I think about it, Mr. Swirlee has a fleet, and the only competitor I can think of in town has two trucks. Anyway, give them a call. Staschio Lydell or Lydella, something like that. Hey look, Dev, I've gotta run. Great chatting. Give me a call if I can be of any more help."

"Yeah, I'll call Sandy."

"Well, that might not be the best idea, but then again you can't really blame her."

"Thanks, Connie."

To be continued...

Many thanks for sampling. Dev's about to make a series of his usual bad decisions and suddenly he'll be in over his head. You can help him out by getting a copy of **Mr. Swirlee** and finding out what happens.

The following titles are stand alone;

Baby Grand
Chow For Now
Slow, Slow, Quick, Quick
Merlot
Finders Keepers
End of the Line

Irish Dukes
(*Fight Card Series written under
the pseudonym Jack Tunney*)

The following titles comprise
the Dev Haskell series;
Russian Roulette: Case 1
Mr. Swirlee: Case 2
Bite Me: Case 3
Bombshell: Case 4
Tutti Frutti: Case 5
Last Shot: Case 6
Ting-A-Ling: Case 7
Crickett: Case 8
Bulldog: Case 9
Double Trouble: Case 10
Yellow Ribbon: Case 11
Dog Gone: Case 12
Scam Man: Case 13
Foiled: Case 14
What Happens In Vegas…: Case 15
Art Hound: Case 16
(*The following titles*
are Dev Haskell novellas)
Twinkle Toes
Dollhouse
The Dance
Pixie

*The following titles comprise the
Jack Dillon series written
under the pseudonym Patrick Emmett;*

Welcome
Jack Dillon Dublin Tale 1

Sweet Dreams
Jack Dillon Dublin Tale 2

Mirror Mirror
Jack Dillon Dublin Tale 3

Silver Bullet
Jack Dillon Dublin Tale 4

Thank You!

Made in the USA
Las Vegas, NV
06 August 2021

27679092R00197